COMPOUND 26

The Makanza Series
Book One

KRISTA STREET

Published in the United States.

ISBN-13: 978-1983461514

www.kristastreet.com

Cover art by Deranged Doctor Design
www.derangeddoctordesign.com

FREE E-BOOK!

Join Krista Street's Newsletter and receive a FREE copy of *Awakened.*

Book 0 – A Prequel – The Lost Children Trilogy

www.kristastreet.com

ALSO BY KRISTA STREET

The Lost Children Trilogy

Awakened: the prequel
Forgotten
Remembered
Reborn

1 – FIRST DAY

Considering my first day at the Compound fell on the ten-year anniversary of the First Wave, I should have felt driven, purposeful, even proud. Instead, I couldn't take my eyes off the wall ahead.

The tall, dark wall stood resolutely. Against the azure sky, it looked menacing and bleak. The wall had to be at least twenty feet tall, maybe thirty. It created a perfect square perimeter around the Compound. The only way in was through the gates ahead.

"Put it into park!"

I jumped, bumping my thigh against the steering wheel. My cheeks heated at my exaggerated response. A guard stood outside of my vehicle. I'd been so mesmerized by the wall I hadn't seen him approach.

His belt buckle gleamed at eye level from my driver's seat. Leaning down, his brown eyes, filled with purpose and efficiency, looked at me expectantly through the window.

"Park. Now!"

"Right, sorry." My voice came out in a squeak.

The guard waved his colleagues over. Four MRRA employees, holding scanning devices and long poles with mirrors, swept my vehicle. They'd told us what to expect in training, but my heart still pounded. While the four guards did their work, the one that barked at me rapped on the window.

"Step out, ma'am!"

I hastily opened my car door and did as he said. A warm, late summer breeze rolled across my cheeks causing my long brown hair to fly in front of my eyes. Pushing it back, I inhaled deeply, but my nervousness didn't abate. I'd never been this close to the Compound before. The wall, with its gigantic steel gates that looked like jaws ready to swallow me whole, waited just a hair's breath away. I couldn't see past the gates. I had no idea what lay within.

"Badge?" the guard said.

Snapping my gaze from the wall, I cleared my throat. "It's my first day… I…"

"What's that?"

I tried to speak more forcefully. "It's my first day. I don't have it yet."

The guard's face didn't crack. He gripped a handheld computer. "Full name?"

"Meghan Janine Forester."

"Place your hand here."

I flattened my shaky palm on the screen. It scanned my handprint and flashed green.

"This way." He led me toward a machine stationed by the checkpoint while the other guards continued to sweep my car.

"Put your chin here and keep your eyes open."

I did as he said. A laser scanned my eyes. Again, the scan shone green.

"Step back and stand here. Legs spread. Arms out."

He held out a metal rod and scanned my body from every angle. When finished, he nodded curtly. "You may get back in your car. Have a nice day."

"Thank you." My heart thumped painfully.

The Compound's gates opened soundlessly. I expected mechanical grinding or scraping but neither happened. Behind me, a trail of cars stood in line on the curving access road, like a snake slithering through a field. Four other checkpoints had guards admitting Makanza Research Institute employees.

I eyed the line of waiting researchers in their silent vehicles. I remembered the days when idling cars, fueled by gasoline, grumbled quietly. Electric cars didn't make a sound.

When the gates opened fully, I slipped back into my car and drove forward. My eyes widened at what appeared.

In the distance, the Compound waited on the flat South Dakota ground. It reminded me of the impressive cliffs at Blue Mounds State Park, just across the border in Minnesota – cliffs I hadn't seen in over ten years. I still remembered them, though. They too jutted from the earth in strong, harsh lines.

The Compound appeared to only be four stories, but its width stretched a quarter mile. Its exterior walls were gray concrete and dotted with windows.

It was huge.

South Dakota wasn't the only state with a Compound. Every state in the lower forty-eight had one, although the bigger states had two, and some even three. Ten years ago, the Compounds hadn't existed. Life had been easy, normal, but then the virus struck. Two years of chaos and death ruled our country until the Compounds were built to help the Makanza Research Institute study the Kazzies – the rare survivors of *Makanza* who remained highly infectious. The Compounds also gave the MRRA, the Makanza Research and Response

Agency, a safe place to quarantine them.

The Compounds were run like correctional facilities and research institutes combined into one, and although the MRI insisted the Compounds were nothing like prisons, everyone knew they were. If the innocent Kazzies inside of them weren't allowed out, and they weren't allowed the basic human freedoms the rest of us took for granted, how could they *not* be prisons?

I pulled ahead to the next checkpoint, my brakes squeaking when I stopped, and did the same procedure as the first. Electronic fingerprinting and retinal scan. Over thirty minutes passed before I completely cleared security.

"Have a nice day, ma'am." The last guard tipped his hat.

I nodded a stiff reply and stepped back into my car. Pulling out my map, I surveyed my location and drove tentatively forward. A large parking lot surrounded the Compound. Now, I just had to find my spot. In training, they told me to park in the north lot and look for section B, but since I'd never been allowed into the Compound before today, it took me a while to find it.

I finally spotted my name in the third row. Pulling in, I turned off the motor and stared at the metal plate in front of me. *Dr. Meghan Forester, MSRG.*

I wondered what MSRG meant.

It was eerily quiet as I sat there. My palms still shook. Now that I was here, finally *here*, I realized my dream was about to come true. As a researcher with the Makanza Research Institute, or MRI, I'd be allowed to study the virus. We were the only ones granted that privilege. With any luck, I would be part of the team that one day discovered a vaccine.

Stepping out of my car, I straightened my suit. Although business suits weren't required, I wanted to make a good impression. I'd be the new kid on the block, with *kid* being the emphasis. At twenty-three, I'd be the youngest researcher to join the MRI. Ever.

I walked across the parking lot, my eyes scanning the Compound. I was supposed to enter at North Door 64. Three doors came into view, but a painted 64 in white caught my attention. My flats clicked on the pavement as I hurried to it.

Two military guards at the door checked me in. I tried not to be intimidated by the assault rifles they held so casually in their arms.

"Full name?" the older one asked.

"Meghan Janine Forester."

His shrewd, beady eyes flicked back and forth between me and his handheld computer. The second guard appeared to be around my age. He was big, meaty looking.

The young one raised his eyebrows. "*You're* Dr. Forester?"

I nodded.

"Place your hand here," the older guard barked. He glared at the younger one.

I placed my palm on the electronic pad. Once again, it flashed green. I hated to think what would happen if it turned red.

"Nervous?" A smile parted the young guard's lips. I glanced at his name badge. Private Williams.

"A little," I replied.

"Most are on their first day." He smiled again, but I looked away.

Jeremy had said to pretend that each new person I met today was him, but…I couldn't. The young guard's eyes were blue, not brown like Jeremy's, and the guard had strong, muscled arms, not wiry ones like my younger brother. I discreetly rubbed my hands on my skirt. I would never be as comfortable with a stranger as I was with my own brother, regardless of how much Jeremy tried to help me with my social anxiety.

"Your bag?" The older guard held out his hand.

I shoved it forward and watched as he searched everything including the zippered pocket containing tampons. I cringed. *How embarrassing.*

"All right." He handed it back. "You're cleared." He sounded disappointed.

I nodded curtly and swallowed my anxiety like a bad cough syrup.

Private Williams inserted a key, typed in a code and pushed a button. With a release of pressure, the door hissed open. A burst of cool air rushed against my face and a bright, interior light illuminated the walls within.

"Welcome to Compound 26."

2 - THE LAB

Holding my breath, I walked through the door. I'd wondered for years what the Compound was like. It had always been this gigantic, clandestine monolith off in the distance. Formidable, domineering and notoriously secretive.

Unfortunately, its grand reveal was anticlimactic. The short hallway opened to a small lobby with smoky blue walls, a small reception area, and two armed guards. That was it.

The receptionist looked up. "Dr. Forester?"

She was an older woman with a ready smile and neatly coifed hair. I hurried to her, my shoes tapping on the linoleum.

She handed me a badge. "Welcome, Dr. Forester. We're pleased to have you."

I took my new access badge and bit back a smile. The plastic card contained my name, title, and the picture they'd taken of me at training. Jeremy insisted I wasn't hideous to look at, but this picture wasn't my best. I'd been nervous and it showed. My long, dark hair was ruffled from running my fingers through it, and my large, hazel eyes were alight with nerves. My nose was small and slightly uneven, thanks to a skateboarding accident as a kid. Tense lips and a clenched jaw topped off the photo, evidence of the anxiety I felt from being around new people. Overall, I looked like a deer caught in headlights.

A feeling of pride rushed through me regardless. I clipped the badge to my suit, my shoulders straightening.

"You'll have to wear that at all times." Her name plaque read Carol Seaburg. Carol waved toward a chair. "Please have a seat. I'll let Dr. Roberts know you're here."

"Thank you."

I sat on one of the hard chairs. The back pressed sharply between my shoulder blades. One of the guards eyed me, his gaze flickering my way for the merest second. I forced myself to relax and take a few deep breaths.

It wasn't long before I heard Dr. Timothy Roberts. Loud, clomping stomps echoed down a hallway behind the reception area. I hastily stood just as he rounded the corner.

As usual, Dr. Roberts wore his uniform. I'd never seen him in anything but his military green cargo pants and button-up shirt. Both were clean and pressed. His hair was freshly trimmed in a traditional buzz cut.

"Dr. Forester, good to see you." His tone wasn't friendly, but it had never been in the dozen times we'd met.

I instinctively straightened. "You too."

"You must be eager to get to work."

"I am."

He did his version of a smile which looked more like a grimace. One of the first things I'd noticed about him, when we'd met three months ago at MRI initiation training, was that his smile never reached his eyes.

"Follow me."

With a click of his heels, he turned precisely and marched

down one of the bright hallways behind the lobby. His loud stomps echoed. I followed him and once again marveled at his gait. It was unusual, even considering his background.

Although the Makanza Research Institute was a branch of the Makanza Research and Response Agency, it wasn't technically part of the U.S. military, as the MRRA was. You would never have guessed it, though, from Dr. Roberts' demeanor. He was a long-retired medical doctor from the Marines and still operated like a soldier. I'd heard he ran his labs like one too.

I sometimes wondered if he made mitered corners on his bed at home, or kept his shoes aligned in measured angles in his closet. Dr. Roberts was obviously a man who valued the precision military life had taught him.

He was also my new boss.

I snapped my gaze away from his feet when we rounded our first corner. The Compound swallowed us whole. Away from the lobby, everything was white. The walls, ceiling, and floor. It was like being lost in a blinding snowstorm, except the harsh fluorescents made everything blindingly visible.

"We'll start with a brief tour." He didn't turn when he spoke. "The MRI is housed in the north, west, and south wings of the Compound. The east wing is for the MRRA. There is no need for you to go there."

From his tone, I interpreted that as, *don't* go there.

"You'll be working predominantly in the north wing. The labs, offices, deep freeze, and Kazzie facilities are all in that portion. However, most of the auditoriums are in the south wing. As for the west wing, it contains separate groups employed by the MRI that have nothing to do with your research. Again, no need for you to go there."

"Okay."

All of this was news to me. So much hadn't been covered in initiation training. The instructors there had seemed more interested in vetting our trustworthiness versus educating us on our positions. All I knew was that I'd be doing lab work to help the MRI find a vaccine or cure for *Makanza*. Other than that, I didn't know much about my new job.

We rounded a corner to a hallway lined with doors. Dr. Roberts marched purposefully past the first one but stopped at the second.

"Your office will be here." A plain, white door stood in front of us. I stared in surprise. *My own office?* My name blazed in a plaque across it, my double degree awkwardly stated.

MEGHAN FORESTER, PH.D. PH.D.

Dr. Roberts slid his access badge through the door's scanner. He then pressed his thumb against the finger pad. With a soft click, the door opened.

"This door will only open to your and my fingerprints and badges. As you know, any sharing of badges is strictly forbidden. Any violation of the rules will result in immediate termination and, if needed, prosecution."

They'd definitely made *that* clear in training.

He nodded toward a desk. "You may leave your bag here."

The office was small, with a desk, laptop, and filing cabinet. Stark, white walls matched the hallway, but the wall opposite the door held a large window. Stepping closer, I set my bag on the desk and looked down. The window overlooked a lab below.

I smiled.

Rows of benches held lab equipment used to study DNA. I easily spotted the liquid handlers, thermocyclers, centrifuges, and sequencers. The lab, however, was empty, not a soul to be seen.

I turned back to my boss. "Will I not be in the lab today?"

Dr. Roberts seemed to force another smile. "Not in your lab." He nodded toward the window. "Your lab is closed at the moment. Normally, there's one research group per lab, but since yours isn't open, I'm having you work with another group. Unfortunately, we've had a setback." A hard gleam lit his eyes.

"A setback?"

"One of the Kazzies hasn't been cooperating. As they may have told you in training, your group works directly with one Kazzie."

I actually *wasn't* told that. I'd never been told who I'd work with, and I definitely hadn't been told I'd work with a Kazzie. My sudden thrill at that revelation dimmed when I processed what Dr. Roberts said. I wondered what he meant by *cooperating.*

He opened the door and marched out of the office. I hurried to follow.

"There are three researchers in addition to yourself in your group. You'll meet them all today."

He led me down another series of corridors to other offices, including his own. When we reached the end of another long hall, windows revealed a second lab. This one was huge, easily four times the size of the lab below my office.

"You'll be working here for now." He swiped his badge and pressed his finger against the pad by the doorknob. The door opened with the same hiss as the others. Cool air washed across my cheeks as stale laboratory air greeted me.

I grinned.

"There are two groups working here, yours included…"

His voice trailed off, mentioning some other details I didn't hear. My smile disappeared the second we stepped onto the metal platform overlooking the lab below.

I walked to the railing and held on. My knuckles turned white. From this height, I could see everything. At least twenty other researchers worked below.

Twenty.

"Dr. Forester?" Dr. Roberts called. He was already at the bottom of the stairs. "Are you coming?"

I forced myself to move, but my stomach twisted into knots. Meeting one or two new people I could handle, but *twenty*? I'd never been comfortable in groups. I'm sure my vagabond, isolated childhood could be partly blamed for that, but twenty? All at once? *Seriously?*

Dr. Roberts watched me with a cool expression. Trepidation was probably written all over my face. I made myself smile. At least, I tried to. "I thought there were only three in my lab?"

Dr. Roberts' eyes narrowed. "Like I said before, your group is working *together* with another group at the moment. And like I said before that, we've had a setback in your lab. You'll be working with this group for the next week."

I clasped my hands tightly together. "Of course."

"Is this the new girl?" a voice called. A researcher walked toward us. He wore khaki pants and a t-shirt that read, *Too Cool for School* under his lab coat. According to his access badge, he had a Ph.D. in addition to his MD.

I smothered a shrill laugh. *Too cool for school. Right.*

"Dr. Forester, this is Dr. Hess." Dr. Roberts waved introductions. "Dr. Hess is one of the researchers in your group."

"Nice to meet ya, Forester." Dr. Hess held out his hand.

"Call me Mitch, everyone else does."

His cornflower blue eyes studied me when I placed my shaky palm in his. His large hand engulfed mine. His skin felt like fire. Or rather, my fingers were ice. That happened when I got anxious.

"First day, huh?" he said.

I nodded and tried to smile. I guessed Mitch to be in his mid-thirties. He had dirty blond hair, a full beard, and although his stance was casual, a keen intelligence glowed in his eyes. He was also huge. At least six-four.

"Not much of a grip there, Forester." Mitch grinned and dropped my hand. "You afraid I'm gonna bite?"

My eyes widened, and I'm pretty sure my mouth fell open.

Mitch laughed.

Dr. Roberts glared at Mitch. I glanced away from both of them and immediately wished I hadn't. The rest of the group had surrounded us. All twenty of them, and they were all dressed casually. I fingered my suit collar.

"Dr. Forester, you'll also be working with Dr. McConnell." Dr. Roberts indicated a woman to my left. "She'll be in charge of your orientation."

"Call me Amy." She stepped forward. Jeans and a button-up shirt under her lab coat adorned her small frame. When we shook hands, her palm felt like a doll's, warm and soft, yet breakable. She was petite and curvy. Her hair, though, was what truly got my attention. The mass of red curls and her flaming green eyes hinted at an Irish background.

Mitch put his hands on his hips. "Amy's the know-it-all. She's only been here five years but thinks she runs the place."

"Dr. Hess, back to work," our boss barked.

Mitch clamped his mouth shut, but I still caught a gleam in his eyes. "See ya around, Forester."

He sauntered back to his station. When he reached it, he turned a knob on a stereo. Heavy metal rock music reached my ears. When he caught me watching, he winked.

I hastily looked away.

Dr. Roberts rattled off introductions of the other researchers. The third member of my group was Charlie Wang – jet black hair, slanted eyes, and a small Asian build made him not much bigger than me.

"Welcome to the Compound, Meghan." He assessed my suit with a raised eyebrow but smiled nonetheless. "We're glad to have you aboard."

I cleared my throat. "Thanks."

The rest of the researchers all came forward. By the time the introductions were done, my palm was embarrassingly sweaty. The blouse under my suit jacket was also soaked. Nobody commented, but I did get a few looks.

As much as large groups rattled me, I still memorized all of their names. My entire life I'd been like that, something that amazed both my parents and Jeremy. My ability to remember anything mentioned to me, or anything I'd read, helped me get where I was today. Even though my unique eidetic memory gave me an advantage, my success was in reality, enabled by two things: ambition and hard work. *Really* hard work.

"You'll be working closely with Dr. McConnell for the next few weeks," Dr. Roberts said after Charlie and the others returned to their stations. "She'll report your progress to me. Once she feels you're familiar with and capable of following our policies and procedures, you'll work independently. Until then, she'll oversee you. Understood?"

"Yes."

"We have high hopes for you, Dr. Forester. Don't let us down."

I swallowed audibly. "I'll do my best."

"Report to me at seventeen hundred this afternoon. Do you remember where my office is?"

"Yes, east corridor, third hallway, the second door down." I'd memorized everyone's office location from our brief tour.

"Don't be late." Dr. Roberts did a precise one-eighty, marched up the stairs and out the door.

Amy cocked her head, a smile on her face. "Friendly, isn't he?"

"Ah… yes?"

Amy grinned. "You'll get used to him. Some of us joke he never got the memo that the MRI isn't military."

I smiled tentatively, trying to judge Amy's demeanor. For all I knew, this was a test. Perhaps she'd report everything I said, good or bad, back to Dr. Roberts. "He seems very capable."

Her eyes twinkled. "That's one way of putting it."

I wasn't sure how to respond so folded my hands together.

"I've been looking forward to meeting you," Amy said.

"You have?"

She nodded. "I heard about you a few years ago. We've all heard about you." She waved at everyone behind us.

"Really?" I ignored the impulse to tug at my suit collar.

"Oh yeah… who hasn't in the MRI? The kid from Vermillion who earned her bachelor degree in eighteen months followed by a masters in one year and two Ph.D.'s within three years." Amy paused. "Even to those of us in here, you're a bit of an anomaly."

"Hmm."

"Not to mention you're the youngest researcher in the MRI at any Compound."

Heat flushed my cheeks.

"Until you, I was the youngest scientist to start here, but I was twenty-six." That made Amy thirty-one. "Given all that, I knew I'd like you." A grin broke across her face, revealing small, perfectly aligned teeth.

Her smile and comment took me by surprise. "What?"

"I knew I'd like you," Amy repeated. "The two youngest researchers to ever be hired in our Compound are both women. How can we not be proud of that?"

The sincere tone of her voice helped calm me. Well, a little. My whole life I'd been different. My uncanny memory and social anxiety could be blamed for that. Whenever someone pointed it out, though, it took me awhile to get over it.

"Come on." Amy nodded toward the stairs. "There's a lot to show you. We can start with the labs. There are a few in addition to the one we commonly use." She led me up the stairs. The metal steps rattled under our feet. "Did Dr. Roberts explain the recent setback?"

I gripped the railing tightly. "He said there's been a problem… with a Kazzie."

"Yeah, but did he tell you *what* problem?"

I shook my head.

Amy stopped at the top and planted her hands akimbo. "Have you ever seen a Kazzie?"

"No."

Of course, Amy had to know that. Unless you worked for the MRI, you were never allowed into the Inner Sanctum.

She smiled. "In that case, we're going on a little field trip. Come on. It's about time you met one."

3 – INNER SANCTUM

I followed Amy out of the lab. My heart pounded. *We're going to see a Kazzie? An actual Kazzie?*

"If you're like most people, you'll be a bit weirded out the first time you meet them." Amy sailed down the hall. Her red hair looked incredibly bright against the stark walls. "But you'll get used to them."

I just nodded, my voice apparently on hiatus.

With each step, my mental map of the Compound grew. Amy led me deeper and deeper into its interior. Dozens of people passed us in the halls, but Amy never said a word to any of them. I wasn't sure if that was because she didn't know them or because we weren't allowed to talk. There was so much to learn.

One thing that soon became obvious was that the blinding white walls extended beyond our labs. It was like being in a snow cave.

"There's a rail system – in the subterranean levels," Amy said after we'd been walking for a few minutes. Humming air filled the hall. A draft hit me. The large vent above looked big enough to crawl through. "It's not entirely necessary to have a rail system. Twenty minutes of walking should get you anywhere in the Compound, but it is convenient when you're in a hurry. Since you're new, though, I'd thought we'd walk so you can see more of the Compound."

"Yes, that'd be good."

We kept walking. And walking. Amy peppered me with questions the entire way. Personal ones. How long had I lived in Sioux Falls? What did I do in my free time? Had I gone to the festival the other week?

I awkwardly answered each one and breathed a sigh of relief when she switched back to work.

"Did they teach you about *Makanza* in training?"

"Not really." I edged to the wall so a researcher could pass us going the other way. I kept my eyes averted. "They thoroughly trained us on the proper procedures for suiting up and how to safely handle the virus in the labs, but we didn't learn much about the actual virus."

"Then that's something we should discuss this afternoon when we have more time."

We reached an access door. She scanned her badge and held her hand up to the fingerprinting screen. I did the same. The door hissed open.

Amy smiled. "Only one more door." A large, double door stood at the end of the hall. Two guards flanked its sides. A sign stating *Inner Sanctum* hung above it.

I took a deep breath. For years, I'd dreamed of meeting a Kazzie, of talking to one. I had no idea who first called them Kazzies, maybe a researcher, maybe somebody in the news, maybe someone at the WHO or CDC. Whoever invented the term, probably hadn't guessed it would stick, but it had.

The first time I'd heard about a Kazzie was when I was

thirteen, approximately a month after the First Wave.

I'd never forgotten that day.

IT HAD BEEN a morning like all the others. Or rather, a morning like the new ones since *Makanza* hit. Jeremy and I sat at the kitchen table, eating breakfast while we watched cartoons. Dad was upstairs, working remotely in his office. Mom was in the basement, ignoring all of us as usual. Everyone was housebound. It had been the weirdest time in my life.

A news flash interrupted our cartoons. A reporter sat behind a desk, her face flushed, her words coming out faster than they should have, all journalistic professionalism apparently thrown out the window in her excitement.

"We're interrupting your program to bring you breaking news. The clean-up in Manhattan has produced an astonishing find: a survivor."

A scene appeared on the TV, showing CDC workers in their biohazard suits helping a man into a van. The man was dirty and haggard, but he was alive and walking. One of the last things *Makanza* took away was muscle coordination and voluntary movement. When that happened, it had moved into the brain. The end was close at that stage.

The scene cut back to the newsroom. The newscaster continued babbling about what a triumph this was for society. *"Now that we know one can survive a* Makanza *infection, we can have hope. Scientists will study the survivor's genome to identify what made it possible for him to survive. This should eventually lead to a vaccine, or perhaps even a cure!"*

Somewhere during that news segment, Jeremy and I clasped each other's hands. I looked into my little brother's dark brown eyes and at his button nose. He still had his baby face then, but already his hands were as big as mine. We both stared in wonder. I could feel his hope as strongly as my own.

In one month, our country had entirely changed, but what I saw that morning gave me hope. The first Kazzie. The very first American to survive *Makanza*. It wasn't until weeks later that the Center for Disease Control understood just how unusual *Makanza* was, when the man began to Change.

"LAST DOOR!" AMY announced.

Her cheerful statement snapped me out of my reverie. The double door approached. I held up my badge to the guard by the scanner. He checked us in, his movements stiff and serious. The door opened with a familiar hiss, revealing a curving hallway. Amy continued talking, as if what I was about to witness was the most natural thing in the world.

"We have seven Kazzies in our Compound, a few less than most Compounds in our region. Minnesota's got nine, Iowa eight, and Nebraska eleven. Montana and Wyoming are the only states with fewer Kazzies than us. Montana has two, Wyoming, four."

I couldn't respond. My heart pounded like a jackhammer. The light grew dimmer with each step.

Amy just carried on. "Due to his altered eyesight, this one is sensitive to bright light. That's why his hall is dark."

A wall of floor to ceiling windows appeared ahead. I knew we were approaching the first cell.

I'd briefly learned about the Sanctum in training. Each cell butted up to the hall, making it easy to see within through the large windows. I also knew there were twenty cells total. They formed a perfect circle with the Experimental Room at the epicenter.

The Kazzies were separated, one Kazzie per cell. However, that was where the details had ended. My initiation training instructor never divulged how big the cells were, what they looked like, if there were windows to the outside or any other specifics. As we walked forward and the first cell appeared, I immediately noticed two things.

The cells were entirely concrete. There were no windows.

Since the hallway was glass, it was easy to study the Kazzie within. His bright, orange shirt made him stand out like a hunter in the woods. I stepped closer, not quite believing what I was finally seeing.

He sat on a chair, at a desk in the corner, his back to us. There was paper, or something like it in front of him. He drew furiously on it. With his head down, his arm moved harshly. The pencil looked like it could snap at any second. For all intents and purposes, he looked like any other human, although there was something heavy about his brow.

I stared at him for a minute, as the enormity of what I watched sank in.

Amy remained silent, letting me look my fill. After a while, she said, "His name's Garrett, but a few of the guards call him Carrots since he can see in the dark."

As if the Kazzie knew we were talking about him, he looked up.

My breath sucked in.

Under his heavy brow, his eyes were huge. They had to be the size of eggs, each of them. Everything else about him looked normal.

Garrett blinked slowly, his expression impossible to read, before he bent back to his drawing.

My breath whooshed out of me. It left a cloud on the glass.

"He's not very happy right now, even though he's usually the laid back one." Amy crossed her arms. "Because of the recent problems with our Kazzie, Garrett's been stuck in his cell for three days. Normally, all of the Kazzies get out to the entertainment rooms each day for a reprieve."

I squinted, trying to get a better look at his paper, but it was too far away.

"Are you trying to see what he's doing?"

I straightened. "Ah… yes."

"He's usually drawing, painting, or sculpting something. It changes every day. Some days it's pottery, other days it's watercolors. Today it looks like charcoal. He's actually pretty good. Before he Changed, he was an artist."

Garrett's agitated movements continued. His lean arm streaked across the desk. The paper tablet in front of him ripped at times. It didn't stop him.

"What happened to him?" I asked. "When he got the virus?"

"For most people that contract *Makanza* and survive, the process is fairly similar, initially at least. They go through the same first symptoms as everyone else: nausea, fatigue, fever, muscle aches, your usual viral immune response. Only, whereas most people move into the second stage of symptoms: high, prolonged fever, delusions, impaired breathing, seizures, loss of muscle coordination and eventually death, the Kazzies don't. They Change. Garrett began his Change when he was in quarantine in Michigan, since he's originally from Kalamazoo. When his entire family was dying in the second stage, he was Changing. The guards at that MRRA facility said it was agonizing to watch. When Garrett's eyes enlarged, it was a slow process. It took several weeks. Garrett screamed the entire time."

I grimaced. "Did anything else Change in him? Other than his eyes?"

Amy shook her head. "Nope, just that. He has *Makanza* strain 19 which primarily affects ocular cells. We have identified forty-one different strains. All cause different Changes since each strain infects different cells. Usually only one or two aspects of the Kazzies Change, but everything else remains the same."

"So Garrett's the same person as he was before he contracted *Makanza*, but he can see better now?"

"Yep. The Kazzies are still completely human. They have the same intellectual capacities, the same memories, the same personalities and so on. They just have added talents now, so to speak." She smiled. "And some of them look funny."

"How many Kazzies are in the country?"

"Around twelve hundred."

I continued watching Garrett. His arm streaked across the paper, like he was taking all of his frustration out in the drawing. I could hardly blame him. Technically, he'd never done anything wrong. His only crime was surviving *Makanza*, but as a carrier of the virus, he could never be allowed to live on the outside since he could infect others. Therefore, he'd be indefinitely imprisoned unless we discovered a vaccine or cure.

Seeing Garrett reminded me why I was here. We needed a vaccine.

"Has anyone figured out why some people Change and others die?" I asked.

"No. The vast majority of researchers employed by the MRI are trying to determine that. If we could identify why the Kazzie's DNA Changed to accommodate the virus, we'd know a lot more about *Makanza*. Unfortunately, that remains a mystery."

"So that's not the research we do?"

"No, we never work with those researchers. They're in a

different wing, and I don't even know who they are. Our group, the Makanza Survivor Research Group, or MSRG, works with the Kazzies, and each sub-group works directly with one Kazzie in particular. You'll get to know ours pretty well."

I thought about my parking lot sign. *So that's what MSRG means.* "Which Kazzie is the one we work with?"

"You'll see. Come on." Amy tugged me away from the window.

Our tapping feet were the only sound in the hallway while Amy explained more about the Kazzies. "There are four males and three females in our Compound. The subject we normally work with, one of the males, is the reason for all of the recent problems."

Another guard sat at the end of Garrett's hall, behind a glass window in a concrete structure. Amy called it a *watch room*, explaining that a guard was stationed in each Kazzie's watch room twenty-four hours a day. She then explained how one could enter a pressurized containment room attached to the watch room. The containment room had access to the Kazzies' cells. However, it was used for emergency purposes only.

"In other words, it's never used." Amy stopped at Garrett's watch room so I could get a good look.

A control panel, with too many buttons and levers to count, sat in front of the guard. Amy explained how the panel operated all of the mechanics inside the cell.

The control panel reminded me of the sci-fi movies Jeremy used to watch. It could have been the inside of a spaceship or cockpit in a high-tech commercial jet. So many buttons and switches. Of course, I'd never been inside one of those jets. I'd only seen them on TV shows. Those days of air travel were long gone.

On the ceiling, large humming vents circulated air in from the outside, unlike the air in Garrett's cell. In training, they'd told us the air circulating throughout the Kazzie's cells went through an extensive process of purification and filtering, but it never actually left the building. It was forever recycled. The MRI didn't trust *Makanza* not to mutate into an airborne virus.

I wondered what it smelled like in Garrett's cell. Stale, was my guess. Probably worse than the lab. I wondered if it bothered him that he never got to smell fresh air or feel the wind on his face. Was he used to it by now? Or not?

A pang of grief struck me for how unfair all of this was. Garrett was a prisoner in the Compound, yet his only crime was surviving *Makanza* and now being a carrier. Regardless, the safety of the public came first.

"Ready to keep moving?" Amy asked.

I followed Amy to the next access door. Once we stepped into the second hall, the overhead lights returned to normal. I blinked a few times. The blinding white walls were back.

"These are the Sisters." Amy stepped in front of the second cell. "Sara and Sophie. They were the first Kazzies to arrive at our Compound, and like Garrett, they're not from South Dakota. As you probably learned in training, most of the Kazzies in the Midwestern Compounds are not from our states, unlike the west and east coasts. When the coastal Compounds filled up, they moved their Kazzies inland. Since the Midwest wasn't as harshly affected by *Makanza*, at least not until the Second Wave, we've never filled up. Of course, that could all change if we get a Third Wave."

I flinched when she said that. Any day, a Third Wave could hit. It's what made the MRI's work so important.

I peered into the cell. The Sisters' cell was similar to Garrett's. It was simple, with two beds, two desks, a few tables, and a small TV. Again, no windows, but it wasn't the room that commanded my attention.

It was *them.*

My eyes widened as I got a better look. On the other side of the glass were two women. Both of the Sisters had pale, blond hair, shiny and straight, like silk from an ear of corn. And their eyes were blue. All of that was normal, except that their eyes were the same color as their *skin.* I stared in awe at the blue hue of their complexion. It was the same blue as a robin's egg.

"Sara and Sophie are twins. Two of the dozen survivors from the Manhattan Disaster," Amy stated.

"You kept them together?"

"Yep. We made an exception for them since they were so young when they came here. They've always lived together in this cell."

"So they've been here eight years? If they came right after the Compound was built?"

"Yep. The Sisters, Dorothy, Sage, and Victor all came here eight years ago. Garrett and Davin, our Kazzie, came after the Second Wave, six years ago. All of the Kazzies in our Compound, except for Davin, were originally from other states. Since the government decided each state needed a Compound, it made more sense to move Kazzies from state to state versus building more and more Compounds in a Kazzie's home state. Better to fill the ones we had versus building more. It's probably the only decision the government's ever made that's financially responsible."

I smiled at her joke just as one of the Sisters stood and walked toward us. Her movements were slow and incredibly fluid. Tall and slender, her frame was reminiscent of a dancer's.

The other Sister stayed sitting on the bed and watched us

warily. When the first Sister reached the window, she held up her hand and pressed her thin fingers against the glass. Her eyes, large and luminous, stared at me. She cocked her head, a curious glint in her eye. I figured it was because I was a new face.

"Strange," Amy murmured.

"What's strange?" I still stared at the twin.

"The Sisters usually ignore everybody. I'm surprised Sara's showing interest in you."

Sara glanced over her shoulder at Sophie before turning back to me. In that second, her skin changed, a subtle display of iridescent colors erupting beneath. My eyes widened. The shimmering quality vanished the second she turned back and met my gaze.

"Anyway," Amy said. "As you can see, their skin is an odd mix of bluish hues. They have *Makanza* strain 31. It's the rarest strain. Less than one percent of Kazzies have it. Only eleven cases in the U.S. have been documented. When the Sisters Changed, we think their gene SLC24A5 changed too. It caused a new pigmentation protein in their skin. It also changes when they talk."

"When they talk?"

"Or at least, that's what we suspect."

Sara continued watching me, but every now and then, she'd turn to Sophie. When she did, the blue in her skin changed, iridescent colors shimmered beneath. Sophie's skin did the same.

"Like right now." Amy pointed at Sara's exposed skin. "You see how their skin's changing? We think they're talking when they do that."

"But their lips aren't moving."

"Exactly. We think they communicate silently to one

another. Telepathically. You should see the EEG readings on these two. It's pretty amazing."

"So strain 31 changed their SLC24A5 gene and also gave them telepathic abilities?" My eyebrows rose. I hadn't fathomed *Makanza* could do *that*.

"Yep, we have good reason to believe that gene changed, however, we *think* it also gave them telepathic abilities. We don't have proof."

Sara still studied me, her expression growing more excited by the second.

I felt like a bug under a microscope. Her look was so intense. I looked away, and as I did, a slight throb hummed at the base of my skull. I rubbed my neck. A headache this early in the day wasn't a good sign.

"How can you tell them apart?" I asked, still rubbing my neck.

Amy nodded toward the one staring at me. "Sara's always been more curious than Sophie, but if you can't tell them apart, look at their wrists."

Since Sara still held her hand up to the window, I could easily see the black mark on her skin. A tiny inscription simply stated, *Sara*.

"We tattooed them," Amy explained. "They kept pulling off their wristbands and switching them, making it hard to tell them apart. It drove Dr. Roberts crazy. He'd go into one of his fits every time it happened." Amy rolled her eyes. "If I didn't know better, I'd say the Sisters did it just to piss him off. In response, Dr. Roberts tattooed them, even though Sophie cried when they held her down."

"Why not sedate her?"

"Dr. Roberts insisted since it wasn't a medical procedure, there was no need to expose her to an anesthetic. For her own benefit, of course."

The sarcastic tone of Amy's reply left me uneasy. Dr. Roberts would never intentionally hurt a Kazzie, surely. *Everyone here does what's best for them at all times. Right?*

After all, it wasn't the Kazzies' fault they'd survived. They shouldn't be punished for that. I shook my head. *Of course, the MRI does what's best for the Kazzies. It would be wrong not too.*

"How old are they?" I asked to stop my wayward thoughts.

"Twenty-two."

"Seriously?" That meant they'd Changed when they were twelve. The Manhattan Disaster was one of the greatest disasters in the last ten years. Everyone knew the date of that one. It meant the twins had been Changed for ten years, almost immediately after *Makanza* struck.

"Young, weren't they?" Amy added.

"Yeah." I rubbed my neck again and groaned inwardly. A headache was definitely brewing.

"Come on. I'll show you the rest."

The guard in the Sisters' watch room waved when we passed. At the end of the hall, we crossed through another armed door to the next cell.

"Dorothy is our other female," Amy said when we reached the third containment cell. "She came over from California after Compound 3 got too full. She was found in Death Valley by the MRRA, wandering around in an area that would have killed most humans in forty-eight hours if they didn't have any water. We have no idea how long she was there, but we know it was longer than two days. Amazingly, she didn't die. She was actually very alive and well. She only needs a tablespoon of water a day to function normally. Give her a whole cup and she's good for two weeks. That's all thanks to *Makanza* strain

8."

Dorothy's cell was different from the first two. It looked like a hospital room. Monitoring equipment surrounded the Kazzie who lay on a bed with her eyes closed, her arms at her sides. She didn't stir when we stopped.

"She's got amazing kidneys," Amy continued. "They're incredibly efficient, and it's not just water her body can conserve. If you starve her for a month, it's like she goes into hibernation."

"Hibernation?"

"She developed pounds of brown fat, also thanks to strain 8, so no matter how much she diets, she'll never be thin."

I knew brown fat was common in newborns and hibernating animals, but for it to be present in a human adult was unusual at best.

"Her researchers haven't given her any food or water for two months now." Amy's head cocked as she studied the Kazzie. "She hasn't woken once."

"Seriously?"

I studied the medical paraphernalia. Dorothy was hooked up to typical ICU monitoring equipment. I stared in awe at the numbers. She had a respiratory rate of four, heart rate of twenty-eight, blood pressure of sixty over twenty, and a temperature of eighty-eight.

Amy leaned closer to the window. "She slows right down when they deprive her, but she never dies. Last year, they starved her for six months, and she was still kickin'."

I was so appalled, the words slipped out before I could stop them. "That's cruel."

Amy nodded, her long, red curls shifting with the movement, but then she shrugged. "Try telling that to Dr. Roberts. He likes to think she's not conscious and tries to tell everyone there's nothing wrong with what we're doing. No one actually knows for sure if Dorothy feels pain or not. She won't tell us, and when she gets low like this, her whole body is like a tomb." Amy rested her forehead against the glass. "She's in there somewhere, and she may feel everything we do, but if she does, she doesn't let on." She straightened, pulling me again. "Come on."

The uneasy feeling returned, even though I tried desperately to shrug it off. At least the headache from earlier had abated. I followed Amy to the next cell, but she walked right past it. It was empty. So was the one after that.

"Sage and Victor are in the Experimental Room," she explained.

My hand stopped mid-air over the scanner at the last access door. The Experimental Room was the place the Kazzies went when research was actively being done on them. Kind of like the back labs in the old cosmetic companies, where rabbits sat lined up to have hairspray squirted into their eyes. Although I was certain it wasn't that bad. After all, the Kazzies were still people.

"I'll bring you back here when they return, but to give you the rundown, Sage came from Canada. He's the only Canadian that I know of in any U.S. Compound. After he became infected, he fled the country, in a panic from what I've gathered. I'm sure if he'd been thinking, he wouldn't have come here."

Canada had also established Compounds for their Kazzies, similar to the ones in the U.S. Unlike our country, though, Canada didn't do research on them. They just kept them confined.

Other countries that had survived the First Wave had taken similar precautions with their Kazzies – all of them were quarantined. However, not all nations had survived the First Wave. Some had ceased to exist completely. The entire continent of India was now a wasteland of decaying human flesh. I still shuddered every time I thought about it.

For over ten years all surviving countries had shut their borders. Importing and exporting had ceased to exist. As a result, Canada didn't have the means to produce enough food for their people. At the moment, all of Canada was slowly starving, and so were their Kazzies.

Amy continued, "Sage probably would have survived if he'd gone up to the Yukon's wild and isolated himself. But since he didn't, it wasn't long before we guessed what happened. All of Washington's border towns got hit with *Makanza*, one after the other. The MRRA had him in no time."

"What strain does he have?"

"Strain 27. He can generate electricity along his skin. Sometimes, when he flicks his fingers, sparks shoot in the air."

Amy chuckled, seeming to find my expression funny. "You haven't seen the half of it. As for Victor, he has strain 40, so his skin's bright red, and he's incredibly durable. His body can withstand temperatures of three hundred and twenty degrees Fahrenheit, and slightly hotter if he's angry."

"Wow."

Amy nodded. "He'll burn eventually. At three-fifty, he starts to cook."

I shuddered, wondering how *that* number was discovered.

"And here's the last Kazzie." We passed through the last access door. The windows to the sixth cell appeared. "Meghan, meet Davin. He's the Kazzie our group normally works with."

If I'd been more alert, I would have been prepared for what happened next. An object hurled at me, traveling at unbelievable speed. It hit the glass wall with enough force to shatter it. And a shattered glass wall linked directly to a Kazzie's cell only meant one thing.

Death.

4 - DAVIN

I instinctively crouched to the floor, covering my eyes, nose and mouth, and immediately stopped breathing. Blood pounded in my ears.

I sat there. Waiting. Waiting for the sound of shattering glass. Waiting for shards to shower over me. As soon as I came into contact with air from Davin's cell, I'd be exposed. Most certain death.

But the sound I expected to hear, the sickening sound of glass creaking and shattering after the thud, never came. I looked at the window. The *intact* window.

A broken chair sat upside down inside Davin's cell. The glass was completely unmarked. As soon as I realized that, my breath came out in a whoosh.

"And now you can see what our setback is." Amy stood casually beside me.

I slowly straightened.

Amy didn't seem the least bit perturbed, or surprised, by my panicked reaction. She just grinned when I straightened my suit. "Scared ya, didn't it?"

"Yes," I breathed. *How embarrassing.*

"Don't worry. It would take a lot more than that to break this window, even with all the force Davin can generate. All of the glass in the Compound is four inches thick, shatterproof, and bulletproof."

I wanted to kick myself. I knew that, from training, but a self-preservation instinct had taken control of me. The chair Davin threw came so fast. And the sound it made when it had hit... My palms still trembled.

"He's pretty pissed off right now, more so than usual." Amy crossed her arms as another piece of furniture flew into the wall. This time it was his bed frame. A second later, his desk flew blindingly fast in the opposite direction. It hit the glass shield over the guard's watch room.

I darted a glance at the guard.

He held a phone to his ear. His mouth moved feverishly as Davin continued throwing things.

Davin's entire cell was a disaster. Not one piece of furniture or object had gone unscathed. The mattress lay in tatters on the floor, the TV, smashed to pieces. Even his clothes were a wreck, or at least they looked shred when he stood still long enough for me to catch a glimpse of him.

"Why is he like this?" I managed.

Another piece of furniture crashed into the glass in front of me. If it had gone through, it would have taken my head off.

"Davin came back from the Experimental Room three days ago. He's been enraged ever since. I don't know why. Dr. Roberts wouldn't allow any of us in the Room. All I know is that Dr. Roberts had him in there longer than usual, but I'm not sure what he did to him."

Just as Davin threw his bed frame again, the access door opened behind us. The hiss of air made me turn. Dr. Roberts strode in with two MRRA soldiers. Both held assault rifles. Dr. Roberts sneered at Davin's cell.

"Damned Kazzie!" he seethed.

When he saw Amy and me, I shrank against the glass, which wasn't a good idea, since another piece of furniture hit it from behind. The vibration made me jump.

"What the hell are you doing here?" Dr. Roberts barked. His boots thumped loudly against the floor with each marching step. He glared at Amy. "Get her back to the lab, McConnell! You're supposed to be working!"

His eyes shot sparks. I resorted to my usual fallback around groups. Muteness.

At least, Amy was coherent enough to say something. "Sorry. Come on, Meghan."

She grabbed my arm, but my legs wouldn't move. I stood frozen in place. Dr. Roberts and the soldiers stepped into the watch room with Davin's guard. Even though I couldn't hear their words, it was most definitely a heated discussion.

Dr. Roberts lifted some kind of plastic cover over a button on the guard's control panel. My eyes darted to Davin and then widened. He wasn't moving. For once, Davin stood still. He stared at the men. It was the first time I got a good look at him.

He looked *normal*, like any other human.

My mouth dropped.

If I had seen him on the street, I would have guessed he was like me or Amy. Healthy, whole, untouched by *Makanza*. Nothing about him screamed that he'd been contaminated.

My eyes traveled up his frame. He was larger than average build, tall, but not so tall he'd draw attention. His skin was tan, like he'd just been out in the sun, which I knew was impossible. The muscles visible beneath his torn clothing were well-defined, but by no means bulky. His incredible strength and speed had to come from something within. When my eyes reached his face, my breath caught. The emotion on his face…

I'd never seen anything like it.

Davin's features, the straight nose, high cheekbones, and deep-set eyes, would normally be attractive, even strikingly handsome, but they had twisted and contorted into an expression that could only be described as absolute rage.

I sucked in my breath, vaguely aware of Amy pulling me again.

"Meghan, come on!"

I held my ground despite Amy's pull. I couldn't leave. Not yet. I needed to see what happened. A second later, a green-tinged gas entered Davin's room. The rage on Davin's face intensified.

Dr. Roberts was pressing a button that had been covered by plastic, his gaze glued to the Kazzie's.

Davin's mouth opened wide as veins in his neck bulged.

Since I couldn't hear him, all I saw was his silent roar. As soon as the green-tinged gas swirled around him, he hurtled himself one last time into the guard's watch room. For the tiniest of seconds, I thought the window bent.

Despite my protests, Amy managed to haul me to the access door.

Davin's face was still plastered to the glass. A snarl covered his features, any semblance to a normal human's expression, gone. His eyes rolled back in his head. He crumpled to the ground.

Dr. Roberts smiled.

The access door closed, cutting off my view.

I DIDN'T REALIZE I was shaking until Amy walked me

into the next hall. The image of Davin falling unconscious to the floor seared my mind. Dr. Roberts' smile came next.

I'd never seen *anybody* treated like that. Ever.

I clasped my trembling palms together. They shook so badly.

"Are you okay?" Amy placed a hand on my shoulder.

I didn't reply.

"Meghan?" she said gently. "Are you all right?"

I nodded automatically, but I couldn't meet her gaze.

"Hey." Amy nudged me. Placing both hands on my shoulders, she turned me toward her. "Meghan?"

I still couldn't say anything.

She frowned. "It's not always like that. In fact, it's usually *not* like that."

"How could he…" My voice broke. "Did he…?"

Amy shook her head. "Davin will be fine. Unfortunately, Dr. Roberts is a bit of a sadistic prick."

My eyes widened at how scathingly she spoke about our boss.

Amy sighed and ran a hand through her curls. "We've all had to accept a few things over the years. Sometimes, I forget how brutal it can appear. Just remember why we're here. Okay?"

I nodded.

"Because without these Kazzies, we'll never find a vaccine for us or them. Keep in mind, our experiments are done as humanely as possible. Usually, they're knocked out and have no idea what's been done to them. We make it as painless as possible."

"Is that why Dorothy's starving?" The question popped out of me before I could stop it.

Amy frowned. She looked like she wanted to say more, but

instead, she hooked her arm through mine. "Come on. We still have a lot to do today."

I followed her out of the Sanctum, and we continued the tour. The long walk helped. Some of my horror abated by the time we reached the Deep Freeze, as if physically distancing myself from Davin kept him mentally distanced too.

However, try as I might, flashes of Davin still crept into my mind. His rage. Him crumbling to the ground. Dr. Roberts' smile. I shook myself and tried to focus on what Amy showed me.

The deep freeze was a huge storage facility maintained at negative fifty degrees to store Kazzie samples. According to Amy, *Makanza* couldn't be stored in normal freezers, unlike most viruses. Researchers had to suit up and go through a middle chamber before being admitted *inside* the frozen storage. It was the only way to keep that temperature constant, yet another way *Makanza* was different.

After that, she showed me the Kazzie entertainment rooms through the various access windows. There was a library, movie theater, gym, indoor soccer field, and pool. The recreation facilities were huge, just like everything else in the Compound.

I took some comfort in the luxuriousness of the rooms. Something like that wouldn't be built if the MRI didn't care about the Kazzies. Obviously, someone cared.

"Until three months ago, they used to all hang out in these rooms together," Amy explained as we walked back to the lab. "The previous director of our department encouraged their socializing. However, Dr. Roberts doesn't agree with that practice." Her words grew bitter.

"So the Kazzies all know each other?"

"Yep, until Dr. Roberts promotion, they spent their free

time together in those rooms. Now, they're only allowed out of their cells individually for two hours a day. Well, that is until Davin's problems arose. Now, they're all in isolation."

I frowned. "Why can't they see each other anymore?"

"Your guess is as good as mine."

"So they haven't had contact with anyone since Dr. Roberts' promotion?"

"Correct."

"And that was three months ago? That doesn't seem fair."

Amy just shrugged. "Welcome to the rules of our notorious Dr. Roberts."

"Hmm." I bit my lip.

Images of Davin's face pressing against the glass flashed through my mind again. I did my best to listen as Amy began explaining all forty-one *Makanza* strains. But no matter how hard I tried to focus, my mind kept wandering back to Davin.

His face. His expression. His rage.

Just what exactly happens in Compound 26?

5 - DINNER

We had lunch with Mitch and Charlie in the cafeteria. I could barely eat. My stomach still churned from being around new people, but it was more than that. Davin's image wouldn't leave me. *What happened to him after we left?* It was a question that kept returning to the forefront of my thoughts.

Similar to Amy, Mitch and Charlie peppered me with questions. Personal ones. I tugged at my suit collar a few times and answered as best as I could. It didn't help that my skirt was tight, like a corset pulled snuggly around my waist. At times, I thought I'd throw up right on the table from nerves and a tight waistline. Luckily, everyone was busy so lunch was fast.

"Okay, let's head back to my office." Amy stuffed the last bite of her sandwich into her mouth. An ooze of mayo dripped off her finger. Real mayonnaise. *When did I last see that?* The din in the cafeteria hummed around us.

So many people. So many new faces.

My stomach lurched as I forced down my last spoonful of soup.

"You two stay out of trouble." Mitch stood. Upright, he

towered over us. "We'll see you in the lab when Captain Roberts deems you worthy." He winked at me.

Charlie brushed a piece of shaggy, black hair from his eyes. "See ya around, Meghan." He ambled off after Mitch.

Amy and I took the rail station back to our wing. The whir and hum of the subway were things I hadn't experienced before. Amy was right, though. It was fast.

Back in her office, Amy propped her feet on her desk and leaned back, crossing her arms behind her head. Long, red curls swirled down her back. It reminded me of satin ribbons.

"Okay, let's talk about the virus. Tell me what you know."

"All of it?" I tried to loosen my skirt as I sat upright, my back ramrod straight.

"Yeah, I'm curious what someone knows who doesn't work here."

The chair I sat on, opposite to her desk, was similar to the chair in the lobby. Hard. Unforgiving. An image of Davin flashed through my mind again. It seemed inconsequential that a hard chair and tight skirt bothered me when he had been gassed to unconsciousness mere hours ago.

"Any day now," Amy said with a smile.

Clearing my throat, I clasped my hands. "*Makanza* originated in Africa a little over ten years ago. It began as a strange viral outbreak in the jungle that nobody could identify. It spread quickly, infecting entire villages and communities. Within a month, the entire continent had outbreaks in every country. By that time, it had also emerged in Asia. Then Europe. Then here. That was all before anyone knew what we were dealing with. The Center for Disease Control and the World Health Organization scrambled, doing everything they could to control it, but since they didn't know what it was or how it spread, their attempts were futile." I paused, wondering if this was what she meant. "Is this what you're wanting me to tell you?"

Amy nodded. "Yep. You'd be surprised how wrong people are about *Makanza*, since the MRI tries to keep all info a secret. I'll correct anything you tell me that's inaccurate."

"Okay." I rubbed my hands on my skirt. My palms were a sweaty, icy mess from having to speak like this. "By the time *Makanza* reached the U.S., only two months had passed since the initial outbreak. Martial law was put into effect, twenty-four hours a day, two weeks after the Manhattan Disaster. Following that, our borders closed. Air travel and trade stopped. The high mortality rate frightened everyone. The major news broadcasters said it was one hundred percent fatal, but that was before we knew about the Kazzies." I paused again, remembering what today was. September 3, the anniversary of the First Wave. The day the first American died from *Makanza*.

The day our country changed forever.

"Considering only 1 in 85,000 people survive Makanza, it can seem like one hundred percent so I can see why the news reported that," Amy said. "*Makanza* is the only virus ever known to be that deadly. Go on."

I cleared my throat. "Things got a little better the second year when the government created the Makanza Research and Response Agency and the Makanza Research Institute, but it still took that entire year before anything was learned about the virus. It was too hard to study."

"Do you know why that is?"

"My professor hypothesized that it was too fragile outside of the human body."

"That's correct. It can only survive on surfaces for around ten minutes, yet it's still extremely infectious. A brush of your hand across a table and then bringing your hand anywhere near your face is enough to infect you. Not to mention, it's also transmitted via droplet. If someone sneezes within six feet of you, you're a goner. Over ninety-two percent of people that come into contact with it are infected."

"I didn't know it was that high."

"Most don't. There's a reason the MRI doesn't want the public knowing the facts. As you remember, panic and chaos ruled our country in the first year, the second year not being much better. The less the public knows about how truly frightening this virus is, and how little we still understand it, the better. We need to make the public feel safe, make them feel that we're controlling the virus, not the other way around."

"Right," I said uneasily.

"Did they teach you anything about the actual virus in training?"

"Only the basics."

"Tell me."

"*Makanza* isn't like any virus we've known. It can be transmitted from host to host through all possible methods: inhaled, ingested, from mother to child, and through sexual contact. It's also not very selective in the cells it infects. Most viruses attack a particular cell in the body, like Hepatitis B which infects liver cells, causing those infected to die of liver complications, or HIV which infects the immune system, or measles which infects lung cells, and so on. Uniquely, *Makanza* infects almost all cells in the human body. No other virus does that–"

"Right… kind of," Amy interrupted. "It *is* somewhat selective, depending on what strain you're infected with. Remember how I told you there were forty-one strains?"

I nodded.

"Each strain targets different cells, but as a whole, *Makanza* can infect everything, so in that aspect, you're right."

For a brief moment, my icy palms warmed as science dominated my thoughts. "Really?"

"Yep. We believe it's an RNA virus, given its characteristics, but since it only survives outside of the human body long enough to travel to a new host, there's no way for us to know more. It literally disintegrates in the sterility of a lab. Both sterile water and saltwater break it down."

I frowned as that implication set in.

Amy just smiled. "What else do you know?"

I wracked my brain for anything else but came up blank. "Um, that's it."

"So you don't know the incubation period?"

I shook my head. "The things I've heard are contradictory, so no."

Amy clasped her hands in front of her and sat forward, her feet making a *thunk* when they landed on the floor. She tucked a wayward curl behind an ear.

"I'll fill you in then. After coming into contact with *Makanza*, it incubates for twenty-one days before a person exhibits symptoms. However, a person is contagious eighteen days *prior* to symptoms. That's essentially why it spread so quickly. People didn't know they were sick until weeks later, so they kissed people goodbye, shook hands when they met, touched surfaces in public, and so on. It spread everywhere. Hence, why so many died so quickly and why our government mandated everyone stay quarantined in their homes until it was under control."

I remembered that time all too well. "That was a weird first year."

The military had brought food to people, leaving it on

doorsteps. Businesses shut down unless the government decided a particular business was critical for survival. If it was, the business ran on a skeleton crew. School was via internet only. Teachers set up "class" in their living rooms, live streaming to students at their personal homes.

That entire year had felt like a prison.

"Where were you living during the First Wave?" Amy asked.

"Vermillion. You?"

"Here, in Sioux Falls."

"Hmm." I hadn't thought about that first year in so long. It wasn't a happy time.

Amy checked her watch. "Crap, we should get moving. Ready to head back to the lab? I want to show you how we study the virus."

I nodded. The sooner I got into research, the better. The entire reason I'd spent the last six years working to achieve the degrees necessary to work for the MRI was to make a difference.

We needed a vaccine. All of our lives may depend on it.

SEVENTEEN HUNDRED ROLLED around faster than I thought it would. Before I knew it, my first day at the Compound was almost over.

I said goodbye to Amy and walked toward the offices for my meeting with Dr. Roberts. I paused outside his door. Sweat dampened the blouse under my suit jacket. I took a deep breath. Forcing myself to raise a hand, I knocked.

"Come in!" a sharp voice called.

I tentatively opened the door and stepped inside.

Dr. Roberts sat at his desk. It was an impressive six-foot long behemoth, with two chairs in front of it and a huge window behind it. The view through the window made me pause. Lush green grass stretched all the way to the Compound's outer perimeter. The sun shone overhead, the sky an endless blue. I didn't realize how much I missed the outdoors until I saw it.

"Please, sit down." Dr. Roberts waved at a chair.

I snapped my gaze away from the window and sat on a chair in front of his desk. I tried not to look around, but it was hard not to. His office was huge. In addition to the desk, a full couch, bookcase, and bar sat in the corner. The décor was browns and blues without a single personal item anywhere. The office was masculine and cold.

Just like my boss.

Dr. Roberts leaned forward and clasped his hands together. Sunspots speckled the backs of his hands. I couldn't gauge his expression. "Did everything go all right today?"

"Yes, I think so."

He eyed me, his gaze cold and calculating.

I tried not to fidget, but his stare made my palms sweat.

"I'd like to hear how your first day went. Do you have any questions about how things work here?"

The hard gleam in his eyes told me he was *really* asking if I had the stomach for how things worked here. Perhaps this was his way of addressing what I witnessed.

I swallowed with some difficulty. "No. Amy's done a good job of explaining everything."

The gleam stayed in his gaze. An aching ten seconds passed before he looked away. Finally, as if satisfied by what he saw, he nodded. "Excellent. In that case, I'd like to further discuss the research you did in grad school that earned you one of your Ph.D.'s."

I let out a breath I hadn't realized I'd been holding. My

Ph.D. thesis had been on RNA viruses and genomic sequencing. I had no problems talking about that.

"Of course."

IT WAS ALMOST six when I stepped into the parking lot. I'd never felt so relieved to be outside.

Since it was the beginning of September, the temperature was mild. I took a deep breath of warm air. Someone must have mowed the Compound's expansive lawn. The scent of freshly cut grass wafted in the breeze. The air that settled around me was like a cloak of normalcy. It was a much needed tranquilizer after the day I'd just had.

My steps sounded on the pavement as I walked to my car. It took roughly thirty minutes to get through security before I hopped onto the frontage road to I-90.

I opened my window. A breeze trailed in. The sweet smell of fresh air helped clear my head. I never minded the stale, processed air that circulated through labs, but perhaps that was because I could always leave. A few steps from my bench lay the freedom of the outdoors, but the Kazzies didn't have that.

They'd be locked up, potentially forever.

My shoulders slumped.

I thought of Davin again, being gassed to unconsciousness and how nobody had batted an eye. For the past six years, I'd wondered what it was like inside the Compounds, for the people who'd contracted *Makanza* and survived, but whatever my imagination had come up with, *that* was not it.

I was about halfway home when my cell phone rang. The image on the screen got a groan out of me. It was my mother. Reluctantly, I answered. "Hello?"

"Meghan, where are you?" Her voice dripped with annoyance.

My mother often reminded me of a cross between The Secretary of Defense and Martha Stewart. She could sound incredibly diabolical while also sounding like she'd just pulled a pan of freshly baked cookies from the oven.

It was a voice that always made me sit up straighter.

"Driving."

"I hope you're almost here. Your father and I have been waiting for over twenty minutes."

I slapped my hand to my forehead. I'd completely forgotten they'd wanted to take me out for dinner. The big celebratory night after my first day. "Right, just heading there now. Luigi's, isn't it?"

She mumbled an affirmation then paused. "You should have called, darling."

"I know. Sorry. Be there in ten."

THE HOSTESS GUIDED me to my parents. Bill and Janine Forester sat quietly at their table. A bowl of bread slices sat in the middle of the booth. My dad was in the midst of buttering a thick slice when I sat.

He wore jeans and a dress shirt covered by a V-neck sweater. His dark brown hair, the hair Jeremy and I had inherited, was parted on the side. My mother, on the other hand, had blond hair, hazel eyes, and a tall, willowy figure.

If my parents were pets, my dad would be the Labrador dog eagerly greeting any visitor that came to the door, whereas my mother would be the purebred Persian cat sitting atop a tall bookshelf while gazing down at everyone with lofty indifference.

"Hi." I kept my gaze averted and slid into the booth.

"Well hi there, kiddo!" My dad grinned.

"Meghan, nice of you to finally join us." My mother picked

up her water and sipped it.

The hostess handed me a menu. "As you can see, we have real French bread this week." She pointed at the bread bowl. "For the menu, we have items two, three, eight, ten, eleven, thirteen, and nineteen. You can refer to the list here." She pointed to a hand-written sheet of numbers clipped to the top. "Your server will be with you shortly."

I glanced down, more to avoid my parents' prying eyes than to actually study the menu. Menu selections were never guaranteed at any restaurant, so I never got too excited about what was available. Restaurants were lowest on the food totem pole, so to speak. The MRI came first, the South Dakota Food Distribution Centers second, and restaurants third. In other words, you could never count on your favorite things being available.

"It's nice to see you, Meg," my dad said.

I glanced up and managed a smile. "You too, Dad."

"What a nice suit," my mother remarked. She sipped her water while eyeing the charcoal gray two-piece. "Although, it looks a bit big in the shoulders."

My initial happiness over her comment vanished. I looked left and right. "Yeah, I guess it is, a little."

"It's a nice color, though."

"Thanks, it was either this or–"

"Waiter!" she interrupted, calling to a passing server. "We're ready to order now."

I bit back my words and stared at the menu again. Lasagna would do.

"How was your first day?" my dad asked after the waiter left.

I thought about what I'd seen. Garrett. The Sisters. Dorothy. What happened to Davin. My breath stopped.

"Fine." I forced a smile and with a shaky hand brought my water to my lips. "It was good."

"So what'd you do? Are you already working in the lab?" he probed.

"Um…"

My mother shook her head. "You know she can't talk about the Compound, Bill. Of all people, you should know that."

He smiled sheepishly. "Of course, sorry."

She continued to look at him disapprovingly.

My dad's degree in structural engineering had helped land him a job eight years ago at Cantaleve Steel, the company that built all of the Compounds. He still traveled regularly, helping to maintain the large structures that were essential for our survival. It was the only way one could travel. Since *Makanza* hit, the states had been sealed off from one another. Checkpoints blocked all border interstates and highways, another way the MRRA was trying to ready us in case another Wave broke out since it would, theoretically, contain the virus to the state the outbreak had occurred.

Of course, people still snuck across state lines. Sometimes you'd hear news stories about the government breaking up smuggling rings or people getting caught selling things between states on the black market. Obtaining a legal permit to leave any state was not an easy feat to achieve.

I often envied the freedom my dad had. Our vagabond childhood had stopped with the virus, not that I liked uprooting and moving every year, but it had been nice to see new things. When *Makanza* hit, my dad's company had him stationed in South Dakota, so that was where we stayed. In the past ten years, I hadn't left the state. My dad, however, had just gone to Florida to work at Compound 48. I'd always wanted to visit Florida. When I was a kid, I'd dreamed of Disney World. Of course, that theme park closed long ago.

I sighed.

I wished I could talk to my dad right now about the Compound. Even though we'd never really had a conversation past the weather or what we were doing for the weekend, it would have been nice to talk to someone. What I had seen today was awful, but we were both sworn to secrecy, whether we liked it or not.

The table remained silent. After I finished eating a bread slice, I sipped my water, wishing I'd ordered a cola. When the silence continued until our salads arrived, I finally said something to break the ice. "So, anything new with you guys?" I picked up my fork.

My mother cocked her head as she cut her tomato wedges into perfectly sliced bites. "Not really. I'm still helping out at South Dakota Orphans, and your dad's going to Cleveland tomorrow. Which Compound are you going to, Bill? Is it 54 or 55?"

"54."

"Isn't South Dakota Orphans that new charity?" I dipped my lettuce in the vinegary Italian dressing and took a bite. "Made to help children who've lost their parents to *Makanza*?"

She nodded. "Yes, the state currently has one hundred and ninety-eight kids in foster care. It's especially hard to find adoptive homes when even their most distant relations have died."

"That's great that you're helping them. I'm sure those kids need all the help they can get."

My mother studied me as if I'd said something peculiar and took a bite of her salad.

I looked down and stuffed a big tomato in my mouth. I

didn't know why I tried. Whenever I attempted to open up to her, it was like I suddenly spoke Japanese.

When our dinners arrived, I breathed an inward sigh of relief. The meal was officially halfway over. We ate in silence, and my mother, as usual, became more occupied in checking things on her phone than actually talking. My dad and I looked at anything but each other.

To pass time, I studied the pattern on the wallpaper behind their heads, and by the time I finished my lasagna, I'd figured out a mathematical equation to determine the pattern of shapes and lines on the paper. My dad had also kept busy. He'd probably readjusted his watch two dozen times and smoothed his hair just as often.

Finally finished, we stood to leave. My dad patted me awkwardly on the shoulder and smiled brightly. "It was great to see you. We'll have to do this again soon."

"Yeah, of course," I replied, even though I knew the next time we'd *do this again* would probably be around Christmas. Most years I got out of Thanksgiving.

"Good luck with work," my mother added, a polite smile on her face as she tucked her phone into her bag. Before I could reply, she looked at her watch. "We'd better go, Bill. We only have an hour before curfew."

I nodded. "Right, of course, drive safely."

"We will, you too!" For a minute, my dad looked like he wanted to say more, but then he smiled awkwardly and followed my mother.

It would take them forty-five minutes to reach Vermillion. Curfew was currently 9 p.m. It would become earlier as winter grew closer. At times, it drove me crazy that curfew was still in place. It had been added, like the state border closings, after *Makanza* hit as a way to control public movement.

Now, with six years passing without another outbreak, it seemed obsolete. However, it was one stipulation the MRRA refused to lift. Their argument being that tracking movement across state lines was harder at night. Therefore, nobody was allowed out of their homes during dark hours.

I headed out after my parents and waved a final goodbye. When they backed out and drove away, I let out a sigh of relief.

AS SOON AS I entered my apartment, I closed the door, leaned against it, and sank to the floor. I hadn't known what to expect on my first day, but utter exhaustion wasn't it. It was awful what I'd seen today. Totally and completely awful. I pictured Garrett and his desperate drawings, the Sisters' forlorn looks, Dorothy's catatonic state, and once again Davin. My stomach lurched.

"How'd the first day go?"

My head snapped up, and I almost shrieked.

Jeremy sat at the kitchen table.

"When did you get here?"

"A little while ago."

I sighed. All thoughts of Davin left my mind. "Thanks for warning me."

He shrugged and crossed his feet at his ankles before uncrossing them and then re-crossing them.

The movement made me smile. Somewhere in Jer's fourteenth year, he'd hit his big growth spurt. It was like a bean stock sprouted in him one morning and up and up he went. He still didn't seem used to his height or long limbs. I shook my head. What had happened to my *little* brother? For years, I'd been the older, wiser, and taller sister, but now, he towered over my five-six.

I stood and walked into my sparsely furnished living room.

The only furniture I owned was a couch, chair, coffee table, and standing lamp. A small TV hung on the wall. I flipped it on.

America News Network, or ANN, still ran coverage on the First Wave memorial, as I was sure they had all day. This year's memorial tribute was a big deal. Six years ago, when the Second Wave struck, a prominent scientist had predicted no one would be alive to see this day.

The Second Wave.

I hated thinking about that day. Up until six years ago, life had returned to some semblance of normalcy. Different, of course, from how life was before *Makanza*, but normal enough. At that time, no traces of *Makanza* had been reported in the U.S. in over two years.

We thought we were safe. We thought the worst was over.

I paused briefly, remembering the Second Wave. How quickly it hit. No warning, no signs of contamination anywhere, and then *wham*! The Second Wave proved just how vulnerable we still were. Somehow, against all odds, the virus cropped up again. It spread like wildfire despite state border closings. It was that outbreak which made the MRI's work so important. Finding a vaccine was critical. Sooner or later, another Wave could hit. Who knew how many would survive that one.

I shook my head. I hated thinking about the Second Wave. *Hated it.* Turning the TV off, I plopped on the couch.

"It's good to see you." Jer stood just at the edge of the room, leaning against the wall, watching me. I knew he was trying to judge my mood.

I nodded, slowly getting pulled from my stupor. Just his presence did that. "It's good to see you too."

"So? How'd the first day go?"

I sank deeper into the couch and thought of Davin. "It was awful."

He pushed away from the wall and sat beside me. "Really? What happened?"

I wished so badly that I could talk to him. "You know I can't tell you."

"Bad though, huh?"

I nodded.

He grinned. "Well, cheer up, you only worked six years to get into that place. No big deal if you quit."

I couldn't stop my smile. "You're right. What are a mere six years?"

"In dog years, it'd only be one."

I chuckled. "Jer, I think it's the other way around."

"Whatever, you know what I mean."

I met his gaze, feeling all of my stress and worry dissipate. "Yeah, I know exactly what you mean."

Jeremy left a few minutes later. He knew I had work to do. A departing gift from my meeting with Dr. Roberts was a pile of research papers to read. Although Jer could have stayed and watched TV, we both agreed TV wasn't what it used to be. It wasn't like when we were kids, when every season held a new program. Now, TV was mostly boring, old reruns. New shows appeared, but compared to how it used to be, they were minimal.

It didn't matter to me. The only shows I actually enjoyed were reruns from National Geographic. It depicted the world as it used to be, before *Makanza*, when people traveled around the globe, freely moving from country to country. I couldn't imagine what it would be like to see the pyramids of Giza, the Great Wall of China, or the Great Barrier Reef. Heck, even seeing the Statue of Liberty would be amazing. Our vagabond childhood hadn't held any sightseeing or vacations. It mostly included small towns throughout the Midwest as my dad moved us from city to city.

Once *Makanza* hit, that all stopped. My dad had been jobless for a while, until Cantaleve Steel hired him. Consequently, the extent of my childhood sightseeing had been Mount Rushmore and The Mall of America.

I sighed. Now, it was every country for itself with trade and travel cut off. Airlines and container ships were a thing of the past. Thank goodness for the Midwest. Without the bread basket, the U.S. would probably be heading in the same direction as Canada. Starving.

6 – STRAIN 11

I held my breath when I entered the Compound the next morning. I didn't know what I'd witness. Torture? Abuse? More drugged Kazzies?

Luckily, nothing like that happened. In fact, the rest of the week passed by uneventfully. We didn't go back into the Sanctum. I spent all of my time studying, listening, and reading. With each passing day, memories of Monday slipped away like a bad nightmare that vanished upon waking.

Throughout the week, if Amy wasn't giving me tours of the various places we worked, we were in an office. My lab work was on hold until I learned everything the MRI knew about *Makanza*.

I soon memorized all forty-one strains. It was mind-boggling what some of the Changes were. The latest one I read about was *Makanza* strain 18. Infected with that strain, a Kazzie's olfactory neurons multiplied. The amygdala, olfactory tubercle, hippocampus, and parahippocampal gyrus grew anywhere from 37% to 52%. In other words, their brains got a little bigger. However, their noses didn't change, but there were increased sensory pathways to the enlarged areas in the brain that processed smell. They also had increased blood flow. The internal and external carotid arteries and sphenopalatine artery usually enlarged by 10%.

The painful part about *that* Change? The skull enlarged. I had yet to learn of any Change that wasn't painful.

Amy's head popped into my open office door. "How's that reading going? Done yet?"

Research papers lay strewn across my desk. I hurried to organize them as she skipped in. They were all on Davin's strain, 11, but I'd finished them an hour ago. After that, I'd randomly chosen a paper on strain 18. "Yes, I'm done. I finished them a while ago so was reading up on strain 18."

"Ah, the bloodhounds." Amy winked.

"Yeah, they could be, couldn't they?"

Amy propped her hip on the desk corner. "Minnesota's got one of them. He can smell his researchers and identify them even if they haven't been in a room for over a week."

"No kidding?"

"Crazy, huh?" She motioned for me to stand. "Come on, let's go for a walk. I want to quiz you on Davin's strain." Since Davin was our Kazzie, most of our time involved studying his variation of the virus.

Standing, I straightened my suit. This one was pure black but had pants instead of a skirt. I knew I was the only researcher who wore business suits, but I needed to do something to appear older and more professional. My lack of crow's feet definitely didn't help.

We walked into the hall. "Hungry?" Amy asked.

"Starving."

"Let's grab the rail system to the cafeteria. You can tell me about Davin on the way."

This wasn't the first time Amy had quizzed me. She'd been doing it all week. Each time, she seemed amazed that I remembered everything she told me or that I'd read.

She only explained complex theories or research projects to me once, and watched to see if I'd remember and comprehend. I did. And she didn't explain the MRI's policies and procedures. Instead, she handed me the gigantic manual and told me to read it. I did, in two nights.

Again, an eidetic memory helped with that kind of stuff. I could recall a page of information if I closed my eyes and concentrated. It was the only way I had excelled in school so quickly. Luckily, it helped with orientation too.

"Right," she said as we rounded our first corner. "Fire away."

Amy also seemed to love my monologues, but I was used to it by now, so jumped in. "Strain 11 is completely internal, which is why Davin appears normal. It only targets skeletal muscle not cardiac or smooth muscle. In other words, his digestive tract works similarly to how it did before his Change, and his heart function hasn't changed much other than its ability to pump blood faster than most since Davin's muscles require higher amounts of oxygen."

"What about the physiology? How are his muscles different?"

"Strain 11 has given him superior tendon and ligament strength. Joint problems will probably never plague him, but the most interesting aspect I've read is how exceptional his muscle activity is. The virus changed Davin's neural pathways, creating more efficient synapses between his muscles and brain, which allows him to be a hundred times faster than uninfected humans. As for his strength, the majority comes from his ability to re-synthesize ATP at a superior level, allowing actin and myosin to maintain a strong binding state. This allows Davin to keep his muscles contracted for much longer than a normal human, and his body's ability to create little to no lactic acid is why he rarely grows tired. Amazingly, his muscles aren't damaged despite the excessive demands."

"Excellent!" Amy grinned.

We pushed open the door to the stairwell and jogged down. Our voices echoed in the concrete structure. "How are you feeling about everything so far? Are there any strains you feel the need to study further?"

I thought for a moment before replying. "No, I don't think so."

Amy cocked an eyebrow. "What does strain 7 do?"

"Allows a Kazzie's lungs to extract oxygen from water, essentially letting them breathe underwater."

"And strain 29?"

"Elongated arms and cupped hands, similar to an orangutan. A Kazzie with that strain can climb nearly any tree and swing from object to object."

"Strain 41?"

"They can see and produce different wavelengths. Radio waves and x-rays in addition to the color spectrum. Researchers working with them must wear lead to protect themselves in case their Kazzies choose to switch their vision."

"And strain 15?"

"Thin skin grows between their arms and latissimus dorsi muscles. When they extend their arms, it looks like they have bat wings. That, along with their bones turning hollow, allows them to fly. They essentially look half-man and half-bat, but like all Kazzies, their intellectual capacities and personalities haven't changed."

Amy raised an eyebrow. "I'm impressed. Perhaps you *are*

ready to move on." She turned a corner in the stairwell. "Since you have the strain basics down, we can move into the genetics stuff next week."

"Really?" I grinned.

"I thought you'd be excited about that."

I almost jumped in anticipation but contained myself. "Very."

"Good. Now, each MSRG group may study their Kazzie specifically, but every researcher in the MRI has one common goal: to figure out a way to keep the Kazzies' DNA stable enough to study at room temp. Until we can do that, we can't identify the genomes for each *Makanza* strain. Without that, a vaccine is unlikely and a cure, impossible."

"So how do we do that?" I pushed the door open and exited the stairwell onto the rail system's platform.

Amy frowned as a loud whir and rush of air surrounded us when the train pulled up. "We're hoping you can help us figure that out. So far, nobody's been able to."

AS MY SECOND week at the Compound began, I continued to slowly learn what my new job entailed. Most of our group's time was spent thinking, brainstorming, and formulating new ways to study *Makanza*. It was very different from everything I'd learned in grad school.

Normally, when studying DNA, we'd shred it up before putting it in a sequencer, and then we'd analyze it, looking for variations and mutations. With *Makanza*, that didn't work since it was so unstable outside of the body. We couldn't even do step one. It disintegrated before it was shred. That made it impossible to study with traditional DNA techniques. Essentially, we needed to create a completely new way to study DNA. It explained why researchers had been working on this project for years.

I bent over an old, decontaminated sample from Davin and peered into my microscope. His muscle fibers were truly fascinating.

Apple scented shampoo flooded my senses. I knew who it was before looking up.

"Did you see the memo Dr. Roberts just sent out?" Amy sidled up beside me at the lab bench.

"No, what'd it say?"

"Our lab's opening tomorrow, which means we'll be working with Davin again."

It felt like the wind got knocked out of me. "Our lab's opening… tomorrow?"

"Yep, no more hiking all the way down here."

Since it was Wednesday, it had been nine days since I'd seen Davin. Nine days. And tomorrow I'd potentially see him again, if Dr. Roberts decided we needed new samples.

It was only on my drive home, that it really sank in. I could see Davin tomorrow, except this time, I'd be working with him. Correction, I'd be working *on* him. And now, I'd truly be one of them. The MRI researchers that treated him like a lab rat. My shoulders tensed while the sun blazed through the windshield. It looked like a ball of fire.

7 – BACK TO THE SANCTUM

I went through my morning routine the next day exactly as I always did. I got up at six. I showered. Made coffee. Watched a bit of the morning show on America News Network. Tried to make breakfast, burned it, and ended up plugging my nose and forcing it down.

The drive to the Compound and the security process didn't take long. I was used to it now. After parking, I stepped out of my car and straightened my suit, pressing out the wrinkles. I hadn't worn it since my first day.

My footsteps paused mid-stride as I groaned. I'd worn the same thing when I saw Davin the first time. *What if he remembers?* As soon as I thought that, I rolled my eyes. *Like Davin would remember what you wore. Seriously, Meg, the guy has bigger things to worry about.*

Cool morning air flowed around me when I resumed walking across the parking lot. It smelled like rain. Private Williams, the admittance guard, waved good day to me after opening the exterior door. I awkwardly nodded in return.

Carol, our wing's receptionist, greeted me warmly at which

sweat popped up on my brow. I knew sooner or later I'd get comfortable with them and my anxiety would diminish, but they were still too new for that to happen anytime soon.

The first thing I did was stop at my office and drop off my bag. The lab below my window was dark, which meant neither Amy, Charlie, or Mitch were in yet. Pulling out my laptop, I sat at my desk and turned it on.

The screen lit up. I stared briefly at the wallpaper photo before pulling up my email. The photo was of Jer and me when we were kids. It was at a local, public swimming pool, about a year before *Makanza* hit. We were both draped over the side of the pool's concrete edge, our elbows nestled on the rim while our lower bodies floated in the water. Wet hair was plastered to our heads. Grins covered our faces. I'd been twelve, and Jer had been nine. Even at those awkward ages, we'd been inseparable.

My email popped up. Two new messages. One was the daily Compound email that circulated each morning. It told of any events or breakthroughs reported at the Compounds nationwide.

Compound 70 in Vermont had lost a Kazzie. It didn't go into details. Instead, it stated she passed away from natural causes. I didn't want to doubt that, but I did. Perhaps she'd been too unruly, like Davin, and during their attempts to subdue her, she'd died.

I stomped down that crazy thought. Surely nothing like that happened. I deleted the email before moving to the next. The second was from Dr. Roberts.

From: Roberts.Timothy@mri.gov
To: Forester.Meghan@mri.gov, Hess.Mitchell@mri.gov, Wang.Lin@mri.gov, McConnell.Amy@mri.gov

Cc:
Subject: meeting

We'll meet in the lab at 9:00 am before going to the Sanctum. Don't be late.

My breath stopped. So I *would* see Davin today.

I checked the clock. I still had an hour before I needed to be in the lab, but I stood anyway. If I didn't want to pace around my office, nervously wringing my hands while waiting for nine o'clock to roll around, I needed to work.

I WAS STANDING at my bench when a hand clamped onto my shoulder. I jumped and shrieked.

A chuckle escaped the culprit. "Forester, how's it going?" Mitch grinned.

The force of his greeting had made my knees buckle. I tried to straighten. He cringed and removed his hand. "Sorry, forgot you were so little."

I shook myself, but my heart still pounded from the surprise. "Um, I'm fine. How are you?"

"I'm good, you know, can't complain. Just livin' the dream." He moved his hand to his hip, causing his lab coat to drape open. His shirt today read, *There Are Three Kinds of People in this World, Those Who are Good at Math and Those Who Aren't.*

I smiled. It was hard to keep a straight face when I read Mitch's shirts. Last week he wore one that read, *A Walrus is Like a Vampire, but Awesome.* I had no idea where Mitch bought his attire, but wherever it was, it wasn't Empire Mall.

He peered over my shoulder. "What are you working on?"

I scooped my notes up. I'd been jotting down ideas about the Kazzie's DNA but wasn't ready to share them yet. "Not much."

He smirked. "I doubt that."

"Morning, Meghan and Mitch!"

Amy sauntered down the stairs into the lab. She waved at us as Charlie and Dr. Roberts followed behind her.

"Excuse me." I inched around Mitch.

Even though our group was small, my nerves still thrummed when we were all together. At times, it felt like the walls were closing in.

I breathed a little easier when a few feet separated me from Mitch's imposing hulk. Smiling tentatively, I approached Amy.

Her red curls were their usual unruly mess, but her green eyes were especially bright. "You ready for today?" Her eyes twinkled.

"I think so."

"Don't worry. You'll see what it's normally like. What you saw that first day is *not* how we usually do things."

Dr. Roberts, Charlie, and Mitch joined us. I took another step back, feeling my pulse leap.

"Let's go." Our boss turned briskly. In his usual fashion, there was no greeting.

The four of us followed him out of the lab. I barely noticed the blinding walls in the hallway and multiple security checks. I kept my folder stuffed under my arm, away from Mitch's prying eyes and thought about Davin to keep my mind off of how many bodies brushed next to me. I hadn't seen Davin in ten days. Hopefully, he hadn't been drugged and kept in the Experimental Room that entire time.

Just the thought of that made me shudder.

When we reached the Inner Sanctum, we filed into the first windowed hallway one by one. I peered tentatively into Garrett's cell, not sure what I'd see.

Garrett sat quietly. He wasn't drawing or painting. Instead, he sat as still as a statue on a small, wooden chair. His back was to us as he looked at something on the wall. I followed his gaze. There was nothing there except gray concrete.

"What's he looking at?" I whispered to Amy.

She shrugged. "No idea."

Garrett's head shifted, seeming to sense that we were there. He didn't acknowledge us. Just like my first day, he pretended we weren't there.

I inched closer to Amy and kept my voice quiet. "Does he always ignore us?"

"Usually."

"Why?"

Amy cocked her head. "Hmm, how do I put this… Most of the Kazzies, to be completely honest, don't seem to like us. Davin even hates us, but I think he's the only one who feels that strongly, so it's not unusual for them to ignore us when we walk by."

I frowned. "Why wouldn't they like us?"

"Because of what we do to them. We experiment on them, Meghan."

"Oh." I felt stupid. Of course, they didn't like us. I would probably feel the same if I were in their shoes.

We continued past Garrett's cell, all of us quiet, the only sounds were Dr. Roberts' loud stomps and the quiet *tap-tap* of the rest of our shoes.

The Sisters were both awake, sitting on one bed, much like they had been the first time. One of them stood when we came into view. Her blue skin stole my attention as a smile grew on her face. I knew it was Sara without looking at her wrist.

Sara approached the window, her eyes glued to mine the entire way. I swallowed as she got closer. She reached the window and held up one fine, blue hand. Just like she had the first day. Her fingers skimmed along the glass surface as we walked side by side. I didn't know why she was looking at me, but I smiled tentatively.

Her face bloomed in response.

"Forester!" Dr. Roberts barked.

I snapped my gaze away from her.

Dr. Roberts stood at the end of the hall, watching me. I felt guilty, like I'd been caught doing something wrong. I glanced back at Sara. Her eyes pleaded with me.

I knew Dr. Roberts was observing everything that went on between me and the twin.

"Forester, what the hell's going on?" Mitch stopped at my side, his head dipping lower.

"What do you mean?"

He nodded toward Sara. "*That.* The Sisters always ignore everybody."

"That's what Amy said."

"Exactly, so what's with you two acting like besties?"

"I dunno," I mumbled, and I didn't.

I felt Sara's eyes follow me as we sailed through the access point to the next cell. I rubbed my neck. A dull ache had started at the base of my skull. *Great, just what I need.*

Dorothy was still on her bed, not moving, when we walked by her cell. Ten days had passed since I'd seen her, yet she lay exactly as she had last week.

I moved closer to Amy. "Are they still starving her?"

"Yeah."

We continued to move deeper into the Sanctum. Sage was in his cell this time. His cell was similar to the others. Simple, sparsely furnished, only the barest necessities, so different for the entertainment facilities they were able to use before

Davin's troubles.

Sage sat on his bed. His back was propped against the headboard, his legs stretched out in front of him while his hands were entwined behind his head. The TV was on. He was watching an old rerun of *The Price is Right*.

The Canadian was a big man, probably the same size as Mitch. He stared at the screen, although I could swear he wasn't watching it. He didn't move, and he didn't look at us, but I got the feeling he was aware of us. I'd be willing to bet he could recite in what order we passed, or recall what each of us had been wearing. It was odd. There was no way I could prove that, but I got the feeling he didn't miss much.

The longer we walked by him, the more I wanted to stop and stare. I knew he had strain 27, which meant he could generate electricity. His skin was made of metal and myelin. The mixture was highly conductive. I tried to sneak subtle peeks, but his skin wasn't overtly different from this distance. From the pictures I'd seen in my readings, photos taken at close range showed Sage's skin looked almost reptilian. Maybe someday I'd get a better look.

"Have you seen Sage yet?" Mitch's deep voice rumbled close to my ear.

"No, not yet."

"He's my favorite. I wish we worked with him. The guy can power a light bulb with a finger."

"Which group has him?"

"The lab two doors west from us."

I peered closer as we walked, and Sage's face tightened. I took the hint that he didn't like being studied and hurried to follow the others.

Dr. Roberts, Amy, and Charlie were waiting for us in the next hall. They had stopped outside Victor's cell. My eyes widened once again. Victor sat at his desk, reading a book, his shoulders hunched over it. He wore jeans and a simple blue t-shirt. I couldn't see his face, but his hair was brown. Quite similar to my own hair color.

Since he'd also been in the Experimental Room my first day, this was the first time I'd seen him in person. Photos had prepared me for what he looked like, but his skin was so bright, the pictures hadn't done it justice. He was beautiful in a way, like a bright poinsettia, demanding attention. However, like the other Kazzies, he ignored us as we lined up in the hallway.

"Do you know what he's reading?" I asked Mitch.

"*Gone with the Wind.* He checked it out last week."

"*Gone with the Wind?*"

"He loves the classics. Prior to that, it was *Paradise Lost.* He's always checking something out from the library."

"I thought they were still in isolation?"

"They are." Mitch crossed his arms. "His guard probably got it for him."

"Let's keep moving!" Dr. Roberts turned and marched to the next door. Amy and Charlie followed. I hurried to catch up, Mitch right behind me.

Every now and then I got a whiff of Mitch's cologne as we moved through the halls. It smelled expensive, and I wondered where he got it. Since the Second Wave, it was harder and harder to come by luxury goods. Those had been the first things to go. Perfume, high-quality coffee, exotic spices, and other products I was too young to really remember, were things of the past. Mitch, however, seemed to know how to get around that. Between the t-shirts and cologne, he obviously knew where to buy things.

We approached the next access door, and my heart rate

increased with each step. Any minute now, I'd see Davin again. I wondered if he was okay and what had been done to him. Neither Amy nor I knew what happened to him after we'd left the Sanctum ten days ago. Only Dr. Roberts knew.

"You okay, Forester?" Mitch stood at my side, holding his palm up to the scanner.

I'm not sure if I answered him. My anxiety had returned full throttle.

When we walked into the hall, the rest of the group already stood lined up outside Davin's cell, facing him. My legs shook so badly.

When I finally stepped in front of the window, my breath stopped. Davin stood motionless in his room. *He looks okay!* Unharmed, healthy. I sighed audibly, smiling as my knees sagged in relief.

As if sensing my reaction, Davin's gaze snapped toward mine. Cold, blue eyes blazed through the glass. He had the bluest eyes I'd ever seen. They were as bright as sapphires.

I took a step back and wished I hadn't. I didn't know if it was something on the floor or just my shaky limbs. Whatever the case, my toe caught and I stumbled. Groping wildly, I tried to stop myself, but it was no use. My left foot caught on my leg and before I knew it...

I fell over.

8 - THE CHAIR

I couldn't believe I'd been worried about Davin noticing my suit. Compared to face planting, wearing the same clothes was trivial. I tried to stand and winced when my leg hurt.

"Jesus, Meghan, you okay?" Mitch knelt down.

"Um… yeah." My face had to be as red as Victor's.

I lay sprawled across the cold, concrete floor. The folder with my notes had flown from my grasp. Papers were everywhere, and my left knee stung. I hoped it wasn't bleeding. Regardless, that was the least of my worries as everyone rushed to my side.

Mitch cupped his hands under my armpits and practically hauled me to my feet, while Amy and Charlie collected all the papers. I brushed off my clothes. My cheeks blazed as I straightened my suit. The first time I'd seen Davin, I'd crouched to the floor, terrified I was going to die. Now, I'd fallen over. *He must think me the world's biggest idiot or klutz. Or most likely, both.*

After I'd brushed my skirt off for what felt like the hundredth time, I tried to subtly sneak a glance at him. That didn't go so well.

A smirk covered his face.

The heat bloomed hotter in my cheeks.

"Are you okay, Meghan?" Amy handed me my folder.

"That was quite the spill." Charlie seemed trying to suppress a grin.

I glared at him as I stuffed the folder under my arm.

"Do you want to clean that up?" Mitch asked, looking at my knee.

I shook my head tightly. "It's fine. Really, I'm fine."

"Dr. Forester, watch where you're going next time." Dr. Roberts' cold voice interrupted.

Our boss stood just off to the side, a few feet behind everyone. The blood drained from my cheeks. "I will. Sorry."

Dr. Roberts wheeled around and marched toward the watch room. I didn't dare look at Davin again. He was probably still smirking or maybe even laughing. I pushed through the group. Ignoring the sting in my knee, I tightened the folder under my arm.

The same guard from my first day was in the watch room. He looked similar to the rest in his military attire, although I guessed him to be middle-aged. His name badge read Sergeant Rose.

"I want to collect another sample today," Dr. Roberts told the guard. "An intramuscular one. The last few have changed too rapidly for us to analyze."

"Of course, sir." The guard swirled on his stool to the control panel. "Should I sedate him?"

Dr. Roberts cocked his head. "No, I want him awake."

I glanced at Amy. "Why aren't we sedating him?" I whispered.

She frowned. "An IM sample is only slightly invasive.

Maybe he wants to use a local anesthetic."

Dr. Roberts hit a button on the control panel and leaned over the microphone. "Davin, we want an intramuscular sample today. Are you going to comply?"

I bit my lip and looked toward the window. My eyes widened.

Davin stood only feet away. He must have materialized in one of his lightning-fast moves. He was directly on the other side of the glass, staring at all of us with such contempt, I could practically taste it.

Our gazes connected again, but his amused smirk was gone. Even though hatred etched his face, I was still struck by his attractiveness. His hair was raven black and curled slightly above his ears. Deep set, sapphire blue eyes shot condemnation. Despite that, they were the most beautiful eyes I'd ever seen.

As hard as I tried, I couldn't look away. There was something compelling about Davin that made me stare, similar to a beautiful piece of art that was intriguing and fascinating.

Mitch brushed against me. "You okay?"

My gaze fell to the floor, my cheeks heating again.

Dr. Roberts tapped his foot. "Well, Davin? What will it be? Are you going to comply?"

Davin shook his head. The movement made his dark hair fall across his forehead.

Dr. Roberts hissed. He snapped his finger off the mike. "Get out the Chair!"

The Chair?

Amy, Mitch, and Charlie tensed, and as if Davin had heard, he took off. He turned into a blur within the cell. It was only then I noticed he had a new bed, desk, and mattress. Everything that he'd destroyed the previous week had all been replaced, like his outburst never happened.

The guard's voice shook. "Sir, are you sure?"

"Of course, I'm sure!" Dr. Roberts yelled.

"Yes, sir." The guard's fingers flew across the controls while Davin dashed manically around his cell.

I nudged Amy, hoping she'd explain, but she shook her head. Pulling my folder tightly across my chest, my fingers dug into it.

Davin's movements were still too quick for me to see him clearly, but something in the middle of the floor caught my attention.

The floor cracked opened.

Something began to emerge, rising from beneath. It was obviously housed in secret chambers below. My eyes widened with every passing second. It felt like I was caught in a bad horror movie, just at the climax when the dumb blonde was chain-sawed.

A brief thought flittered through my mind. *My dad works for the Compounds. He helped build them. Does he know about these cells? Did he help design them?*

I shook those thoughts off as the metal chair rose to its full height. It looked like something out of a deranged psychopath's lab. Metal cuffs stood open on their hinges, draped across the metal slats that would hold down someone's limbs. A metal bar waited to clasp someone around the head… and neck.

Once it had risen to floor height, the floorboards sealed around it. Davin still flew around the room, barely stopping anywhere long enough for me to see him. Part of me waited for furniture to fly again.

It didn't.

I glanced at Dr. Roberts. He watched everything with a

satisfied smile.

"What are you going to do?" I asked.

Dr. Roberts' smile vanished. "What do you think, Dr. Forester? What do you suggest is the best way to collect an intramuscular sample from an unwilling Kazzie?"

I stood dumbstruck. *Davin doesn't have a choice?* Dr. Roberts was really going to make him get in that… *thing*?

Dr. Roberts pushed the button on the microphone again. "Davin, we can do this the hard way or the easy way, but you *will* get in that Chair."

Suddenly, Davin stopped. He stood just off to the right, almost out of view. Even though he'd been tearing around the room at breathtaking speeds, he didn't appear winded.

He balled his hands into tight fists. Sinewy muscle rippled in his forearms. "Make me."

It was the first time I'd heard him speak, or truly acknowledge us. The deep challenge echoed in the small room. My eyes darted to the ceiling where speakers hung in the corners.

Dr. Roberts smirked. "If you insist."

A compendious, silent exchange took place between the two men. It was as if each was inviting the other to a duel, even though we all knew who the victor would be. Davin didn't stand a chance against the Compound.

My stomach twisted as I watched Davin ready himself for whatever was to come, yet something deep inside me clenched in admiration. Despite everything that had been taken from him – his freedom, his dignity, any semblance of a normal human life – he still fought. That sudden realization dawned on me like being doused with a thousand gallons of water. Davin still fought. Fought for the only thing he had left.

His own free will.

"Can't we do this some other way?" I blurted.

My boss eyed me coolly. "Dr. Forester, I suggest you keep your mouth shut and learn a thing or two today."

I pressed my lips together, but my fingers curled tightly around my papers.

"Cuff him," Dr. Roberts said to the guard. "Now."

Sergeant Rose tensed and seemed reluctant to do his job. Regardless, he complied.

Panels opened from within the ceiling of Davin's cell, and long, snakelike protrusions emerged. They looked like metal cords, but they moved and twisted as easily as organic rubber bands. Open cuffs waited at their ends.

I could only guess their intent.

Davin's chest rose heavily before he took off, his movements once again a blur as the snakelike cuffs sprang into action. They followed his blurred movements but couldn't catch him.

"Damn, Kazzie!" Dr. Roberts hissed.

I internally cheered Davin on. Minutes passed as he whizzed around the room. No matter how quickly the cuffs moved and grabbed, they couldn't snare him.

"Electrify the room!" Dr. Roberts barked.

"Sir?" the guard replied.

"No!" Amy whispered.

Her barely audible exclamation dashed any hope I had for Davin's escape. Amy hung her head, closed her eyes, and crossed her arms tightly over her chest. Alarm bells warned within me. If Amy reacted that way, it must be bad.

I glanced at Mitch and Charlie. Charlie stood silently, staring into nothingness. I got the feeling he was in a world of his own, not really seeing what was going on around him. As for Mitch, he frowned and shook his head.

The guard lifted a plastic cover over another button. There were several buttons covered in plastic. I guessed that meant they were the worst ones.

"Are you sure, sir?" The guard's tone was pleading. He obviously didn't want to do what Dr. Roberts asked.

"Just do it!"

The guard's finger shook as it hovered over the button. He hesitated another moment before pushing it down.

What followed next happened too quickly for me to fully comprehend. Metal rods emerged from each side of the room. A millisecond of light flashed. A second after that, Davin stopped. The grim picture it revealed was not something I wanted to remember.

The electricity contorted his limbs into unnatural angles as he barely maintained a standing position. His head was thrown back, his mouth open in a silent cry. My brain registered all of that in the split second before the cuffs descended. Each snakelike, twisting metal contraption wrapped around Davin's wrists and ankles.

He didn't fight. He couldn't.

Forcing his limbs to bend, the cuffs lifted him off the ground. It must have been excruciatingly painful. Davin's entire body was stiff and contorted from the electricity, but the cords bent him onto the Chair. Tears pricked my eyes. I imagined the muscle fibers in his body breaking and snapping at the cruel angles the cuffs demanded.

Once Davin was in the Chair, the hinges closed over his legs, arms, head, and neck. I could barely watch as recognition filtered back into his face while the last clamp settled tightly against his throat. As soon as he was contained, the snakelike cuffs released him and pulled back into the ceiling. The panels in the corners closed over them, once again smooth.

Fully restrained by the cuffs, Davin couldn't move. A blank expression replaced the ferocious snarl that had been there only moments before.

Dr. Roberts put his hands on his hips and nodded curtly. "That's better. Now, about getting that sample…"

I didn't watch.

I couldn't.

Closing my eyes, I ducked my chin just the way Amy had. I understood her reaction now. Once again, a deep growing shock settled inside me over the horrors that happened within these walls. Nothing had changed from my first day. *Nothing.* This wasn't any better than what I'd seen before. It was worse. Much worse.

A part of me felt betrayed. I'd believed Amy when she'd told me I'd see what a normal day was like, but from what I'd seen, there were no normal days. Not back here. Only days full of torture and cruelty.

My fingers dug so tightly into my papers they crinkled and ripped. This wasn't what I'd signed up for. This was *not* what I'd spent the last six years working toward. I hadn't known what the Compounds did. If I had, I never would have dedicated my life to this.

9 - SEAN'S PUB

Just like he ordered the guard to remove intramuscular samples from Davin without anesthetic, Dr. Roberts ordered us to spend the rest of the day in the Inner Sanctum. Saying it was awful wouldn't do it justice. Watching the *drip-drip* of Davin's blood pool on the floor made my stomach roll. Davin, however, tightened his jaw and stared straight ahead. He didn't flinch when the machines cut into him.

Watching someone abused and subjected to blatantly barbaric practices ranked as one of the most disturbing and twisted things I'd ever witnessed. I could tell Amy, Charlie, and Mitch felt the same. They kept their eyes averted and stayed quiet. The guard seemed to feel similar. Sergeant Rose did as he was told, but the sideways, angered glances he gave my boss, portrayed feelings that went much deeper than one day's work.

When we finally, thankfully left the Sanctum, we bumped into a few researchers working with the Sisters on our way out. Normally, the introductions would have made me sweat like a glass of ice water on a hot summer day, but since I was still so sickened by what I'd seen, my usual response faded. I barely felt anything, much less nervousness, as I met a dozen others.

Only one researcher penetrated the fog blanketing my mind. She was a woman close to Amy's age. Her access badge stated her name was Geraldine Krause, but she introduced herself as Gerry. Her olive skin glowed in the bright hallway, accenting her dark hair and slanted eyes.

Gerry stood with us outside of the Sisters' cell, explaining the research currently being done on the twins. I stood by the windows, peering inside, wondering if Sara would approach me again.

She didn't.

Instead, she acted very differently to how she'd been only a few hours before. She didn't look at me or stand up. Instead, she sat on the bed with Sophie as each gripped the other's hand tightly. They looked like they'd been crying. My stomach sank. *Were they hurt too?*

It was late afternoon when we returned to our wing. My stomach grumbled, reminding me I hadn't eaten anything when we'd taken a short lunch break. But I couldn't eat, not then and not now. For the past few hours, only one thought had steadily crossed my mind.

I need to quit my job.

As agonizing as that was, I did not want to be a part of the Compound. Not at this cost. It was a sobering, heartbreaking realization. I'd dedicated the last six years of my life to obtaining a job with the MRI, and now, it was about to end.

When we reached our lab, Mitch and Charlie shuffled to their benches. I paused beside mine and let my long, brown hair cover the side of my face. It helped shield me as I bit my lip. I needed to send in my resignation. Now, it was just a matter of how.

"I need a drink," Amy exclaimed.

My head snapped up. "What?"

Amy twisted her hair into a ponytail. Her hands shook, and her skin looked paler than usual. "A drink, as in an alcoholic beverage."

"Oh, um…" I shook myself back to the present. "Won't that be hard to find?" Since the Second Wave, alcohol was almost nonexistent in the South Dakota Food Distribution Centers, and most of Sioux Falls' bars had closed. Those that stayed open weren't always reliably open.

"I know a place. It's kind of a well-kept secret. Want to join me?"

An image of Davin in the Chair flashed through my mind. His blood. His pain. *Drip-drip.* "Ah… sure," I replied shakily. I had no intention of working anymore today anyway.

"Great, let me grab my purse."

I glanced at the clock as Amy gathered her things. Dr. Roberts was still in the Sanctum, but I'd need to tell him my decision. I supposed I could always return after Amy and I finished our drinks. Or I could email tomorrow. It was the coward's way out, but at the moment, I didn't really care. I was about to dump six years of schooling and hard work down the drain. *Does it really matter how I quit?*

Amy appeared at my side again. "Let's go."

We didn't say anything to Charlie or Mitch. It was easy to sneak out without them noticing. Heavy rock music blasted from Mitch's CD player and muffled any sounds as we escaped out the door. Once we cleared security and exited the building, we both went to our individual cars.

"Do you know about Sean's Pub?" Amy called.

"No."

"Didn't think so. You better follow me."

I rolled down my window once on I-90. The windmills, our city's main power source, whirled in the distance. Warm air flowed around me, and autumn sunshine streamed overhead. A dip in the jet stream brought warm air from the south, making the day unseasonably pleasant.

It did little to warm me inside, however. I still felt like ice. Quitting would alleviate my guilt over being part of an institution that subjected people to torture, but it wouldn't help the Kazzies.

Their abuse would continue.

More than ever, my feet itched to move. I really needed to go for a run.

Amy exited on East Tenth Street and drove down to North Summit Avenue. She parked in front of a house in Sioux Falls' historic neighborhood. It was a large two-story with a red brick exterior. Flower boxes hung from the windows, and hydrangeas dotted the landscape. It looked occupied. The grass was cut, the windows intact. All of the surrounding historic homes were crumbling and neglected, obviously abandoned. I parked on the street behind her, trying to figure out why we were here. *Maybe this is Amy's home and she needs to grab something.*

Amy stepped out of her car and waited on the sidewalk. She waved for me to join her. Grabbing my purse, I got out.

"Deceiving, isn't it?" Amy crossed her arms.

"What is?" I slung my purse over my shoulder.

"This!" She waved at the house. "This is Sean's Pub."

"Seriously?"

She merely nodded and pulled me up the cracked concrete walkway, nervously chatting the entire way. "When my dad first took me here, I thought it was a joke. I pictured some little, old lady opening the door, but this place is legit. It's even legal. The guy who owns it is a family friend of ours. He bought this house a few years ago, fixed it up, and got a permit from the city to turn it into a pub. He's originally from Ireland and brews everything himself in the basement."

"How come I've never heard of it?" We climbed creaky, sagging porch steps.

"Sean doesn't advertise. Those of us that know about it, tend to keep it to ourselves. The beer's good and reasonably priced. If everyone knew that, this place would be busting at the seams."

There weren't any signs or hours listed in the window. Amy opened the door without knocking and stepped inside.

I followed her into an entryway and was greeted with the smell only found in old homes. It wasn't bad, just *old*.

Folk music played from further inside. I didn't recognize the tune. A dozen hooks and two coat trees cluttered the entryway.

I followed Amy into what was probably a living room and kitchen at one point but was now a large, quiet seating area and bar. The design was simple. Several stuffed chairs and couches circled a small, cold fireplace. Dining chairs and tables were scattered throughout. A long, mahogany bar ran the length of the back wall. Faded wallpaper was covered with a smattering of Irish décor. An old Irish flag hung next to us with a blackboard beside it. Chalked numbers on the board read, *183 days till St. Paddy's Day.*

I probably would have found the place charming if my mind wasn't so preoccupied with Davin and knowing my days at the Compound were over.

"Amy, my dear, it's good to see you, love!" An older gentleman with a bushy white mustache appeared through a door from a back room. He wiped his hands on a towel and positioned himself behind the bar. I guessed he'd once had black hair to go with his blue eyes. A dark Irish.

Amy ran a hand through her curls. "You too, Sean. This is my friend, Meghan."

Sean smiled as Amy and I settled on the bar stools. "Any friend of Amy's is a friend of mine." His soft accent lilted pleasantly.

I did my best to smile, but my anxiety cranked up a notch.

He slung the towel over his shoulder. "What can I get you girls?"

"Do you like beer?" Amy asked me.

"Um, sure." I didn't dare tell Amy I'd never had a beer in my life.

"Two lagers." Amy held up two fingers.

"Comin' right up." Sean pulled out chilled glasses from below. A moment later, the drinks sat in front of us. "You girls want to start a tab?"

Amy nodded. "Definitely."

Sean wiped down our part of the bar, set out coasters, and retreated to the far end.

Amy picked up her drink. "Bottoms up." A forced smile spread across her face before she took a long, deep swallow. I'd barely lifted my beer to my lips before she took another drink. After her third gulp, she set her glass down. "That's a little better."

I tentatively tasted the beer. Cool, frothy liquid flowed into my mouth. Surprisingly, it tasted good. I took another drink, a longer one this time, swallowing it in a large gulp. The beverage hit my empty stomach like a water balloon splattering on the sidewalk. I wasn't sure if that was a good thing or not.

We sat in silence. Each of us seemed lost in our own thoughts. I was about to take another drink when Amy blurted,

"Meghan, I'm sorry."

I set my drink down. "For what?"

Amy glanced at Sean. He remained at the end of the bar, but she lowered her voice anyway. "For today. Everything about today. It was awful what we saw this morning. And I promised that you'd see what it's normally like. You must think we're monsters." The quiet anguish in her voice was genuine.

A spark of hope shot through me. "So that *wasn't* normal?"

"No. I've never seen Dr. Roberts do anything like that. I mean, I knew about the Chair. He had them installed a few months ago, but before that, we never treated the Kazzies that badly. It's always been humane, mostly at least, up until now. Really, I swear."

"So the *Chair*," I could barely make myself utter the word, "that's *not* something that was used all of these years?"

She shook her head. "I've only seen it once before today, but Davin was never electrically shocked, or forced to get into it like that. The one other time I saw it used, he was tranquilized beforehand. He didn't know he was in it."

I grimaced. That didn't seem much better. *Since when is it okay to drug someone and do whatever you want with him?* Outside of the Compound, that would be illegal. "And that's okay with you?"

She looked down and fiddled with her fingers. "I know how it looks, the things we do, but remember what I said before. We've all had to accept a few things. It's the only way we might find a vaccine."

I paused, contemplating that. Amy didn't strike me as a sadist. Neither did Mitch nor Charlie. But nobody in the Stanford prison experiment thought they would abuse others either. People could do things they never imagined if they were put in the right circumstances. We all had a Mr. Hyde lurking in us somewhere, or so psychology had us believe. I wondered if I would become like the others if I stayed at the Compound. Passively watching the going-ons, not speaking up, even though it was wrong.

My stomach dropped. Passively watching and not speaking up is exactly what I'd done this morning. I stood by while Dr. Roberts took Davin's samples. Other than my initial question of doing it some other way, I'd kept my mouth shut, just like the others.

That realization made my stomach heave.

I'm no different than anyone else. My hand shook when I brought my beer to my lips. "But what happened today is not okay. No vaccine or cure is worth that."

Amy frowned and shrugged. "You might be right, but then I think about the millions of lives we could potentially save. Sometimes, I don't know anymore."

We were both quiet again, our beers slowly disappearing. A splinter stuck up in the bar. I picked at it, and finally asked something I'd been wondering all day. "Do you know why Dr. Roberts would torture Davin like that today, after all of the problems we've had with him lately? Wouldn't forcing him into the Chair and not giving him sedation only throw him into another rage?"

Amy shook her head. "Davin's usually pretty controlled. Dr. Roberts has done some awful things to him, but usually, Davin takes it. His rage last week was the first time I've seen him like that."

I picked at the splinter again as Davin's restrained form flashed through my mind. *Drip-drip.* I clenched my jaw. "All I wanted to do this morning was leave. I hated watching that."

"Yeah, we've all felt that way at times over the years. What we did to Davin this morning wasn't easy for me either."

I took another drink, thinking of the last six years. All of the hours and hours, countless hours, I'd spent studying and researching. I'd done it all for one reason: to join the MRI and stop the virus.

Something inside of me shattered.

I gasped it hit me so hard. It felt like my heart was dropped into liquid nitrogen and then thrown against a brick wall, breaking into a million, tiny shards. *What am I supposed to do with my life now?*

I gulped down another mouthful of beer and picked more fiercely at the splinter. *Without my job, what can I possibly do to help society? To stop the virus?* I muffled a hysterical laugh. In one morning, my life goal had been destroyed.

Even so, I couldn't return to the Compound. I wanted to think I wouldn't become like Amy, Mitch, and Charlie, grudgingly accepting the atrocities the Compound committed. That next time I'd stand up to Dr. Roberts, stop him, or at the very least make an attempt to. But considering how I'd acted this morning, I wasn't so sure I'd do that.

And I couldn't live with myself if I didn't.

My shoulders drooped, as the enormity of my decision sank in. Leaving truly was my only option. I cleared my throat and took a deep, shaky breath. "Amy, I have to tell you something. I'm not going back to the Compound. I can't. I'm going to quit."

Her eyes widened.

"I can't be a part of the things Dr. Roberts does to the Kazzies."

Amy just stared at me. She eventually nodded, but the surprise was still evident on her face. "Okay, I get it. I can only imagine what you think of us, but if it were up to me, treating Davin like that would never happen again."

"I know." I took another drink. My lager was already over half gone. "What about you? Are you going back?"

She hesitated a moment. "Yes. I have to. If we all left the Compounds, we'd potentially be dooming the human race to extinction."

"Even after what we did this morning? You still want to return?"

She was quiet again. Eventually, she nodded. "Yes, even after what we did. You've got to remember the good days in our job. They still outweigh the bad."

I frowned and gulped down another mouthful of beer. *Can I do that? Focus on the good and ignore the bad? Turn the other cheek, so to speak?*

No, I couldn't.

But then an idea came to me, and a spark of hope, so strong it took my breath away, coursed through me. "Why has nobody said anything to Dr. Roberts' boss? Somebody must oversee him, right? Couldn't his boss stop what he's doing?"

"Dr. Roberts' boss got promoted to a Director position at another Compound three months ago, which is why Dr. Roberts was promoted to head of all research at our Compound. At the moment, his only boss is the Compound Director, Dr. Sadowsky. He's the head honcho. But I don't know if Dr. Sadowsky even knows what goes on in the Sanctum. There's a lot of other stuff he deals with."

I sat up straighter, my words rushed. "Did anybody try reporting what was happening to Dr. Roberts' boss before he left?"

Amy nodded, averting her eyes. "A few people did, but they got demoted or moved to other positions in the Compound."

My mouth dropped as my shoulders slumped. I picked

angrily at the splinter again. "In other words, they were fired for speaking up."

"Something like that."

"But Dr. Sadowsky might not know? You said nobody's ever gone to him?"

"Not that I know of."

"So we could talk to him? Maybe he would stop what's being done?"

Amy frowned, an uneasy expression flitting across her features. "You could try, I suppose."

Her hesitation was as palpable as the splinter between my fingers, which made me wonder how bad the consequences were for the others who *had* spoken up. If Amy was hesitant, the problems at the Compound ran deeper than I'd initially thought. I picked the splinter aggressively, my mind going one hundred miles an hour.

Maybe quitting wasn't the answer. Maybe the best thing I could do was try to have Dr. Roberts demoted, even fired. Perhaps then the Kazzies would be treated humanely. *And if I get fired in the process, so what, right?* That wouldn't be any worse than quitting. Regardless, I'd still be out of a job, but at least then, I'd have tried.

"Maybe I won't quit," I murmured, more to myself than to her.

Amy nodded emphatically. "Exactly, don't quit. Think of all the good that could come from what we do. Think of what we could contribute, especially you, Meghan. You're so young and have so many years ahead of you. What if *you* found the vaccine?"

I took another drink as a second thought struck me. *If I find a vaccine, the Kazzies won't be locked up anymore.* A vaccine would stop Dr. Roberts for sure. That was another route I needed to contemplate. Since I didn't know Dr. Sadowsky, I didn't know how he'd react if I went to him with my concerns, *but* a vaccine was virtually a guarantee that the abuse would stop.

"You girls want another round?" Sean called.

I looked up sharply and immediately regretted it. The room spun. I was once again surprised at how much I'd drunk. My glass was empty.

"Yeah, bring us two more," Amy replied.

Sean refilled our drinks before returning to the end of the bar. He seemed to sense Amy and I wanted privacy.

I took another sip as my mind shifted to Davin, imagining him in the Chair. *Drip-drip.* Anger rekindled in my core, but with it, came a new sense of purpose.

Since Davin was a Kazzie, our research apparently had no limits. His 'Kazzie' label seemed to be all he was, but that could change. *I* could help make that happen. In a way, it was sadly ironic. In all the reading I'd done on Davin and his strain, there had been no information on him before he became infected. It was like his life hadn't started until he came to the Compound.

"How did Davin contract the virus?"

Amy looked up from her beer. Her second was already half gone. "Do you remember when *Makanza* hit South Dakota?"

"Yes." I remembered all right. Although it was something I did my best to forget.

"Do you remember where it hit first?"

"The reservations."

She nodded. "There's a reason he's so tan you know, even though he never gets outside."

My eyes widened as a memory came crashing back.

I WAS SITTING on the couch at my parents' house in Vermillion. I'd been seventeen at the time and was home alone. Jeremy was at a friend's house, my parents, at work. The TV blared, a rerun playing in the background as I studied calculus in the living room.

The *Makanza* alarm sounded outside. My hand stilled, my pencil hanging midair. I'd never forgotten that sound. When I'd been young, those sirens meant a tornado was close, but now, it meant something else.

It sounded shrilly, all around, as if I was in a sphere, the sound everywhere.

My eyes snapped first to the outside and then the TV. The rerun vanished, and our local news anchorwoman appeared. Her voice trembled as she sat at her desk and discussed how an outbreak had possibly erupted on the Cheyenne River Reservation.

I sat motionless, my heart pounding.

Makanza was supposed to have been wiped clean from the public, but her words spoke otherwise. Three Native Americans had reported to the local IHS hospital with symptoms.

My stomach sank. If they were having symptoms, that meant they'd been contagious for over two weeks. Who knew who else had been exposed.

I glanced out the window to the quiet street, anxiously watching for Jeremy and my parents to come home. If the alarm sounded, that meant everyone in the city had sixty minutes to return to their houses. After that, martial law would be in effect. We'd once again be prisoners in our home as we monitored ourselves for symptoms, isolating ourselves from our neighbors. The next four weeks would be crucial.

If we were still healthy in a month, we'd stay alive.

I CLOSED MY eyes. That's how it had all begun. The Second Wave. On the Cheyenne River Reservation.

"Are you okay?" Amy asked quietly.

"Um, yeah." I brought my beer shakily to my lips and took another drink.

"So you remember when they reported on Davin?"

"Yes." It had been weeks later, after *Makanza* truly reared its ugly head. Davin was the only Kazzie in Compound 26 who came from South Dakota, the only infected South Dakotan to survive the virus wildfire, which swept through the reservations first, wiping out an entire race of people, before sweeping throughout the state and region.

The Sioux Indians had been annihilated by the virus. All except one. I vaguely recalled a haggard, young man dragged out of Mobridge by MRRA workers. Even then, he'd fought. I shook my head.

Until now, I'd completely forgotten about him. Davin must have only been eighteen when he'd been admitted to the Compound. He was only twenty-four now.

I hastily took another drink and realized how alone Davin must feel. I'd always been an outsider, different from everyone else, but I still had family. Davin didn't. He had no one, and he was now doomed to a life of torture and isolation… simply because he'd survived.

"I can't believe I didn't realize that sooner," I said shakily.

Amy shrugged. "Yeah, I just assumed you knew who Davin was. It was all over the news back then."

I picked again at the scratch in the bar, remembering the details the news reported. Davin was only half Sioux. His father was Native American, but his mother was Caucasian. He'd been visiting the reservation, seeing family, when the outbreak occurred.

More details returned to me. He hadn't lived on Cheyenne River. Rapid City was his home. He had two brothers and two sisters. All of them had been together on the reservation when the outbreak happened.

I shook my head at the irony. If Davin hadn't been visiting the reservation at that time, if he'd chosen to postpone his trip until the following month, would he have contracted the virus?

"He's only half-Sioux," I stated.

"Yeah." Amy took another drink. "His mother was married to a guy in the tribe for about twenty years, but they divorced and his dad moved back to the rez. Davin grew up in Rapid City but would occasionally visit his father and relatives on the reservation after his parents split."

"And he had siblings," I added. "Two sisters and two brothers. They were all with him on the reservation when the outbreak occurred."

"Yes, they all died, along with his dad, but his mom's still alive. She lives in Rapid City."

My head shot up. "She does?"

"Yeah, she never contracted the virus since Davin and his siblings were quarantined on the reservation. She was at home throughout that period."

"Does she ever visit Davin? At the Compound?"

A frown briefly marred Amy's features. "No, never."

Of course. How stupid of me to even ask, but a part of me had hoped. Maybe, just maybe, they'd allow him that one, small gift. "What about contact with her? Do they keep in touch?"

"They used to." Amy turned on her stool to face me better. "Before Dr. Roberts was promoted, Davin was allowed to recite letters to a social worker. All of the Kazzies were. Of course, nothing they touch could ever be removed from their cells, but the social worker would listen and record letters while sitting in the watch room. Davin and his mom wrote weekly to one another."

"They used to allow *social workers* in the Compound?"

"Yeah, until Dr. Roberts took over. Things have really changed under his rule."

I sat quietly for a minute, processing everything. "How come none of this is in his file?"

Amy's brow furrowed. "Um, I don't know. I guess we didn't consider it relevant to the virus. Maybe we should add it in."

"We should. All of us should know where he comes from. It's important."

"You're right. It is."

I took another drink, my mind whizzing as I thought about all of the sources I would need to find to compile a more well-rounded record of Davin. Birth records, school records, community rosters, even tax returns. All of it would give us a broader understanding of why Davin was the way he was.

Maybe it would help us get through to him better. Maybe he'd *cooperate* more, as Dr. Roberts called it.

"Do you think we could allow social services back into the Compound?"

Amy shook her head, her red curls bouncing. "I doubt it. Dr. Roberts seemed to enjoy taking that privilege away."

"But is that standard practice? Do all of the other Compounds allow social workers? Maybe Dr. Roberts is breaking the rules?"

Amy frowned. "I honestly don't know. Beyond 26, I don't know much about how the other Compounds are run, but I'm assuming it's somewhat similar to ours. Even though state law dictates how each facility is individually governed, we all have to follow the federal guidelines. So, maybe?"

We sat in silence for a minute.

A warm, dizzying feeling swept through me. I looked down at my mostly empty second glass. *Am I intoxicated?* Crap. I didn't want to be drunk. I needed to think clearly right now, but since I'd never been drunk, I didn't actually know if that explained this feeling.

I finished my beer and ran my finger through the wet ring it left on the bar. My vision swam in and out of focus. *Yep, I must definitely be drunk.*

Another beer appeared in front of me. I looked up at Sean's retreating form. *Great, just what I need.*

I crossed my arms on the bar and rested my head on them, hoping the spinning feeling would stop. Another image of Davin flashed through my mind. I pictured him and Dr. Roberts staring at one another, the blatant animosity apparent to anyone. I lifted my head. "Why does Dr. Roberts hate Davin so much?"

Amy sighed. "I'm not sure, but I think it really pisses him off that Davin defies him. Davin doesn't submit like the others do. He never has."

Another dizzy feeling swept over me. I fought to stay focused. "So none of the others ever fight?"

Amy shook her head. "Not anymore. I guess Sage did initially, but that only lasted a few weeks. As you saw from today, it's much easier for them if they submit."

"Right," I muttered darkly.

"And if you haven't noticed, our boss doesn't like his orders being questioned. He's particularly hard on Davin because of his defiance."

"I've noticed." I took another deep breath and shakily brought my third beer to my lips.

I UNDERSTOOD NOW why some people drank as a way to cope with *Makanza*. It really did make the world disappear. When I woke the next morning, my head pounded like a drum beating to a bad techno song. Hard, loud, and steady.

But it didn't stop my mind from shifting to Davin and everything Amy and I talked about last night. Dr. Roberts was a cruel sadist, and Davin paid the price because of that.

But that could stop. If enough of us worked together, we could stop what was happening in the Compound.

My cell phone rang, getting a wince out of me. I picked it up, wondering if I had any acetaminophen in my apartment. Drugs were always hard to come by, even over-the-counter ones. Only a few pharmaceutical companies still functioned.

"Hello?" I croaked.

"Are you coming back?"

The voice sounded familiar. "Amy?"

"Yep. I'm driving to work right now. Are you coming in today? Do you want me to pick you up?"

I suddenly remembered *why* she thought I may not come in. I never told her my ultimate decision on quitting. "Oh."

"Meghan, I know yesterday was horrible, but please don't give up. Fight for the Kazzies. The sooner we find a vaccine, the sooner they'll go home."

She was right, but I'd never told her I wasn't giving up. My real work had only just begun.

"I'll be ready in twenty minutes."

10 – WAITING

I felt differently about work over the next few weeks. The horrors were still there, but my purpose for working had changed. I became focused and driven, just like I'd been in grad school for the past three years. We needed a vaccine and soon. Except now, it wasn't just the public I thought about. I wanted it for the people infected with *Makanza* too. It was the only thing that would set them free.

Working judiciously with Davin's samples helped. Holding a part of him anchored me to my new goal. It made leaving each night hard.

I'd make myself go home, only because working twelve to sixteen hours a day, five days a week, required routine sleep to maintain that kind of schedule. As annoying as it was, my mind wouldn't stay sharp if I got less than six hours in the sack each night.

My work ethic was something I'd adopted in grad school, so my body was used to the long hours. My co-workers, however, weren't. Charlie and Mitch joked that I made them feel old.

When five o'clock rolled around, they'd pack up and go home. However, their teasing slowly turned into begrudging smiles and grunts of admiration. With each day, as I got to know my group more, I became more and more comfortable. Consequently, my anxiety calmed to a slow, trickling stream, versus the raging river it had been on my first day.

"Are you almost done?" Amy asked. She plopped down on the stool beside me, crossed her arms on the lab bench and collapsed her head on top of them. "We've got to get something to eat. I'm starving. And coffee, I need coffee." She groaned, rubbing her eyes on her arms. "Thank God the latest coffee bean crops from Arizona have been good. Otherwise, I'd be passed out. I seriously don't know how you keep up these hours. I mean, I know I said I'd help in any way I could, but this is killing me. Too bad I don't have kids. Then I'd have an excuse to leave before nine every night."

I grimaced sympathetically. It was Friday afternoon. Amy had worked with me late until the end of each day. By the time we'd leave tonight, it would be an eighty hour work week. She'd told me this morning it was the most hours she'd ever worked in one week at the Compound.

"Just let me finish this, and then we can go to the cafeteria." I carefully put the specimens away. They'd need to incubate anyway, so it was probably a good time to have lunch. Besides, I felt a little guilty that I was to blame for the dark circles under Amy's eyes.

"Thank God," she mumbled. "I feel like I could fall asleep right here."

Amy yawned several times before we left our lab coats on the stools. Once out of the lab, we headed to the rail station and took the stairs at the end of our wing, disappearing into the subterranean levels. Other researchers waited on the rail system platform.

Among the researchers, I spotted a familiar face. Amy did too.

"Gerry!" Amy called, perking up.

The tall woman stood out amongst the men. Her olive skin and slanted eyes gave her an exotic look.

Gerry grinned broadly when she saw us. Walking over, she stuffed her hands in her lab coat and assessed us warmly. She looked similar from when we'd first met on that afternoon following that horrible morning in the Inner Sanctum. Tall and intimidating, yet there was a warmth about her.

Gerry gave Amy the once over. "Jeez, you look tired."

Amy groaned in response.

"And… it's Meghan, isn't it?" Gerry cocked her head.

Gerry's tone was friendly so I smiled tentatively. Regardless, my anxiety still cranked up a notch. I just wished everyone else would stop watching us.

"How's everything going in your lab?" Gerry asked.

"Pretty good." Amy yawned again. "We just started some new work on Davin's samples. How about you?"

"Same. We've spent most of the week in the Experimental Room. Sara and Sophie have been hooked up to the EEG almost continuously. It's fascinating. Did you know the other day we isolated the area in their brains where they communicate? Or at least we think we have…"

She trailed on. I was relieved to hear their group wasn't hurting the Sisters. The EEG was painless, just time consuming. It was probably excruciatingly boring for the twins but nothing worse.

I tapped my foot and wrapped my arms tightly around myself as we waited for the train. The people around us seemed to be closing in. Since Gerry, Amy, and I were all women, we made a unique group. Men still dominated most of the staff at the Compound. I'd never felt more aware of that than I did right now. They kept looking at us.

A whoosh of air swirled around the platform as the train pulled into the station. I exhaled in relief.

"Did you hear about the teleconference with Compounds 10 and 11 on Monday, Meghan?" Gerry asked.

I cocked my head. "What teleconference?"

"Didn't you see the email?" she asked as the train's doors slid open.

I shook my head. "No, I haven't checked my email since this morning."

We sat in the back of the train, at least three rows away from the next researcher. I relaxed into my chair.

"I didn't see it either." Amy propped her elbow against the window and leaned into it. "What's up?"

"Dr. Roberts emailed the memo an hour ago." Gerry angled her body to face us. "Apparently, 10 and 11, the Compounds in Washington state, have discovered something."

"Really?" Amy turned toward me. "Anytime a Compound makes a breakthrough, of any kind, there's a nationwide teleconference between all of the Compounds. Following that, we also do an international one."

The doors closed. With a soft shift in movement, we were off. "Do you know what discovery they've made?" I asked.

Gerry shook her head. "No, we'll find that out Monday, but I'm not surprised. Compounds 10 and 11 are making a lot of progress out in Washington. They run their facility very differently from ours."

I perked up. "How so?"

"For one, they allow visitors to see the Kazzies."

"They do?" My brow furrowed. "But how can they do

that? And keep things a secret?"

"Each Compound creates their own rules, which is fine as long as they're following the federal guidelines," Gerry explained. "A certain level of secrecy is always maintained, but Dr. Roberts has recently decided, here in our Compound, absolute secrecy is mandatory. Hence, why the Kazzies were cut off from their loved ones almost four months ago. However, some states are different. Washington is one of them. Dr. Hutchinson, the Director of Compounds 10 and 11, decided visitors were fine as long as their Kazzies didn't divulge any information about *Makanza*. Their visits are monitored, but they're still allowed."

Since Amy had slumped against the window with her eyes closed, I scooted closer to Gerry. "How do you know so much about Washington?"

"I spent a summer out there a few years ago, on an internship."

My eyes widened. "You spent a summer… in Washington? How did you do that?"

"Researchers can travel between the Compounds if it's granted by the federal office. I've spent a number of months at four different Compounds now. The last one I worked at was 46, down in Alabama. It was seventy degrees in the middle of winter. It was bliss."

I laughed at her expression.

Gerry smiled. "There's a lot they don't tell you in training."

My thoughts drifted to Compounds 10 and 11 as the train sped along. The research papers I'd read, coming from Dr. Hutchinson's Compounds, were more progressive than any others in the country. She was known for pushing the limits and trying new things. Her work was highly respected and distinguished. I'd give anything to meet her. Even if I stood tongue-tied in front of her, I'd love to be in her presence, just to see what she was like.

"I wonder what they've discovered."

Gerry flashed me another smile. "We'll find out Monday."

THE WEEKEND CAME quickly, but all that meant was that it would be two more days of waiting for the teleconference. More than anything, I wanted to know what Washington's Compounds had discovered. However, I had a lot of things to do to keep myself occupied. Everything had been neglected in my apartment since I'd started my job.

Piles of laundry sat in my room. My sheets hadn't been washed in weeks. Food-crusted dishes sat forgotten on the kitchen counter. My entire apartment was a mess.

I'd also grown lazy about grocery shopping so opted to kill a few hours doing that. Anything to procrastinate on cleaning.

First thing Saturday morning, I dressed and hopped in my car. The South Dakota Food Distribution Center was a ten-minute drive from my apartment. When I arrived, I grabbed a cart and perused each aisle in my usual fashion. Planning a grocery list or menu ahead of time was impossible since one never knew what would be available.

Distribution Centers were in every city throughout the country, but the selection was never guaranteed. Food was not something any state had in abundance. A lot of times, shelves were bare or the produce section was pathetically lacking. Given it was only the beginning of fall, we still had a fair amount of fresh fruits and vegetables. Come winter, that would change.

Even though I hadn't shopped in weeks, my weekly food allotment hadn't changed. I was allowed three staples, seven items from the carbohydrate shelves, three from the meat counter, two from the dairy section, six from the produce area, and one free item. The free item I could choose from any section in the store, and I always chose the same thing: coffee. Staples never changed, though. They were always flour, sugar, and salt. Everybody needed those.

The Compound's cafeterias were completely opposite from how most families lived. My eyes bulged every time Amy and I ate there. Not only were our meals free, but the selection was huge. There was a deli counter, a salad bar, two rows of hot items, and even a dessert bar. I felt guilty the first time I'd loaded my plate. Few were ever accepted into the MRI, but still, it didn't seem fair that we were treated like royalty while some families scraped by on their food allowance week after week.

I rounded a corner in the store, my cart squeaking. Scents of yeast filled the air. The bakery section was only two aisles over.

Stopping my cart, I assessed the selections. A young girl and a woman stood a few yards away. The woman's brow furrowed as she contemplated the options. However, the girl raced to a package on the third shelf. She held it up to her mom.

"Can we get this?" A large smile spread across her face.

From the shiny wrapper, I knew what it was. A true luxury. Cocoa powder.

The girl couldn't be older than five or six. Her dress looked like it had been handed down. She held up the small bag of cocoa. "Please, Mommy? Please? Can you make chocolate cake?"

Her mother frowned and squatted down, gently extracting the cocoa from her daughter's hands before placing it back on the shelf. "We don't have enough in our allowance. I'm sorry, sweetie."

The girl didn't argue. She just nodded and hung her head. I guessed this wasn't the first time she'd asked for something they couldn't buy. It definitely wouldn't be the last.

I waited until they left the aisle before putting my coffee back and grabbing the cocoa. At the checkout, I pointed out the woman and child to the cashier. "Can you give this to them?" I handed her the bag.

Dalia was working today. She was one of the only workers I'd grown comfortable talking to. I also knew she'd do as I asked and not keep the cocoa for herself. "Sure, Meghan."

As I left the store, guilt still pummeled me. Images of that little girl filled my thoughts.

Maybe I won't pile my plate quite so high this week in the cafeteria.

I checked my watch. It was only mid-afternoon. In other words, there was still a day and a half until the conference. I sighed. More than anything I wanted to know what Compounds 10 and 11 had discovered.

11 – CONFERENCE

When Monday morning finally rolled around, I bounded out of bed before my alarm went off. The teleconference was here. By the end of the day, I'd know what Compounds 10 and 11 had discovered. With any luck, we'd be closer to a vaccine, which meant the Kazzies would be closer to freedom.

A dusky sky shone overhead when I pulled into my parking spot. I'd put a jacket on before leaving my apartment. The warm spell over the weekend had disappeared. Since it was the end of September, the nights had grown colder. The temperature hovered just above forty when the sun crested the horizon.

Private Williams was his usual polite self when he admitted me, and Carol nodded a hello when I passed. I managed a smile for both of them.

I first went to my office to check my email. The lab below my window was dark. It seemed everyone was in the same mindset. Conference first, work later. My laptop popped to life, the screen harshly bright in the dark room. I didn't bother to turn on the overhead fluorescents since I didn't intend to stay.

The usual morning note from the MRI popped up at the top. I skimmed past that and pulled up Dr. Roberts' email.

> *From: Roberts.Timothy@mri.gov*
> *To:MRI.list.geneticresearchgroup@mri.gov;*
> *MRI.list.biomedicalresearchgroup@mri.gov*
> *Cc:*
> *Subject: Conference*
>
> *The conference will be Monday morning in the auditorium in Unit B, second level. Start time 0800.*

Unit B, second level. That was a good fifteen to sixteen minute walk from my office. It was almost 7:30. The rail system would get me there fastest. I shut down my computer without bothering to check the other emails. The lid *snapped* when I closed it before I hurried out.

I caught the train, wind from the tunnel blowing long strands of brown hair around my shoulders. When I stepped onto the platform in Unit B, three men were ahead of me. I followed them up the stairs from the subterranean levels. Since everyone was invited, I knew we were all going to the same place.

One of the researchers glanced at his colleagues as his hand trailed along the stair railing. "I lived in Washington a few years back, on an internship. It's very different there. Their Director is known for being a bit radical."

"Who's presenting today?" another asked. "Do you know?"

The first guy shook his head. "Could be Martins or Zheng. They run the two research groups. Or if it's big enough news, it could be the Director, Dr. Hutchinson."

On the second level, I followed the men down the hall. Groups of people already flowed into the conference room. Scents of coffee and breakfast foods from inside the auditorium wafted out.

I stood in line and looked for Amy. We hadn't coordinated a meeting point, but I guessed I'd sit with her, Mitch, and Charlie. For the first time in my life, I was part of a team that I actually felt like I belonged to.

But when I entered the auditorium, I faltered. The room was huge.

The dim auditorium held a large projection screen hanging above the stage. Several workers hurried around the front, getting things ready. Hundreds of researchers filled the space.

My pulse leaped. *Calm down, Meg. Just find Amy and take a seat.*

I searched for Amy, my palms growing damper with every second. Since I didn't spot any red curls, I looked for a seat instead. My wandering gaze stopped when I saw the tables of food and beverages in the back. Everyone was going there first, helping themselves to generous portions of the catered breakfast. Mouthwatering scents drifted my way. I remembered my resolve to not be so glutinous and walked cautiously back to take a closer look.

"Meghan!" a voice called. "There you are!"

Amy pushed her way through a group clustered in the aisle, Mitch and Charlie on her heels. "We've been looking all over for you." She stopped when she reached my side. "I waited outside the lab for you, but you never showed."

A flush crept over my cheeks. I hadn't considered she'd wait for me. "Oh, sorry. I should have thought to go there first."

She shrugged, looking bright and alert. I guessed she'd spent her weekend sleeping in. "No worries. Should we grab some food?"

"Sure." I glanced at Mitch and Charlie. "Good morning."

Mitch grinned. "Morning, Meg." His t-shirt read – *If at first you don't succeed, don't try skydiving.*

I bit back a smile.

"Hey, Meghan." Charlie waved. "Have a good weekend?"

"Yes, you?"

"Well, I wasn't here, so can't complain."

I laughed softly.

We all walked toward the back. The buffet was loaded with food. Eggs, bacon, sausages, pancakes, waffles, fresh fruit, muffins, donuts. The list went on. There was so much food, it easily could have fed my entire apartment building ten times over. I swallowed as I remembered the promise to myself.

I stared at everything, my stomach grumbling. Ignoring it, I scooped a small portion of eggs and a few orange wedges onto my plate. My mouth watered at the sight of fresh oranges. *When did I last have these?*

"That's all you're taking?" Amy eyed my plate.

I shrugged. "I'm not that hungry."

She raised an eyebrow when my stomach grumbled again.

Carrying our plates, we hurried to the front. The other three had left their lab coats and bags in four seats, effectively reserving them. Mitch removed his coat from one and waved for me to sit. I settled between him and Amy.

Amy started chatting. I smiled a few times when she said something funny, but for the most part, I was too distracted to listen. The oranges were partly to blame. The sweet juice coating my tongue created a joy in me that was hard to describe. Until one lived without certain things in life, it was so easy to take them for granted. I remembered having orange juice every morning when I was a kid, never thinking anything of it.

Now, I knew better.

I finished my small meal just as the lights dimmed. A hushed silence fell over the crowd. Pale light gleamed from the sconces lining the auditorium's walls. Above, the projector's stream glowed like a tunnel. Everything else was dark. I checked my watch. 8:00. *Right on time.*

Mitch continued to eat his toast, the *crunch, crunch* amplified a thousand times in the quiet room. Amy gave him a pointed frown when Dr. Roberts appeared on stage. Our boss' clomping steps echoed as he marched toward the center. He stopped when he reached the middle.

"Good morning." His booming voice echoed in the enclosed space. He didn't need a microphone. "We're connecting with Washington's Compound now. When the conference is finished, report back to your labs." He turned a sharp ninety degrees and marched off. A hum of conversation bubbled up in the room.

A moment later, a picture flashed on the screen showing a woman sitting behind a desk. The projector was as high quality as the city's movie theatre. The woman's complexion was completely smooth, no pixels present. She didn't look old, maybe in her late forties. Short blond hair was tucked behind her ears, and thick, dark-rimmed glasses adorned her eyes. Her demeanor seemed casual yet confident. Serene yet steely.

It was Dr. Hutchinson.

"Good morning, Compounds," she began. "I hope this morning finds everyone well. We want to thank all of you for joining us today. It has been a truly exciting time here at Compounds 10 and 11."

I didn't realize I was sitting forward in my seat, an eager smile on my face until Mitch chuckled.

"Careful Forester, you might fall off your chair," he whispered.

A flush crept over me. He chuckled again, but I didn't care. I'd been waiting for this moment since I'd heard about the breakthrough.

A presentation slide filled the screen. Dr. Hutchinson started by reviewing the latest research and the most recent discoveries. From there, she moved onto what they'd found.

"As you all know, despite our efforts with the deep freezes, and keeping conditions uniform, *Makanza* still disintegrates too rapidly outside of a host. However, we think we may have discovered a way around that."

Murmured whispers erupted.

"Quiet!" Dr. Roberts barked from the back.

The room stilled. Dr. Hutchinson carried on, oblivious to the reaction in our Compound, and I was sure, every Compound nationwide.

"As you all know, we've spent years trying to find a way to stabilize the virus so that a weakened version can be used in a vaccine. All attempts have proven unsuccessful. However, no one has ever tried stabilizing the virus *before* samples were taken."

Before? My brow furrowed as I leaned forward once more.

"Some of you may have heard of mind-body genomics, a relatively new field. Research has shown how emotions can affect telomeres. As you all know, telomeres act as protective caps for DNA strands. The longer the telomere, the longer a cell can survive. Mind-Body Genomics has shown that telomeres respond to behavioral and emotional cues. Negative environments, chronic stress, mental unwellness, and an entire host of psychological effectors can shorten telomere length. Whereas, stress-reducing environments and mental wellbeing can maintain telomere lengths. So we began experimenting. We started taking samples in different scenarios. We removed samples from Kazzies infected with *Makanza* in various conditions. We always asked those infected for their permission to remove a sample. If they said no, we didn't. However, if they said yes, we varied the collection process. We placed them in cold rooms, hot rooms, peaceful atmospheres, chaotic atmospheres, awake, asleep, while they were happy, sad…" Her voice trailed off. "We varied the collection process as much as we could, and what we've discovered is astounding. The samples taken from willing participants in peaceful atmospheres, in which they rated their happiness as high, have remained stable longer than any samples we've previously collected. Stable enough to study at room temperature for twenty minutes."

A commotion erupted in the room.

"No way…" Charlie murmured.

Mitch dropped his toast on his plate. "Even for twenty minutes, that's huge."

"If we can get the samples to last longer, a vaccine *is* possible," Amy exclaimed excitedly.

I gripped the armrest of my chair so hard my knuckles turned white. A grin spread across my face. Samples collected from happy Kazzies, willingly given. *Who would have thought that would make a difference?*

Everything Dr. Hutchinson proposed was so opposite from everything done at our Compound. So different from how Dr. Roberts operated our labs. My mind shifted to Davin. The Chair. The absolute anger and despair I sensed in him and the other Kazzies imprisoned in our facility. *Is it possible that will change? That their treatment will improve now that we have proof it's necessary?*

Dr. Hutchinson kept talking, detailing the specifics of their research. I listened to each word, while my mind leaped to the future, envisioning all of the changes that could take place. With a guaranteed vaccine, the Kazzies would no longer be a threat to others. They could be free. And without the fear of a Third Wave, society might return to the way it used to be. The borders could reopen. We could become a global community again.

I knew it was a long shot, that there was still so much work to do, possibly years of work. But for the first time since I began my job with the MRI, I felt something I'd never felt before.

Hope.

12 – CHANGES

The conference finished an hour later. The four of us hurried back to our lab.

"Can you believe this?" Amy chatted beside me as we raced down the hall. "Mind-body genomics? I've heard of it but always thought it more voodoo than actual science."

"Don't knock voodoo." Charlie pushed through a door as a draft hit us from one of the large vents. "I happen to be a big believer in playing with dolls."

Mitch chuckled as I bit back a smile.

We all stopped at the next access door and waited to be scanned. From the curious look the guard gave us, I felt fairly certain it was the first time he'd ever encountered giddy researchers.

The elated high coursing through me seemed to also be coursing through my colleagues. I could feel the hopeful energy bubbling around us when we entered our lab.

Study the Kazzies in positive environments. Stabilize the virus before *it's removed.* I shook my head. *Who would have thought?*

Dr. Roberts was nowhere to be found as we all moved to

our lab stations. I wasn't surprised. He and the other department heads were probably convening. The proposed new research techniques would require significant changes in our facility.

Mitch cranked up his stereo until heavy rock music blasted around us. I couldn't help but grin.

Things are going to change!

It was hard to concentrate for the rest of the day. My mind buzzed with the conference. The same thought kept running round and round inside my mind, like a hamster running on a wheel. Stabilize the virus *before* we removed it. It seemed so absurd, yet at the same time, so simple. I felt sure I wasn't the only one kicking myself for not thinking of it.

Toward the end of the day, Dr. Roberts finally made an appearance. Mitch shut off the music as soon as our boss entered the lab. From Dr. Roberts' dark expression, I guessed whatever he had to tell us, it wasn't good.

My hand stilled mid-air over the test tubes I was dropping solutions into. I set my supplies down and snapped my gloves off. A pit formed in my stomach.

After all of us had gathered around our boss, Dr. Roberts put his hands on his hips. "I know you all heard from the conference what Dr. Hutchinson proposes we do."

We all nodded.

Dr. Roberts scowled. "Dr. Sadowsky has outlined a few changes as a result of what's been learned."

I swallowed audibly. Dr. Sadowsky. The Director of Compound 26. Dr. Roberts' boss.

"Dr. Sadowsky wants us applying the techniques done at Compounds 10 and 11, with one added change." Dr. Roberts clenched his teeth. It looked like it pained him to continue. "One person from each group will be entering the cells to work with their Kazzie directly. We wish to see whether close contact has a measurable effect on the virus when samples are taken."

"What?" Amy's head snapped back causing her curls to shift. "Go *in* the cells?"

"Yes. Those are direct orders from Dr. Sadowsky." Dr. Roberts seethed. "He wants to see if we can obtain more productive results than Compounds 10 and 11."

Mitch shoved his hands in his pockets, a frown on his face. "That's extremely dangerous. The risk for exposure to the virus increases dramatically out of a controlled environment. The Kazzie's cells are completely contaminated."

"I'm quite aware of that," Dr. Roberts replied dryly.

"So why risk that?" Mitch persisted.

"Let's just say that Dr. Hutchinson's discovery has caused some sparks of competition in our Director."

I'd never met Dr. Sadowsky. However, I imagined it wasn't a laid-back personality that had earned him the most coveted position in our Compound.

"So who's going in?" Charlie asked.

"And how do we know Davin won't attack him… or her?" Mitch added.

Dr. Roberts took a deep breath. "We'll confine Davin to the Chair, and I've decided Dr. Forester will go in."

My eyes widened. "Me?"

"Meghan?" Amy said at the same time.

Dr. Roberts nodded. "Yes. Dr. Forester will be the designated researcher conducting the experiments for your group."

My heart pounded. "Why me?"

"Dr. Sadowsky feels that females will be best for this project, since overall, women are seen as less threatening than men."

Amy guffawed. "If that's not sexist, I don't know what is."

No kidding.

"Despite your opinions on this." Dr. Roberts gave Amy a sharp glare. "Those are my orders."

"But why *Meghan?"* Mitch put his hands on his hips. "She's the newest one here. Shouldn't it be Amy?"

Dr. Roberts' tone dropped. "Are you questioning my orders?"

Mitch's nostrils flared. "Perhaps."

As nervous as I felt, I almost pointed out the irony of the situation. Dr. Sadowsky felt women might make the Kazzies more comfortable. Considering the hostile amount of testosterone flowing between Mitch and Dr. Roberts, I had to admit, he had a point.

"So when does this all start?" I shuffled my feet while wringing my hands. "When do I go in?"

"Tomorrow."

THAT ONE, LITTLE word left me reeling. Tomorrow I'd be going into a cell. With Davin. Just the two of us. The thought was enough to make me sick.

At home that night, I tried to block the memories of the first time I'd seen Davin, when he'd been in a rage, throwing everything. The blindingly fast crash of his chair, the splintering of his bed frame. Everything had cracked or broke the moment it made contact with the wall or ceiling. Thinking about that was bad enough, but knowing he was powerful enough to make the glass vibrate every time he'd launched *himself* against it…

That made me grow cold.

Davin was so powerful, and he *hated* me. He hated

everything about the Compound and every researcher in it. I wondered what he would do if he wasn't restrained. As much as the Chair repulsed me, I was suddenly thankful for it.

Since I needed to be fresh and alert for the next day, I made myself go to bed early. That backfired. I had a fitful night's sleep. Perhaps it was the smoky air floating in through my open bedroom window. A few neighbors, in the houses surrounding my apartment building, had fires going. The wood smoke was heavy and sweet. It settled around me as I tried to doze off.

Normally, I liked the coolness autumn brought, but the sickly, fiery smell was like sticky tentacles wrapping themselves around me, forcing me to plug my nose and cover my head. I eventually gave up and closed the window. It did little to help. The smell and frigidness hung in the air, refusing to dissipate.

Once I finally fell asleep, I tossed and turned. Vivid, haunting dreams of Davin and the Chair plagued me. In each of them, he broke free from his restraints and launched himself at me, wrapping his impossibly large, incredibly powerful hands around my throat, my biohazard suit nowhere to be seen.

Each time I woke, I was gripping my shirt and gasping for breath. *How is it possible for another human to hate like he does?* His rage consumed him in my dreams, making him barely human.

WHEN I WALKED across the Compound's parking lot the next morning, I took deep gulping breaths of fresh air. Nothing but beautifully empty air, lacking any distinct taste or smell surrounded me. The next time I'd smell that, it would be the end of the day.

I hoped I would still be alive to enjoy it.

The first place I stopped was my office. I checked my

email, dropped off my bag, and did all the normal things I did every morning. An email appeared on the computer screen. It was from Dr. Roberts. He reminded all of the chosen researchers, that had been handpicked to study their Kazzies, that they were expected to enter their Kazzie's cell first thing this morning.

They're definitely not wasting time.

I snapped my laptop closed and paced my office. *You can do this. You know what you need to do. Just do it!*

But as soon as I left my office, moving deeper into the Compound toward my lab, that confidence disappeared. It was like I was no longer there. My mind didn't feel connected to my body. Like a part of me trailed behind myself, watching my movements from above, completely disconnecting from what was about to happen.

Everyone convened in our lab. Amy came to my side as soon as she saw me. "Are you doing okay?"

I just stared at her.

She tried to smile. "It'll be fine. You've been through training. You're perfect at following procedures, and the guard will double check everything. It'll be okay. Really."

Even Mitch's joking demeanor failed him. For the first time since I'd met him, he didn't have a comical t-shirt on. Instead, it was plain black.

How fitting. They're already preparing for my funeral.

From there, the four of us marched to the Inner Sanctum. Amy chatted nervously the entire way. I had no idea what she said. Her voice was like a hum in my ears, the words and sentences stringing together into a never-ending tone of nothingness.

The nerves fluttering through me made it impossible to comprehend what was going on. I barely noticed the other

Kazzies as we passed them. I briefly registered Sara's reaction. She stood again when she saw me, a sad smile on her face. A strange thrum filled my head, but I was too distracted to pay much attention to it.

Davin was already in the Chair when we entered his hall. I didn't want to know how he'd been put in it. Guessing it had probably been done similar to how it had happened before, I couldn't meet his gaze. I was too afraid of what I'd see. Afraid of that rage, that hate. Soon, all of those emotions would be directed solely at me.

Before I knew it, Sergeant Rose ushered me into the pressurized containment room attached to the watch room. The door opened with the familiar hiss of all the doors in Compound 26. I wondered whose job that was, to make sure all of the doors sealed properly and never leaked.

Someone has that job.

With the guard's help, I slipped into the biohazard suit. At least I'd had the foresight to wear pants and not a skirt. After I secured my hood and turned on the respirator, a rush of air entered the suit. It blew softly against my ear, blowing a few loose tendrils around my cheek. The guard helped me through the remaining safety checks. One mishap and my suit wouldn't be airtight.

If this suit fails, I'll surely die.

That realization crashed upon me like a baseball shattering through a glass window.

It became real what I was doing which forced me to focus. At least it squashed my other worry. The worry that I would enter Davin's cell, tongue-tied, and not be able to do my job. Again, I didn't understand why Dr. Roberts chose me. I was the least socially apt in our group. *Has he not picked up on that?*

I took a deep breath and pushed that thought away. Right

now, I needed to concentrate on one thing and one thing only.

Survival.

With the safety checks complete, Sergeant Rose gave me a reassuring smile. His kind brown eyes softened before he squeezed my gloved hand and exited the containment room. The door separating us sealed behind him like the lid closing on a coffin. I stood alone in the small, white chamber with nothing but my breathing and pounding heart for company.

A moment later, Sergeant Rose's voice sounded in my hood. His words rang loud and clear through the earbud. "Test, test. Can you hear me?"

"Yes." I fiddled with the volume and turned it down.

"Are you ready?"

Ready? Is that a rhetorical question? "I guess so."

"On my mark. Five… four… three…"

The green light still shone above the door.

"…two …one."

An alarm sounded. Red light replaced the green.

Red.

The universal color of danger.

The color of warning.

The color of blood.

For a second, I froze. On the inside, I was slamming myself into the door, even though it hadn't opened yet. Just having that seal broken was enough to make me panic.

Makanza particles covered every surface in Davin's cell. Right now, some virons were creeping their way into this room, like warriors stealthily inching across the battle line, ready to attack given the slightest opportunity. Never had I been in a situation like this. Not the lab, not the deep freeze, certainly not at school. In none of those situations was I out of control in my environment. Now, I would be the visitor in a cell controlled by *Makanza*.

"Are you okay?" Sergeant Rose asked.

I knew my suit conveyed my vitals to him. I could only imagine what my heart rate read. "Yeah." I took a deep breath. "I'm fine."

"I'm opening the door now. Are you sure you're ready?"

I forced myself to nod. "Yes."

The door hissed as six-inches of solid steel swung outwards. I waited until it was completely open, but I still didn't move. *Am I really only a few steps from Davin's cell? Is there really nothing between him and me but my suit?*

With a deep breath, I stepped forward.

13 – GOING IN

I didn't know what I expected. Maybe some change in the air color or a subtle difference in the cell's interior. Something that alerted me to *Makanza's* contamination on every surface.

Of course, nothing like that happened.

After I was completely in Davin's cell, the door swung closed. I faintly heard the hiss as it sealed. I turned and watched the decontamination process through the window. Dials inside the room turned as a mist sprayed from all angles and coated every millimeter of every surface. The purifying process didn't take long. A minute later, the light above flashed green. Any potential particles of *Makanza* that had entered the room in those few, short moments, were gone.

I knew Davin was in the Chair, but I still hadn't looked at him. I couldn't. I needed to compose myself and get my lines rehearsed one last time. As I internally stated my introduction, I studied Davin's cell.

The furniture was intact. I took that as a good sign. I searched the back of his room. A toilet sat discreetly in the far corner behind a half wall. A single shower stood beside it. *So that's how they bathe.*

My entire lab group and Sergeant Rose watched me through the window. My gaze met Amy's but then a flash of movement caught my attention.

Dr. Roberts stepped into the watch room. He crossed his arms and positioned himself close to the glass. It was impossible to read his expression.

I briefly realized an observing audience was what Davin lived with day in and day out. His life was forever on display. My gaze traveled to the hall with its floor to ceiling windows. I balked. His life truly was lived under *complete* exposure.

After I'd looked everywhere but at Davin, I knew I couldn't put it off any longer.

Finally, I turned toward him.

He came into view, millimeter by millimeter in the hood's viewing shield, like a slow-moving assembly line of inanimate body parts.

He sat calmly in the Chair, his relaxed posture in complete contradiction to the metal bands secured around his chest and limbs. His blue irises blazed. He had such beautiful eyes.

In fact, his entire face was striking. High cheekbones, a proud straight nose, deep set eyes, firm lips, that smooth skin a mixed shade of honey and fire. Beautiful. Truly, he was, but his look held such contempt. It distorted his natural beauty.

Absolute hate filled his gaze. I could almost *feel* the hatred emanating off him.

Sweat trickled past my ear. I suddenly felt very hot.

Davin obviously had no intention of breaking the ice. We stood looking at one another for a full minute, maybe longer, and then Dr. Roberts practically burst my eardrum. "What the hell are you doing, Dr. Forester?"

I jumped when his barking voice filled my earbud.

In the watch room, my boss stood with his hands on his hips, a scowl on his face.

Amy stood by his side, slowly nibbling fingernail after fingernail off all of her fingers, while Mitch and Charlie stood with their arms crossed over their chests, worried expressions on their faces.

"Get on with it, Dr. Forester," Dr. Roberts growled.

I wondered what it was like for my boss. To not be in control. It didn't take a genius to see that it didn't suit him. Moistening my lips, I turned back to Davin and opened my mouth to begin my carefully rehearsed introduction.

I walked closer, my feet heavy in the suit. "Do you mind if I sit down?" I waved at the chair by his desk.

He just looked at me, the hatred pulsing off of him.

With awkward movements, I pulled Davin's chair over. The dragging sound along the concrete echoed in the small cell. I positioned the chair a comfortable four feet away from him and sat. Swallowing, I folded my hands in my lap and began the process I'd memorized from the research done at Compounds 10 and 11. The process where I developed Davin's trust.

Or tried to.

"Hello, Davin. My name's Meghan Forester. I'm a researcher here at the Compound. As you probably noticed, I've just joined your group."

He didn't reply.

"I'm here today to talk to you. That's it. I won't be taking any samples."

His gaze narrowed. I could practically feel his suspiciousness meshing into the hatred.

I licked my lips again and continued. "As of yesterday, we're trying something new. We've learned…" I waved my gloved hands toward my research group and turned awkwardly in my suit. Nobody had moved. Except for Amy. She was now biting the cuticles off the sides of her thumbs.

I turned back to Davin. "We've learned that the way we've been doing things isn't very effective."

He still didn't reply.

"So from now on, we're not going to take samples from you unwillingly."

His eyebrows shot up like fireworks on the Fourth of July. "And you expect me to believe that?"

My heart thumped. *He replied!* "Well… um… not right away of course, but over time, I hope you see we're serious."

He didn't say anything further, but that suspicious look remained.

"You see, we've learned that the virus responds better when it's taken willingly. I know that sounds crazy, but some other Compounds have discovered very promising results when they've varied their collection process. I can assure you that you won't be…" I almost said *tortured* but stopped myself just in time. "Ah, you won't be *subjected* to anything that you don't consent to from now on." I smiled encouragingly. I figured if he knew the reasoning behind this change, he might actually believe it.

Unfortunately, the opposite seemed to happen. Davin's eyes hardened. "You must really think I'm stupid," he muttered so quietly I almost didn't hear him. I opened my mouth to reply, but he beat me to it. "Do you really think I'd believe you're never going to take samples from me again, just because I say no?"

"I–"

"You really think that sadist," he glanced toward Dr. Roberts, "won't cut into me again?"

"No, you don't understand–"

"Oh, I understand," Davin interrupted, his voice growly and deep. "I understand that you're a naïve, young researcher who believes everything she's told, but I know more about this place than you ever will."

My mouth dropped. A minute passed where we just stared at one another. I finally managed to force a few words out. "Davin, please… Just give me a chance to prove this to you. Please, let me try."

For a second, I thought he looked at me. *Really* looked at me, and saw me. Not some phony researcher covered up in a ridiculous suit, but *me*. Meghan. But as quickly as that look flashed across his face, it disappeared.

"Dr. Forester…" Dr. Roberts' voiced warned in my ear.

I ignored my boss. "I know you don't believe me, and I don't expect you to. But please, give me a chance. Let me prove to you that things are going to change."

"Do you know how many times I've been promised things in here?" he said quietly.

"I… I know. I know what's been done to you."

"Then you'll excuse me for not wanting to spend another minute listening to this bullshit. Now, *get out* of my cell." He said the words so quietly yet with such burning intensity, I flinched.

"Please, Davin…"

"Get out!" he roared.

I stumbled to standing, feeling like the biggest idiot in the world. "I'm sorry, Davin. I'm sorry for what's happened to you, but if you would just let me explain…"

He closed his eyes, a muscle ticking in his jaw.

My stomach plummeted as I realized what he was doing. He was taking control of the situation in the only way he could, by closing himself off. He was defenseless in the Chair.

My heart sank.

I stumbled back to the watch room, feeling like a complete fool. *Did you really think he'd react any other way?* He was right.

I was naïve. I was foolish.

I'd actually thought if I explained everything to him, he'd see that I was serious, that we weren't going to hurt him anymore.

Right. Since when has he not been hurt? Of course, he wouldn't believe you!

My shoulders slumped when I stepped into the containment room. *How am I supposed to get through to him? How am* I, *of all people, supposed to do this?*

He hated us.

He hated me, and I didn't see how anything could ever change that.

BACK IN THE containment room, I tried not to look as horrible as I felt. Once I was out of the biohazard suit, the lasers scanned my body. The light in the containment room flashed green.

The only good thing about the entire debacle was that I wouldn't be dying of *Makanza* in the next few weeks. *I suppose I should be grateful for small miracles.*

When I stepped into the watch room, my boss assessed me coldly. "That was quite the performance, Dr. Forester."

Humiliation made my cheeks burn. "Yeah, it's not what I hoped for."

"Cut her some slack." Mitch glared at our boss. "I'm sure none of us would have done any better."

"Yeah," Amy added. "Davin hates us. You can't expect that to change anytime soon. I'm surprised he even talked to her. He usually refuses to speak to any of us."

"That's gotta be a good sign." Charlie shoved his hands in his pockets. "She's probably the one he hates the least since she just started." He grinned after he said that. As if anything about this situation was promising.

"Hmm," Dr. Roberts replied.

I sighed, feeling a little better that everyone leaped to my defense. As much as I hated how the interview went with Davin, if you could even call it that, Charlie may be right. Since I was the newest to the group, Davin had barely interacted with me. Although considering he lumped us all into the 'hated researchers' group, maybe it wouldn't matter.

Still, I had to cling to some hope.

We left the Inner Sanctum shortly after that. As we walked down the windowed hall, I peered into Davin's cell. I did it cautiously, trying to respect his privacy. He was out of the Chair, at his desk, his back to us. He never looked up.

His blatant action to ignore us stung. I knew I meant nothing to him, but still, I cared. I cared about him and all of the people in this country infected with *Makanza*. It wasn't right what had been done to them, and I wanted to be part of the team that stopped it. Maybe someday he'd see that. Maybe someday he'd wave goodbye to me, instead of turning his back.

Right, and maybe someday I'll see the pyramids of Giza.

I frowned and kept walking.

I nibbled my lip as my mind raced for how to continue. Maybe I'd be able to get through to him with a lot of patience and a lot of time. If there was one thing I was good at, it was persevering. I hadn't gotten to where I was today for lack of determination. If I just worked hard enough, if I didn't give up, maybe I'd make progress with him.

My resolve grew fiercer as we approached the lab. With a

goal in mind, I set about planning how to achieve it. That didn't make working very productive. I spent the majority of the afternoon replaying my conversation with Davin, analyzing what I did well (very little) and what I needed to work on (pretty much everything).

I kept second guessing myself too, which didn't help. *If I had used a different tone, would it have gone better? If I'd given him more time to engage in the conversation, would he have said more? Should I have been so upfront with him for why we were changing procedure?* Maybe I should have eased into what Compounds 10 and 11 had discovered at a later time.

I shook my head as soon as I thought that. No, that was probably the one thing I'd done right. If I ever wanted to gain Davin's trust, I had to be one hundred percent transparent, about everything. I had a feeling if he ever found out I lied, about anything, he'd shut me out like the borders to Canada.

Forever.

LATER THAT AFTERNOON, Dr. Roberts returned to our lab. I was so lost in thought I didn't realize he stood right beside me until his voice barked in my ear. "Dr. Forester. I'd like to speak to you."

I jumped. "Um. Okay."

He led me out of the lab, into the hallway. When he turned toward me, his cold eyes pierced mine. He had gray eyes. I'd never noticed that before. Right now, they looked like sharp, metal bullets shooting right through me.

"I told Dr. Sadowsky how poorly today went and how entering Davin's cell was a complete waste of time."

My stomach dropped.

"Unfortunately, he disagrees. Dr. Sadowsky wants you to keep working with Davin. I suggested we try Mitch, but he's insistent it's a woman."

My heart pounded. It never occurred to me that they might stop this experiment, or give up on me so quickly. "I'm sure I can do this." I rubbed my icy palms on my pants.

He raised his eyebrows. "You are?"

"Yes. I won't let you down."

"Let's hope not. You have one month to obtain a sample. If you fail, I'm sending Amy in."

I balked. *A month?* "Is that the time limit Dr. Sadowsky gave?"

"No. That's the time limit I'm giving. The sooner we end this hippy nonsense, the sooner we return to real research."

Hippy nonsense? *Real* research? I stood up straighter. "But Compounds 10 and 11 are the only Compounds who've made progress. Don't you consider that real research?"

His eyes narrowed, and his voice dropped to a deadly quiet tone. "Are you questioning me, Dr. Forester?"

I opened my mouth to acquiesce but then stopped. "Yes. I am. Dr. Hutchinson's labs made a huge discovery. I think we all need to work together and give these new techniques a try. It's the only lead we have right now."

Dr. Roberts' head cocked. "Well," he finally said. "We'll see." With that, he turned and marched down the hall.

I stood looking after him, my breathing coming fast. I couldn't believe I'd done that. I thought I'd never have the guts to stand up to my boss.

I smiled. Jer would be proud of me. Taking a shaky breath, I turned back to the lab.

I SPENT THE evening reviewing textbooks on the human psyche and traumatic events. That was kind of how I viewed what the Compound had done to Davin. Continuous psychological trauma.

"You gonna read all night?" Jeremy lounged against the wall in my living room, sitting on the floor beside me, his feet crossed at the ankles. Books and papers were strewn everywhere.

"No, not all night. Just most of it," I replied without looking up.

He thumbed through one of the books I'd checked out from the Compound's library. "Interesting stuff," he said dryly.

I gave him an annoyed look before turning back to my paper. "It is interesting, at least to me."

"Why are you reading this?"

I bit my lip. He knew I couldn't talk about the Compound, although I wanted to. It would be such a relief to talk to him. To tell him about my fears and anxieties. I was terrified of failing at this. *This*, being the one thing that mattered to me now more than anything.

"Um, no reason." I let my dark hair fall across my cheek, hiding my face. He could always tell when I was lying. He'd said often enough my face was like an open book.

Jeremy guffawed. "And you expect me to believe that?"

I just shrugged, letting him know the topic was closed for discussion.

Miraculously, I fell into a deep sleep that night. Perhaps all of the reading had done it. Maybe my exhausted mind and body had decided enough was enough. I needed sleep. Period. Consequently, when my alarm went off at 4 a.m., I awoke invigorated and ready to get to work.

Part of my earlier than usual rising was due to the plan I'd thought up before bed. It required me getting in early today, at least, earlier than my boss.

THE COMPOUND WAS dark when I pulled into my parking space. It wasn't even five in the morning. Curfew wouldn't lift until six. The only people allowed out after curfew were people with jobs requiring travel at odd hours. Medical personnel, security officers, law enforcement. They had to carry permits stating their work schedule. Days off didn't entitle even them to be out as they pleased.

The MRI, however, was in a class of its own. I always had an excuse to be on the roads, in Sioux Falls and Brandon at least. After a flash of my MRI badge, stating I was in the midst of conducting important research, any hefty fines would be waived, and I certainly wouldn't go to the detention center.

However, the patrol officer may still follow me, to ensure I was telling the truth. In other words, if I was out, it better be because of my job or I *would* get in trouble.

It was so early, I beat even Private Williams to work. The night shift guard checked me in, and I hurried to my office to drop off my stuff. From there, I took a different route than we usually took to the Sanctum. I highly doubted Amy, Mitch, or Charlie would be in this early, but I couldn't risk encountering them. They might insist on joining me. That was the last thing I wanted.

When I reached the Inner Sanctum, the dim glow of nighttime lights barely illuminated the halls. I hurried through each access point. All of the Kazzie's cells were dark. I checked my watch and kept walking. It was just past five.

When I reached Davin's hall, I peered into his cell through the floor to ceiling windows. His cell was as dark as the others. *Of course, it is.* I smacked my hand against my forehead. I forgot one, itsy, bitsy, tiny little detail in my grand plan.

That Davin may still be sleeping.

I cursed silently and tiptoed to the guard's watch room. I

stopped just outside when I heard voices.

"...he went to bed at nine. Didn't do much during the night. Got up around one to use the toilet and that was it. He's been sleeping soundly since."

From the sounds of it, Sergeant Rose had just come on his shift. He was getting handover from the night shift guard.

"He asked for his breakfast to be delivered at six. Scrambled eggs, toast, and bacon with a cup of coffee."

"Not his usual," Sergeant Rose commented.

"Nope, mixing it up today."

They kept talking so I waited. When the night shift guard stepped out of the watch room, he jumped when he saw me.

I tried not to look guilty. "Good morning," I mumbled.

Sergeant Rose's head peeked out of the watch room. "Meghan... I mean, Dr. Forester."

The other guard's shoulders relaxed. "Ma'am." He nodded his head before he passed.

I smiled tightly, feeling a slight thrum of anxiety before wishing him a good day.

After he left, I stepped into the watch room. The smell of coffee greeted me. A steaming cup sat beside Sergeant Rose on a small table by the control panel.

He cleared his throat. "Um, you'll have to excuse me. I didn't realize anyone was coming at this time. What can I do for you?"

I stepped forward, thinking of what I'd heard between the two guards. It gave me an idea. It would require talking to Sergeant Rose. A lot. But it seemed worth it. I took a deep breath, telling myself to suck it up and to forget my nervousness around new people. I was doing this for Davin.

"Well, nothing right now," I replied. "I didn't realize Davin would still be sleeping."

"Yeah, it is pretty early."

I blushed, realizing how stupid that sounded. "I mean… I just didn't consider how early it was when I came down here. I should have known better."

Sergeant Rose smiled. "Well, you won't have to wait long. He's always up by six. He's been an early riser ever since I've been here." He sat down on his stool and motioned to the stool beside him.

I hesitantly sat.

"Want some coffee?" He held up his cup. "It's right down the hall in the breakroom."

I shook my head. "No, that's okay."

We were silent for a moment, both of us peering into Davin's dark cell. It seemed now was the perfect opportunity to break the ice. From what I'd overheard during their handover, Davin's guards knew him better than anyone.

I took a deep breath. "So, he sleeps pretty well?" I continued peering into Davin's cell.

"Yeah, most nights. Although when he returns from the Experimental Room, that's another story."

I winced. I could only imagine why that was. Amy had shown me the Experimental Room once when we were passing by the Sanctum. It looked like something out of a sci-fi movie. Four beds with robotic equipment surrounded each. Technicians worked in a separate room, controlling the equipment. Each robotic arm held sinister looking tools: scalpels, drills, hammers, chisels, pinchers. I could only imagine the number of scars each Kazzie had.

"Has Dr. Roberts had him in the Experimental Room lately?"

"No, not since about the time you started."

I sighed in relief. "How does Davin usually spend his days?

When he's just… hanging around here?" I waved at his cell. "When we're not doing research on him?"

Sergeant Rose took a sip of his coffee before crossing his arms and leaning back on his stool. "It's kind of the same most days. He always eats breakfast at six and then he watches the news, or reads the newspaper, and sometimes does sit-ups and push-ups. After that, he usually reads. The guy's read more books than anyone I know." He said that bit admiringly, a smile breaking across his face.

It was then I picked up on something I'd never noticed in my previous visits to the Inner Sanctum. Sergeant Rose *liked* Davin, or at the very least, respected him. I wondered how that affected his job, when he had to do cruel things, like put Davin in the Chair.

"After lunch, he usually exercises in his cell," Sergeant Rose continued.

"He does? But there's no exercise equipment."

"It's mostly body resistance stuff. Push-ups, sit-ups, jumping jacks. That kind of stuff. You know, the stuff anyone can do in a small space."

A small space. The confinement that all the Kazzies lived in right now.

"It wasn't always like that," Sergeant Rose added. "Before all of the changes a few months ago, he'd go to the gym after lunch and then go to the lounge to be with the other Kazzies. And some mornings, he'd read in the library, not stay in his cell. But since Dr. Roberts took over, that's stopped. Now, each Kazzie gets out of his, or her, cell two hours each day. That's it. Well, at least, they *did*, until recently."

"And they're not now because they're still in lockdown?"

"Right."

"So… Dr. Roberts is punishing them? Because Davin got

angry at how he was treated?"

"I guess." A bitter edge clung to Sergeant Rose's tone.

"Any news on how long this is going to continue? They haven't left their cells for… what… over four weeks now?"

"Correct," Sergeant Rose replied grimly. "But no, I haven't heard anything about when he's going to lift the ban."

"How long has it been since Davin's had any interaction with anyone? Socially, I mean, not with us?"

"Not for months." Sergeant Rose took another sip of his coffee. "You going in his cell yesterday was the closest contact he's had with anyone since Dr. Roberts stopped allowing the Kazzies to socialize."

I glowered. That was four weeks of isolation, and that kind of treatment was in no way conducive to happiness. If anything, it bred insanity. No wonder our Compound hadn't made any progress.

I tucked a long strand of hair behind my ear. "What else can you tell me about him? You know… what kind of books he likes to read or what kind of news he prefers? Or his favorite foods? You said he orders the same things most mornings? Does he have other habits?" I cut myself off, realizing I was asking too many questions at once.

Sergeant Rose cocked his head and smiled. "Do you really want to know that stuff?"

I nodded.

He shook his head.

"What?" I asked warily.

"None of the researchers have ever asked anything like that before."

"So what do the other researchers want to know?"

"About the Kazzies?" Sergeant Rose shrugged. "Nothing really, all they worry about are samples."

I thought of what Amy had told me, how they'd all had to accept a few things, for the sake of research. I wondered if distancing themselves from the Kazzies made it easier to do their jobs. If by not having a connection with them, they didn't feel as guilty.

I was about to ask Sergeant Rose another question when movement came from Davin's cell. My head snapped toward the glass. A light turned on, illuminating the room. Davin had turned the lamp on beside his bed. He sat up slowly, his chest bare. I hadn't considered he may be undressed.

I quickly averted my eyes.

Sergeant Rose chuckled. "Don't worry. He's got pants on."

I glanced up, but I was still cautious. Davin swung his legs over the side of his bed, his back to us. He had broad shoulders and a tapered waist. Chiseled muscles shifted under his skin when he moved.

I swallowed audibly.

Sergeant Rose leaned down and pushed a button on the control panel while speaking into a microphone. "Your breakfast will be in soon."

Davin didn't acknowledge that he'd heard. Instead, he stood and stretched.

I tried not to notice the sinewy muscles that rippled in his back and arms, or the way his golden skin was perfectly flawless and smooth. Wherever they took samples from, it wasn't his back.

Davin finished stretching and padded to the bathroom. I averted my gaze again. Not that I could see much since a half wall blocked him from view. Still, he had no idea I was there. Just as I had that thought, I once again wanted to smack my hand against my forehead. I suddenly realized my grand plan could end up being the biggest disaster of my career.

Here I was, wanting to gain Davin's trust while forming a therapeutic relationship, and instead, I'd snuck into the watch room and watched him sleep without him knowing it. Yeah, not creepy at all. *Way to go, Meg, definitely hit a home run with this plan.*

"Um, I think I'll go grab that cup of coffee after all." I jumped off my stool and almost bumped it over in my haste to escape.

IT DIDN'T TAKE long to find the breakroom. It was past the tenth cell. Each Compound had twenty cells. Since Compound 26 only had seven Kazzies, we had a lot of empty space. Hence, why so many Kazzies from the coasts had been transported to us. None of the Midwestern Compounds were full.

It was almost creepy walking past the empty cells. They stood like silent, vacant ships in a harbor waiting to be loaded. It was an ominous feeling. Like it was just a matter of time before they were occupied.

I had to use my access badge to enter the breakroom. The digital clock on the wall read six in the morning. If Dr. Roberts was already at the Compound and decided to check up on my whereabouts, my digital fingerprint would tell him exactly where I was. I just prayed he wasn't feeling curious this morning.

The small breakroom held a half kitchen including a sink, bar sized fridge, microwave, and coffee pot. A few tables and chairs were farther back. There wasn't a couch, but there was a vending machine. One of the nice things about vending machines at the Compound was that they didn't require money. Like the cafeterias, everything in them was free.

I opened a cupboard in the kitchen. White, porcelain cups

sat lined up neatly. I grabbed one and took my time pouring a cup of coffee before adding cream from the fridge.

I sipped it slowly, my fingers wrapping around the hot mug. It was flavored coffee, a true luxury. Scents of hazelnut wafted up to greet me. I closed my eyes and savored the creamy richness.

Usually, I had my coffee black, but that was only because I never used my rations for real cream at the SDFDC. There were so many things in the Compound those on the outside never experienced.

I glanced at the clock again.

Ten minutes had passed. I figured that was enough time for Davin to have gone to the bathroom and maybe dressed. Unless he decided to shower. Frowning, I settled onto one of the chairs.

Better to make sure I give him enough time to fully get up.

BY THE TIME I left the breakroom, almost half an hour had passed. Even if Davin took long showers, I figured he'd be done by now.

When I approached the watch room, bright light streamed into the hallway from the floor to ceiling windows. Peeking my head around the corner, I peered cautiously into Davin's cell. He was sitting at his desk, a tray of food in front of him. I breathed a sigh of relief and joined Sergeant Rose again.

"Looks like he's up." I settled on the stool.

"Just started breakfast."

I clasped my hands together and waited. Davin still didn't know I was there. Once again, his back was to me. "Does he always eat facing away?"

"Yeah, he usually ignores me. Most of the time, it's like I'm invisible. I've gotten the impression it's easier for him to pretend I'm not here."

"So he can't talk to the other Kazzies, and he doesn't talk to you either?"

"Right."

My brow furrowed. "It's a wonder he hasn't gone crazy."

Sergeant Rose shrugged. "Davin's pretty… resilient."

A few minutes later, Davin stood with his empty tray. He was fully dressed, wearing a plain t-shirt and jeans. His feet were bare. That must have felt cold on the concrete. He walked to the back corner with his tray and waited.

Sergeant Rose pushed a button on his control panel. A small portal opened in the cell's wall, and Davin set his tray inside it and the portal closed.

"Is that how he gets his food? Through that system in the wall?"

"Yeah, all three meals."

Davin returned to his bed. A newspaper waited on his covers.

"How'd he get that?" I watched Davin sit and open it.

"It always comes down with his breakfast tray."

"Hmm," I mumbled, intrigued. Our city newspaper wasn't large by any means. It was usually ten pages at the most with news as exciting as watching water boil. I bought a paper every now and then. Just to see what was in it.

It usually reported events in the state. Most were community outings and fundraisers. The actual news aspect was minimal. Classifieds took up another large portion of it. Since new things were hard to come by, some people made a living off finding old junk and refurbishing it.

The dresser in my apartment was a perfect example. I'd bought it from an old farmer who had turned his cow barn into a woodworking shop after the government took away his farming privileges. I still got a faint whiff of hay every now and then in my bedroom.

I leaned forward and watched Davin. He sat calmly on his bed, reading the paper. He still had no idea I was there. *This would be so much easier if he just looked at me.*

"Did you want me to put him in the Chair?" Sergeant Rose asked.

I could tell from his tone that he didn't want to. "No, no of course not. I don't want him in that thing again unless he chooses it."

"I can't let you in the cell, Dr. Forester, unless he's in the Chair."

"I know. I have no intention of going in again unless he's okay with it."

The guard's eyebrows rose. "I thought researchers entering the cells was the new protocol ordered by Dr. Sadowsky?"

"It is, but he also ordered that we follow Compound 10 and 11's techniques. They wouldn't force themselves upon any of their Kazzies without consent."

I gave Davin a few more minutes of peace before asking, "Can I talk to him? On the microphone?"

"Of course."

"Would I be able to do it… in private?" One thing I learned from my readings was the necessity of confidentiality. If Davin was going to trust me, he had to know whatever we talked about was between him and me only.

Sergeant Rose shook his head. "No, ma'am, I'm sorry. That's strictly against policy. I have to stay in this watch room at all times."

I sighed. I knew it was against policy but thought it was worth trying. "In that case, do you mind waiting just outside the watch room?"

Sergeant Rose frowned. He looked truly apologetic. "I can't, Dr. Forester. I have to stay here."

"That's all right. I understand."

We traded spots, and he showed me what button operated the microphone. I pushed it and leaned down. *Here goes nothing.* "Davin? Can you hear me?"

Davin's head shot up. His gaze immediately swept to the watch room.

"Would it be all right if I talked to you?" *At least my voice isn't shaking.* "It's Meghan Forester again. I visited with you yesterday."

Davin didn't say anything. Instead, he turned away and continued reading his paper. It would have been easy to feel dismayed by his silence, but I'd expected it. I knew it could take days before he spoke to me again.

"I know you don't believe what I was saying yesterday, but it really is the truth. I'd like to get to know you more and help make some changes around here. Positive changes."

He still didn't say anything, but I thought his eyes rolled.

Sergeant Rose chuckled. "Did I mention he's stubborn?"

I sighed. "I'd already figured that out." I waited a few minutes and then tried again. "I'd like to tell you more about our new theory. Would that be all right?"

Davin simply turned a page in the paper.

"As I was telling you yesterday, the Compounds in Washington state, Compounds 10 and 11, have made a startling discovery about *Makanza*. They've learned the virus is more stable when it's removed in positive circumstances. It's related to mind-body genomics."

Davin turned another page.

"The Director of our Compound, Dr. Sadowsky, is hoping to learn what reaction the virus has when it's removed using close contact, human to human contact. That's why Dr. Roberts had me enter your cell yesterday."

At the mention of Dr. Roberts, Davin's face tightened, but he still didn't say anything.

"I'd like to enter your cell again, Davin, but I won't unless you tell me it's all right." I thought that would get a reaction from him, but all he did was put down the paper and turn on the news.

I leaned back on the stool, my finger leaving the button. Sergeant Rose cleared his throat awkwardly. I could tell he didn't want to highlight how spectacularly I was failing, but it was hard not to notice.

"He likes word puzzles," Sergeant Rose suggested. "Maybe if you brought him some new ones, he'd be more likely to talk."

Word puzzles? It was worth a try.

I pushed the button again. "Davin, would you like me to bring you some new word puzzles? Or new books you haven't read?" It seemed like a rather condescending question, like I was trying to bribe a kid with candy, but I had to start somewhere. Anything to get him talking.

Unfortunately, it didn't work. That question got an annoyed look, exactly as I'd feared, as if I was treating him like a bribed child.

Sergeant Rose shrugged. "Sorry, that wasn't much help."

I smiled encouragingly. "It was worth a try. Do you have any other ideas?"

"He also enjoys movies. Maybe we could get him a DVD player?"

I hesitated, trying to figure out how to word my reply tactfully. Sergeant Rose only had good intentions. "Well, I'm hoping to get him talking without bribing him. I don't want him to feel like I'm treating him like a child."

Sergeant Rose actually blushed. "Oh, right. That makes sense."

"But keep telling me your ideas. I need all the help I can get."

"Will do."

I leaned back down to the microphone, opting for a more direct route. "Would it be all right with you if I enter your cell again, right now?"

Nothing.

Sergeant Rose looked sheepish. "I did warn you he was stubborn, right?"

I sighed. "Yes."

I SPENT THE next hour trying different angles to get Davin's attention or to bridge the distance between us. I tried all of the techniques I read about but failed time and time again. I was either met with stoic silence or an icy stare. I counted the icy stares as victories.

At least, he'd looked at me.

When seven in the morning rolled around, I called it quits. It felt like I'd been interrogating him for hours with nothing to show for it. If I continued, I'd probably just annoy him further.

Davin had moved from his bed to his desk at some point in the last twenty minutes. I couldn't tell what he was doing since his back was to me. Regardless, I still said, "Thank you for your time today, Davin. I'll be back again tomorrow morning. If there's anything you think of that you'd like to talk about, you can tell me then."

"Right."

The comment was muttered sarcastically.

Startled, I stared at him. He was still bent over his desk, his broad shoulders straining against his t-shirt. I glanced at Sergeant Rose.

The guard was grinning. “At least he replied to something.”

I guess I hadn’t imagined Davin’s response after all. I turned to hide my smile.

One day down, twenty-nine to go.

14 – PTSD

Since I arrived at the lab a little before eight, I beat everybody else in. Thankfully, that meant nobody knew where I'd been.

I spent the morning working, but it was hard to concentrate. I kept wondering how I would get through to Davin. Two days in a row, I'd struck out.

Around noon, Amy approached. "Lunch?"

I sighed. It's not like I was getting much done. "Sure."

After lunch, we returned to the lab. My breath stopped when I saw who waited for me.

Dr. Roberts.

He stood ramrod straight by my lab bench, dressed in his usual cargo gear, the picture of military perfection.

"Dr. Forester." He spoke in clipped tones. "Are you ready to speak with Davin today?"

I bit my lip. I'd known this was coming. "I already have."

He frowned. "Excuse me?"

I clasped my hands tighter. "I already saw Davin today. I went in first thing this morning since I know how important it is to obtain a sample as quickly as possible. I didn't want to waste any time."

His eyes turned glacial. "You did this without telling me?"

I shuffled my feet. "Yes."

"Well, did you get a sample?"

I wanted to roll my eyes. *Seriously?* "No. Not yet anyway, but Davin talked willingly to me again." So technically that was a white lie, but it was partially true.

"Hmm." The momentary anger in his eyes vanished. "And you plan to do this every day?"

I felt, rather than saw, Amy, Mitch, and Charlie approach behind me. "Yes, unless you have an objection. I feel like I've already made progress."

His hard gaze studied me. I had no idea what swirled in his mind behind those irises. "I suppose that's fine," he finally replied. "However, if anything changes in his behavior, I want to know immediately. Is that clear?"

I nodded and added, "Yes, sir," for good measure.

With that, Dr. Roberts marched out of the lab.

When he was gone, all three of my colleagues swarmed around me. "You already went into Davin's cell this morning?" Amy asked.

"I talked to him." I hoped she wouldn't notice that I avoided her question.

"What did he say?" Mitch's cologne wafted to me as he stepped closer.

I shrugged, my stomach flipping now that I'd become the center of attention. "Not much, but he didn't break any furniture."

Mitch and Charlie both chuckled.

"Keep it up, Forester." Mitch clapped me on the back. Both guys returned to their work stations, but Amy lingered at my side.

"What?" I tucked my hair behind my ears, but then made myself stop fidgeting.

She just watched me with her head cocked. "There's something different about you."

I turned toward my bench, pretending to get to work. "What do you mean?"

She was quiet for a moment. "I don't know. You just seem more sure of yourself lately."

I laughed softly, hoping she wouldn't see the sheen of sweat that erupted across my forehead.

I BEGAN THE evening at home similar to the one before. Reading, reading, and more reading. It wasn't as easy to concentrate. I kept thinking about Davin and the other Kazzies.

I speed-read through the latest group of articles I'd checked out from the library. Most of them were on PTSD. They were grim, highlighting how severe PTSD could be a psychiatric disorder. I hadn't seen evidence of that in Davin. Not yet anyway. He slept soundly. He ate. The only sign of psychological trauma was his intense rage. But that rage, according to Amy, was something he rarely showed. Normally, he was very controlled. But still…

Is he really as resilient as everyone thinks?

I tried to shrug those thoughts off and consume myself with work, but no matter what I did, images of Davin kept working their way into my mind. Like a persistent solicitor who kept knocking on the doorstep.

Davin's image readily appeared every time I thought about him. His cold stare, his lofty indifference. The way his muscles rippled in his back when he climbed out of bed.

I dropped the magazine I was reading. *His rippling muscles?*

Really, Meghan?

I jumped from my living room floor and jogged to my bedroom. I threw on my running clothes faster than I ever had. A few steps later, I was out of my apartment.

The streets were quiet. The air cold. Within minutes, I'd set my pace. The only sound was the rhythmic slapping of my shoes on the pavement and my rough exhales as I ran on the road. Every now and then, a car would pass, otherwise, it was silent.

At this time, most families were sitting down for a supper of carefully measured rations. As for me, when I wasn't holed up in my apartment reading research, I was usually going for a run. Sometimes that was hard. Curfew got earlier and earlier as winter approached. I checked my watch. I only had an hour before I needed to return to my apartment.

I'd started running six years ago as a way to cope with all that was happening. Running helped clear my head and allowed me to just… *be*. When I ran, I felt still. Quiet. The irony wasn't lost on me. Regardless, tonight I needed the peace that running evoked.

I was thinking about Davin more than I should.

I returned to my apartment just before 7:30 p.m. One of my neighbors was getting her mail when I entered. Ameena was one of the few apartment residents I occasionally interacted with.

"Hi, Meghan." She locked her mail cubby and stuffed the key in her pocket. "How was your run?"

Rivulets of sweat trailed down my temples. "Pretty good."

"It's getting cold out there. My mother's already complaining about it."

I smiled. Ameena's mother had grown up in India, when India was still an alive and functioning country before the First

Wave. She had only moved to South Dakota fifteen years ago. She swore she'd never get used to the winters.

"Are you two doing all right?" I put my hands on my hips as my breathing calmed more.

"Oh, yes, we're just fine, couldn't be better." Her smile was big.

Too big.

Ameena's mother had a permanent injury from an accident several years ago, and Ameena cared full-time for her. I knew she struggled at times although she was too proud to say it. And despite claiming they were fine, her thin face spoke otherwise. I knew she was either giving her mother most of her food portions or the stress was getting to her.

"You know I've been meaning to stop by." I wiped sweat from my forehead. "I've got a whole loaf of bread that's going to mold and there's no room in my freezer. Would you take it? I'll just have to throw it out otherwise. I don't want to waste it."

Ameena frowned. "Can't you find some use for it?"

I shook my head. "I'm so busy at work right now. A lot of times, I'm not even home. Some of my fruits and vegetables are spoiling too."

Ameena's mouth dropped. Food was such a precious commodity. Nothing in our society went to waste.

"Will you take it?" I asked. "Please? I don't want to throw it out."

She sighed. "All right, only to keep it from going to waste."

"I'll bring it over after I shower."

"Sure." She stuffed her mail under her arm and strolled down the hall.

I managed to shower, drop off the food to Ameena, and

have dinner in my apartment without once thinking about Davin. That all changed when I climbed into bed. In my darkened room, with the moon shining through the window, his face swam in my mind. As much as I tried to stop it, I couldn't.

He dominated my thoughts.

I told myself it was purely because I was working so closely with him now. It was only natural to think of him. Still, it was unnerving how easily every detail of his face appeared, his features etched into my memory. Those bright, blue eyes that almost glowed. The proud nose and cheekbones. Dark hair that curled around his ears. His broad shoulders and well-defined muscles.

My breath caught. *Meghan, seriously! Stop!*

I did my best, but it was hard. I buried myself under my covers and tried to sleep, but Davin was not someone easy to forget.

WHEN MY ALARM went off the next day, my body protested. I hadn't run in a while, and I could feel it in every muscle. When I stood in front of my closet, I instinctively reached for a suit.

At the last minute, I faltered. I pushed the hanger aside and instead pulled out a sweater and slacks.

The blue sweater was something I found about two months ago at Empire Mall. It was from one of Ralph Lauren's clothing lines from over ten years ago. When the First Wave hit, and our population had died off at a rapid rate, a surplus of goods was left. The government now had all of those items: clothes, shoes, furniture, electronics, appliances, vehicles, tools, etc. Everything was carefully stored in warehouses throughout the country.

Each year, every state was rationed a percentage of those items to put on shelves. Newly manufactured items were available as well, but without world trade, supplies were limited. Consequently, prices were high, choices were low, and quality uncertain. It was one of many changes our society had grown used to.

I pulled the thick sweater on, marveling at the luxurious quality. It was a material called cashmere. I smoothed it against me, realizing how lucky a find it had been. I frowned, though, when I slipped my pants on. They were loose. Perhaps my vow to not be so gluttonous was going too far.

I made a mental note to eat more today. While food in the Compound was plentiful, that didn't mean it always would be. Getting too thin could be dangerous. There had been more than one rumor in the community about people dying from starvation, especially during the winter.

IT WAS BLACK as tar when I pulled into my parking spot in the Compound. The setting moon barely illuminated anything. I hurried through security, dropped my things in my office, and strode straight to the Inner Sanctum.

It was around 5 a.m. again when I entered the watch room.

"Morning," Sergeant Rose said when I peeked my head around the corner. He was talking to the same night guard. "Have you met Private Paulson?"

The night guard's eyes widened in surprise when he saw me. No doubt seeing the same researcher at five in the morning, two mornings in a row, was a record for him. He appeared to be around my age with bland features that weren't unattractive but also not attractive. His eyes though seemed kind. I liked that.

"Ma'am," he said when I just stood there.

My anxiety kicked into overdrive even though I told myself I was being ridiculous.

With a pounding heart, I stepped back. "Sorry to interrupt. I'll wait in the hall."

I escaped to the comforting solitude of the empty hallway. Davin's cell was so dark I couldn't see anything. The nighttime lighting in the hall created a mirror effect on the cell's glass.

My hair looked unsightly. It was only then I realized I'd forgotten to brush it. I ran my fingers through it, straightening the dark tendrils billowing around my head. Perhaps I needed to be a little more conscientious from now on if I was going to wake up at four in the morning every day.

Private Paulson exited the watch room a few minutes later. He politely nodded. I returned the gesture as best I could and stepped back into the watch room.

"Back again," Sergeant Rose remarked as I sat on the stool beside him.

"You sound surprised."

"Well, to be honest, I kind of am."

I gave him a confused look. "I told Davin I'd be back this morning."

He shrugged and hesitated before saying, "Intentions don't always equate to action."

"Maybe, but I try to keep my promises."

"I can see that." He smiled and leaned back on his stool before reaching for his coffee. It smelled liked vanilla today. "Do you have kids?" he asked, after taking a sip.

Here it was. Small talk.

As much as it made me squirm, I took a deep breath. *You can do this!* "No… and not married either… since I'm guessing that's the next question you're going to ask?" *That sounds good. Right?*

He chuckled.

"Um, do you have kids?" I wrung my fingers together.

He pulled out a wallet from his back pocket. "Two boys." He fished their pictures out. They were both dark haired, like him, and looked close in age. "Shawn's twelve and Cooper's ten. Cooper was born just before the First Wave."

"They're good-looking kids."

He smiled. "My wife and I think so too."

"No girls?"

His smile evaporated. "No…"

I mentally slapped myself. I knew better than to say something like that. I had a fairly good guess what he was holding back. His look said everything. It was the look everyone got when *that* subject came up.

"We had a daughter once," he finally said. "McKenzie. She would have been fifteen this year. She died in the Second Wave."

A heavy ache settled in my chest. "I'm sorry, really, I am."

He shrugged. "We've all lost someone, right?"

I swallowed thickly. "Doesn't make it any easier."

"No, it doesn't."

We sat quietly after that. I felt awful, and I also felt like a complete fool. Small talk was something I was eternally working on. Sometimes it was hard, sometimes it was easy, but never was it comfortable, especially when it revolved around families.

Now, small talk about the weather, I could handle. Nothing like a good discussion on the jet stream to really get a conversation going, but families, I struggled with that. It was too personal. Too intense.

Some people loved talking about their dead loved ones and *needed* to talk about them. As if their name was never mentioned again, that they'd cease to have ever existed. I got that and I was good at listening.

If Sergeant Rose wanted to talk about McKenzie, I would have listened, abandoning my plan to get more information from him about Davin.

But Sergeant Rose appeared to be in the group that didn't like to talk about dead loved ones. It might still be too raw, even though it had been six years. I'd heard once that losing a child was a pain one never got over. It was simply a pain one was forced to endure.

"I think I'll get a cup of coffee." I slipped off my stool. "Would you like another?"

He glanced at his cup, as if surprised it was empty. "No, I'm okay. One cup's enough."

As quietly as I could, I slipped out of the room.

VANILLA COFFEE BREWED in the breakroom. I poured myself a large cup and added an extra dollop of cream. That would add at least fifty calories. I also grabbed some food from the vending machine. As I pushed the button, the food whirled around inside. An egg salad sandwich would do.

Unlike beverages, food wasn't allowed out of designated eating locations so I sat at the table and ate the entire sandwich. When finished, I procrastinated on leaving. Part of me dreaded returning to the watch room, wondering if Sergeant Rose would still be feeling the painful memory of loss, the loss that *I* provoked, but I wanted to see if Davin would be more talkative today. It was getting close to six so he'd be up soon.

Luckily, when I returned, Sergeant Rose seemed back to normal. "You were gone awhile." His friendly smile was back in place.

"I had breakfast. I keep forgetting to eat at home."

"Best not to get too thin. Winter's coming."

"Yeah, I know." I sat on the stool. The digital clock on the control panel stated 05:49. "Do you think he'll be up by six?"

"Always is."

"Is he… um, like that? A routine kind of person?" I fiddled with the stool height.

"He is now, but when he first arrived, he wasn't."

"You've known him since he came here?"

"Yeah, I've been working here since the Compound opened." He moved his empty coffee cup to the side.

My mouth went dry. Here it was, the perfect way to precede a *real* conversation about Davin. Sergeant Rose had to know him better than anyone else here. "What was he like when he first arrived?"

He chuckled, although there wasn't much humor in it. "In a nutshell: he was angry."

"Right away?"

"Yeah, before anything was even done to him. Just the fact that he was here made him mad."

"Do you know why he felt that way?" For some asinine reason, I assumed everyone would be happy to be here, at least initially. If they weren't, they'd be dead, having died of *Makanza*.

He paused, looking thoughtful. "I wondered about that, when he first arrived. He'd just lost all of his siblings. That couldn't have been easy. When his mother's letters arrived, up until a few months ago, they wrote weekly," he explained, "he'd seem a bit better, at least for a couple of days. I don't know what she said to him, but whatever it was, it seemed to help."

"So he's close to his mother?"

"Yes. That's one thing I'm certain of."

"Was he close to his siblings?"

He shrugged. "I really have no idea. He's never spoken of them, to anyone."

"But he did… in the letters?" I knew a social worker had dictated correspondence for Davin. Although from what Sergeant Rose just said, I gathered that only Davin had seen the letters from his mother.

"When he first came here, yes, he did talk about his brothers and sisters to his mom, or at least I think he did. I guess I don't actually know because whenever he spoke of people, he'd only use an initial, never directly saying who it was. After years of corresponding with his mother, they practically spoke in code. It was like they spoke another language to one another. It didn't make sense to any of us."

That made me pause. "Is that why Dr. Roberts put an end to it?"

He sighed and scratched his chin. "I'd like to think that was the reason, but just between you and me," he lowered his voice, "I think he stopped it because those letters made Davin happy."

My jaw clenched. *That's why he stopped it?* Of all the reasons to stop something, killing someone's happiness should not be the primary one. I tried to stop the anger that rose within me.

Clearing my throat, I said, "Do you know what her name is?" I still needed to compile a more rounded background on Davin. Knowing the names of his family was a good place to start.

He cocked his head. "Karen… no, Sharon, I think. Yeah, that's it. Sharon Kinder. Same last name as Davin."

Davin's light turned on.

I snapped my head up so fast I pulled a muscle in my neck.

He was shirtless again. A long tanned arm was visible as he'd reached for the lamp by his bed. He swung his feet over the side, his back to us. The sheets fell to his waist.

My breath stopped.

It was like déjà vu from yesterday.

"When will his breakfast arrive?" I squeaked.

"Fifteen minutes."

Davin didn't glance our way. Once again, we were invisible. I wondered if that was a coping mechanism. *If he pretends hard enough, does it feel like he's alone? That his every move isn't scrutinized?*

I averted my gaze when he went to the bathroom, even though I couldn't see anything.

"He won't shower today. He only takes one every other day." Sergeant Rose adjusted a few controls on the panel. "Right now, he'll just take a piss." He cleared his throat after he said that. "Uh, I mean, use the restroom."

I bit back a smile.

"Then he'll brush his teeth. After that, he'll probably do a set of push-ups and then wait at his desk until his breakfast arrives."

Just as Sergeant Rose predicted, Davin picked up his toothbrush after he finished in the bathroom.

I watched, amazed. "He really does follow a strict routine."

"Now he does. When he first arrived, he had no structure to his day. He spent a lot of time pacing."

"Do you think he has the routine now as a way to deal with the monotony of the same day, day in and day out?"

"Maybe."

Sure enough, after Davin brushed his teeth, he returned to the center of the cell and got down on his hands and knees. Kicking his feet back, he balanced on the balls of his toes and started doing push-ups. I counted at first, but with each one, he went faster and faster and faster. He was up to fifty when his movements turned to a blur.

"Wow…"

Sergeant Rose grinned. "Amazing, isn't it?"

It went on for a few minutes. When Davin finished, there was only the slightest sheen of sweat on his skin.

"Any idea how many he did?"

Sergeant Rose grinned. "Around two thousand."

"You could count that?"

He chuckled. "No, of course not, but we've set up a camera a few times to record him and then watched it back in slow motion. Each time his push-up routine averages around two thousand, give or take a hundred."

I was so stunned I couldn't speak.

Davin next sat at his desk. He glanced toward the watch room almost as if he didn't realize he was doing it. When his blazing blue eyes met mine, he stopped cold.

I hastily leaned over, almost falling off my stool in the process, and spoke into the microphone. "Good morning, Davin. Did you sleep well?"

His only response was a narrowing of his eyes.

I sighed internally. I knew it was too much to ask for him to be happy to see me. I was about to say something else when Davin turned his chair so his back was to me.

Directly to me.

Taking the hint, I murmured, "I think I'll wait until he's done with breakfast."

Sergeant Rose tried to smile, but try as he might, I still caught the appeasing sympathy in his gaze. "Yeah, I'm sure it'll go better then."

Davin's breakfast arrived a few minutes later. He stood,

retrieved his tray, and somehow managed to keep his back to me the entire time.

I cleared my throat when he sat back at his desk and told myself it wouldn't be that bad once I started talking. I just needed to be consistent and patient. I could do that even if it meant waking up at four in the morning for the rest of my life.

Or rather, for the rest of the month.

15 - VISITOR

During the next week, my spirits fell more and more each day. Davin didn't talk to me. At all. Every day it was the same. Cold stares, icy indifference, and looks of contempt. Granted it was only week one, but I'd made zero progress.

The only thing I'd accomplished was that Davin seemed to expect me in the mornings. Consequently, he made a point to keep his back to the watch room the *entire* time I was there.

In other words, my grand almighty plan was, in reality, a complete and total disaster.

It was well past nine in the evening on Friday night as I walked to my car. I was alone since Amy had left, complaining of too many late nights and needing a break. Charlie and Mitch had cleared out too. But not me.

I couldn't leave the lab when everyone else did, not even when my stomach cramped in pain from lack of food or my eyelids hung heavy. The Kazzies were still imprisoned and experimented on. That needed to stop, and the only way that would happen was if we discovered a vaccine.

And I'd made a promise to myself. The only reason I'd

continued my position at the Compound was to vigorously work toward achieving that goal. Without that anchor grounding me in my purpose, I was merely a complacent bystander – supporting the atrocities that were committed in these walls.

That wasn't a position I was willing to support.

ON SATURDAY MORNING, I woke early and spread the dozens and dozens of articles I'd accumulated on PTSD on my living room floor and got back to work. I needed to learn more. If I was going to break through to Davin, I needed to better learn how to communicate and heal victims of traumatic events. It was my only hope.

Jeremy made an appearance mid-morning. As always, his presence eased my anxiety and allowed me to continue working despite the fear of failure looming. When he left, I felt more grounded. More sure of myself.

I can do this!

A heavy psychology text was propped against my knees as I leaned against the couch when a knock sounded on my door. At first, I kept working, thinking I'd imagined it, but then the knock came again.

Pushing to a stand, I cautiously padded to the door. While crime was low, there was still the rare story about someone being assaulted during a home robbery. Usually, it was teenagers in a tiff with each other or someone looking for alcohol. Still, it was enough for me to pause at the door and peer through the peephole.

Amy's distorted image stared back.

I pulled the door open. A rush of air flowed across my cheeks. "Amy?"

She waved. "Hi."

"Is everything okay?"

She stepped into my cramped entryway and placed her hands on her hips. "Yes, sorry, it's nothing like that. I just wanted to talk to you."

I ran a hand through my hair. "Um… sure. Come in."

Amy didn't make any move to further enter my apartment. Instead, she studied me, a curious gleam in her eyes.

Since that look made me want to squirm, I looked anywhere but her face. Tall leather boots covered her lower legs. I cleared my throat. "Nice boots."

She bent her leg so I could get a better view of them. "I know, right? I got 'em two years ago when the state released that double quantity of footwear. They're real leather. When do you ever find that these days?"

I stuffed my hands in my pockets. "They look comfortable… and stylish."

I cringed after I said that last part. *What do I know about style?*

Fashion trends these days were non-existent. Nobody really cared about that anymore, except for the odd few who probably would have been fashion designers before *Makanza*. For the rest of us, clothes and footwear were viewed more practically. *Is it warm? Will it last? How much does it cost?* Those were the only questions I ever asked when I bought something.

Amy ignored my stumbling words and grabbed my coat. She held it out to me. "Can I take you out for lunch?"

"Lunch?"

Amy tapped her watch. "Yep. It's what people usually do around this time, you know, eat something?"

My cheeks heated as my stomach grumbled at the mention of food. I'd missed breakfast. I'd been too consumed with work. "You don't have to do that. It would cost a fortune."

Amy waved a dismissive hand. "Don't worry about it. I'll take you back to Sean's. He serves reasonably priced food if you're willing to go back there?"

I hadn't been to Sean's Pub since my disastrous first encounter with alcohol. My trepidation must have shown because Amy added, "Don't worry. He also serves non-alcoholic beverages."

"Um… okay, just give me a minute while I change."

TEN MINUTES LATER, we were in Amy's car driving to the pub. The sky was gray and overcast. She turned the heater on as soon as the motor started.

We were both quiet. The only sound in the car was the air flowing through the dash.

I tried not to fidget, but it was hard not to. Amy said she wanted to talk to me. That couldn't be good.

"Meghan, can I ask you something?" She turned onto a residential street.

I threaded a hand through my hair. "Uh…sure."

"Have you gone into Davin's cell at all this week?"

My stomach jumped into my throat.

"I asked his guard." Amy's green eyes met mine when she paused at a four-way stop. "He said you've tried talking to Davin through the microphone, but you haven't entered his cell."

I took a deep breath. *So that's why she wanted to talk to me.* "Um, no, I haven't gone it." I wrung my hands. "Does Dr. Roberts know?"

She shook her head and drove forward. "Not as far as I'm aware. Believe me, he'd confront you, so I think you're safe in that aspect."

I sighed. "Good."

"Are you scared to go in his cell? Is that why you haven't? Are you afraid you'll catch *Makanza*?"

I shook my head which caused my long, brown hair to fall over my shoulders. "No, it's nothing like that. I mean, of course, I'm a little scared, and I'd definitely take all of the precautions, but that's not the reason–"

"Then why haven't you gone in? You could be in a lot of trouble if Dr. Roberts or Dr. Sadowsky found out."

"I know."

"Then why?"

She pulled up to the street outside Sean's and cut the motor but made no move to step out. The silence in the car as she waited for my answer was deafening.

I shrugged. "I'm trying to respect Davin's wishes. The whole objective of this new experiment, in which we enter the cells while following Compound 10 and 11's policies, won't work if we do it against a Kazzie's wishes. Right now, Davin doesn't want me in his cell, so I'm not going in."

Amy smiled. Her smile then turned into a grin.

"What?"

"Nothing. I just like what I'm seeing." She opened her door. A rush of cool air entered.

I wasn't sure what to make of that comment as I stepped onto the sidewalk.

We strolled up the cracked concrete walkway, neither of us speaking. The stairs creaked again when we climbed them. Judging from the muffled noise coming through the front door, I wasn't surprised what we encountered when we stepped inside.

The pub's atmosphere was the exact opposite of my first visit. For one, it was almost full. Dozens of people filled the rooms. Laughter and conversations flowed through the air.

I stopped short when I saw how crowded it was. *Just breathe, Meghan.*

A fire roared in the fireplace, taking the chill out of the home. Wood smoke swirled around, bringing with it its rich scent. It appeared to be the only source of heat for the place. I walked closer to it and concentrated on the dry warmth.

Amy nodded toward the wall. "Looks like there's an open table over there." She had to speak loudly over the din.

I followed her to it. The din of the small pub was like noise traveling under water, quiet and muffled. When we reached the table, we slung our jackets over the seatbacks before sitting.

I felt a little safer against the wall since I wasn't surrounded on all sides. The heat from the fire warmed my back, and its quiet crackling was oddly relaxing. It helped calm my racing heart.

A waitress appeared, a smile on her face. "Care to look at some menus?"

I took the outstretched menu. They were simple pieces of paper with *Sean's Pub* printed at the top. Decorative Celtic designs swirled around the heading while handwritten items were listed beneath. There were ten food items to choose from. Most had similar ingredients in them. In other words, those were the surplus items in the nation right now.

"How you been, Amy?" The waitress pulled out a pad as she turned to my co-worker.

"Pretty good, Rach, you?" Amy replied.

"Can't complain. Dad's only got me working four shifts a week right now, so I can concentrate on school. Tips have been pretty good today."

"You can count on a good one from me." Amy placed her menu on the table and rested her elbows on top of it.

Rachael laughed. "If you stiffed me, I know where you live."

"Exactly!" Amy smiled.

"So what can I get you for drinks?"

"I'll take a lager." Amy raised her eyebrows at me. "What about you, Meghan?"

"Water's fine."

Rachel jotted it down before leaving to tend another table.

"Old friend?" I asked when Amy and I were alone again.

"Probably one of the oldest ones I've got. We grew up together. My parents and Sean have known each other forever." Amy picked up her menu again. "Rachael's a few years younger than me. She's still in school, working on her masters and hoping to work for the state one day in Child Welfare."

I cocked my head and wondered if Rachael knew my mother.

Following Amy's lead, I studied the menu. My eyes widened when I saw the prices. No wonder this place was packed. The prices were half that of most places.

"Do you know what you want?" Amy asked.

"Um, I'll get a burger and fries." It was the cheapest thing on the menu.

"Are you at least going to add cheese and all the fixings? I know they still have tomatoes and onions. Not sure about lettuce, though."

"Um, a plain burger is fine, really."

When Rachael returned, Amy intercepted before I could order. "We'll both have cheeseburgers with fries and all the fixings, and ketchup if you have it."

"We've got tomato sauce. We ran out of ketchup last week, and the next shipment won't be in till next month."

Rachael took the menus from our outstretched hands. "And we're out of lettuce, but we still have tomatoes, onions, and pickles."

Amy shrugged. "That works."

After Rachael was out of earshot, I avoided the urge to run a hand through my hair. *There are so many people in here!*

Of course, Amy was oblivious to the anxiety that strummed through me like disjointed music chords. She leaned forward and clasped her hands on the table. "So, tell me what's going on with Davin. We've all been wondering."

Her straight forward question help dampen the anxiety that wanted to consume me. I debated sounding optimistic and diplomatic, telling her everything was fine, but the bigger part of me wanted to say exactly how bad it was going. It would be such a relief to get it off my chest.

"Well…it's…" I tried to smile but failed. "Honestly, it's going terribly."

She cocked an eyebrow. "Really?"

"He hasn't said one word to me all week, except for that second day, and that's all I got. One word."

Amy's mouth dropped. "But the first day went so well."

I shrugged helplessly. "Maybe I caught him by surprise."

"Is that the real reason you're not going in his cell? Because it's going so bad?"

"No, I wasn't lying earlier. It completely contradicts what Compounds 10 and 11 discovered to enter his cell uninvited. I firmly believe that."

"So tell me what's going on."

I told her.

Everything.

How I'd started waking up so early and had arrived at the Compound all week before everyone else. How all of my free time was spent reading about psychology and PTSD and ways to encourage Davin to open up. How I'd spent an hour of every morning in the watch room with absolutely nothing to show for it.

"He won't even look at me now. If anything, I've made it all worse. He makes a point to keep his back to me."

"I didn't realize it was going that bad." Amy leaned back, frowning. "Okay, so you obviously need to change tactics. What you're doing isn't working." She leaned forward again, a keen light in her eyes. "Maybe it's something as simple as he's not a morning person, so you need to talk with him at a different time."

I raised an eyebrow.

"Okay, I know. It's probably not that. If the guy chooses to wake up at six every morning, he's obviously a morning person."

"I need to get through to him somehow, though, make him *want* to talk to me."

"Right." Amy pursed her lips.

Our drinks arrived a minute later. I took a sip. The water was icy cold, but the warm fire still roared against my back.

"So what else could you do…" Amy said, more to herself than me. She drummed her fingers on the table. "Bargain? Barter? Blackmail?"

I sputtered. "Are you stuck on the letter B?"

She laughed. "I'm brainstorming out loud. I could move on to C. Con? Conspire? Cultivate?"

I laughed again. "I've been trying to cultivate a relationship all week. It's not working."

"Okay, so I suppose you could continue doing what you're doing and hope that he eventually talks to you."

"I can't. I'm on a time limit. Dr. Roberts gave me one

month, and if Davin hasn't given any samples by then, he's sending you in."

"A month?" Amy's eyes widened. "That means you only have three weeks left."

"I know."

"So what we need to do is think up an incentive. Something that would persuade Davin to talk to you, or at least, listen to you."

"I suppose I could pump Sergeant Rose for more information on Davin, find out more about his interests, maybe find something that's important…"

Something that's important to him.

My words caught in my throat. I already knew what was important to him. I'd known for weeks.

Amy continued talking, oblivious to my epiphany. I thought about mentioning my idea but decided against it. If I were to pursue something like that, it was very much against MRI policy, but it was the only thing I could see working in the short time I had.

Our burgers arrived a minute later.

Amy chewed a french fry, not seeming to notice my silence. "What if we get Dr. Roberts to approve you giving Davin something from the outside? New shoes maybe? Or some kind of clothing?"

"Hmm," I mumbled, taking a bite of my burger. I'd definitely be bringing him something from the outside, but it wouldn't be a pair of shoes.

AMY DROPPED ME back at my apartment an hour later. I stepped out and leaned down, talking to her through the open door. "Thanks for the burger and for stopping by."

"No problem, and don't worry about Davin. We'll think of

something. I still think you're the best person to work with him."

I tried to smile but felt like I was lying to the one friend I had, besides Jeremy, but I couldn't tell her my plan. She'd get in trouble, just by knowing it if I ever got caught.

"Yeah, I'm sure we will." I waved goodbye and watched her drive off.

As soon as she rounded the corner, I sprinted toward my building. It was almost two in the afternoon. If I wanted to make it to Rapid City before curfew, I had to leave, *now*. It was at least a five-hour drive going at top speed. That didn't leave much room to spare. With a trip like this, I couldn't claim Compound business so I couldn't be out after curfew. It was too risky. If it got back to Dr. Roberts what I was doing, I'd be fired.

An old suitcase was buried somewhere in my closet, and I cursed when it took me five minutes to dig it out. Once it was on my bed, I packed a set of clothes, a toothbrush, a hairbrush, and some soap and shampoo.

I almost closed it but then hurried to my dresser. I threw in an extra set of clothes, just in case I needed to add layers. With any luck, I'd find accommodation somewhere near Rapid City. If not, I'd have to sleep in the car. Either way, it was best to be prepared.

Realizing that, I also pulled the comforter and pillow off my bed. I'd never slept in my car before, but I supposed there was nothing like trying it for the first time when it dropped close to freezing at night.

After packing some food from the kitchen, a few water bottles and a hat, I was almost ready. The last thing I needed was her address.

I pulled up the internet and searched for *Sharon Kinder* and

Rapid City. It took a while to find her. I cursed the entire time. There was so much data to scroll through, all pre-First Wave stuff that never got cleared from servers.

Luckily, I finally found her. With suitcase in one hand, and my bedding awkwardly stuffed under the other, I carefully walked down the back stairs to the parking lot. Thankfully, the battery in my car was new, so a 350-mile trip wouldn't be a problem. I just hoped there would be a station to recharge it when I arrived.

I briefly contemplated how smart this entire plan was as I packed my car. I'd never done anything impulsive like this before. Let alone something impulsive, against my job's rules, and at such late notice with curfew coming.

Perhaps I wasn't nearly as smart as everyone thought I was.

Fearing I'd changed my mind if I thought any more about it, I pulled out of the parking lot and headed for the interstate. I-90 connected the cities, so there was no worry of getting lost.

When I turned onto the interstate junction, I accelerated down the ramp to I-90 west. A tentative smile crossed my face as the speedometer climbed. I'd never gone west on the interstate before. Only east.

Open land sailed past me as I cranked the speed up to seventy. It was a bumpy ride. Road maintenance was the bottom of the list for our state's funding, but the hard jostles and dips didn't stop the euphoria that coursed through me. It felt like I was on an adventure, even if that adventure could lead to the end of my career.

16 - TRIP

Rolls of hills covered the land, like gentle waves in the ocean. The land stayed consistent for the first couple hundred miles. Empty, barren fields as far as the eye could see. Nobody lived out here. The small towns that once dotted the interstate were now ghost towns, except for the odd few.

Rough bumps and uneven patches on the road made it hard to keep a consistent speed. Large cracks also appeared. Luckily, none of them were big enough to cause problems.

By the time the sun blazed red and the Badlands appeared, I'd only encountered two other vehicles during my long drive. It was an uncomfortably isolating feeling. The Badlands didn't help. Their small peaks of striated stone jutted up against the land like shark fins cutting through water. They were beautiful but in a harsh, deathly sort of way.

The clock on my dashboard glowed 7:01 p.m when a sign appeared stating Rapid City was twenty miles away. Anxiety strummed through me like ocean waves crashing on the shore. The sun was close to setting. Curfew was coming.

I'd never been out past curfew. If I didn't find a place to

stay, I'd have to look for a residential street to park on and hope any patrol that passed didn't look into my car. Once again, I couldn't believe how impulsive I'd been. A well-planned out trip within the state could have gone well if it had been just that.

Planned.

The sunset faded with each mile. Lights from the city glowed faintly in the distance. I kept my eyes peeled for any accommodation. My heart leaped when I saw the first hotel, but as I got closer, it sank. It appeared all of the hotels entering the city were closed, no longer in business for who knew how long. Shingles were blown off roofs. Debris, caught in neglected landscaping, fluttered in the breeze. *So much for beginner traveler's luck, but at least I made it to Rapid.*

I sped up as I approached the town. 7:19 p.m. I didn't have much time, and my battery was low. Lights glowed in some buildings, but so far, all of the hotels were dark. I chewed my lip as I scanned for any sign of life in the skeletal structures. 7:24 p.m. Curfew was currently at 7:30 p.m.

Just as I began scouting for a place to pull over and spend the night, a sign appeared. *Motel 6.* The 'vacancy' sign blazed bright and promising.

It was 7:28 p.m. when I pulled in front of the motel. They also had battery charging stations in their parking lot. Someone was definitely watching over me. I looked up at the sky when I stepped out of my car and mouthed a silent thank you to the only person I'd ever count as my guardian angel.

A GIRL, YOUNGER than me, manned the check-in desk. Gum snapped in her mouth as she leafed through an old paperback. She blinked when I approached, obviously surprised to see someone.

"Can I get a room for the night?" I pulled my wallet from my purse.

"Did you make a reservation?"

"No, but the sign said vacancy."

"Oh yeah, we've got tons of rooms. It's just that nobody's come in for a while without a res, especially just before curfew."

The clock behind her read 7:34 pm. If she denied me a room, I'd be spending the night in my car. In the parking lot.

The check-in girl leafed through her paper forms. "Smoking or non?"

"Non-smoking."

"King or queen bed?"

"Whichever's cheapest."

She lifted a sheet. "I've got a queen bed at ground level for $439 tonight."

$439! "That'll be fine."

She gave me the key and instructions on how to find the room. Before I turned, I asked her if she knew where Franklin Street was.

She pulled out a paper map from behind the desk. "Twenty bucks for one of these."

I grudgingly bought that as well.

Since I had everything I needed from my car and had already plugged the battery in to charge, I didn't need to go outside again. While I probably could have gotten away with sneaking out to grab a forgotten bag, even if a patrol drove by, I didn't want to chance it. I was in an unknown city, with unfamiliar law enforcement. I was playing it safe from here on out.

It didn't take long to find my room. The drab décor left a lot to be desired. The bedspread was thin, the carpet threadbare, and the furniture looked at least thirty years old. That said, it was warm, safe, and most important, legal.

I SET THE bedside alarm for seven the next day. Surprisingly, I didn't wake once during the night. Perhaps the long drive and anxiety had left me too exhausted to do anything other than sleep.

Once I rolled out of bed, I didn't waste any time. After dressing, brushing my teeth, and tidying my hair, I was ready to go.

A different person was at the front desk when I checked out. He barely looked up from his book when he took my key. That suited me just fine. Small talk was not something I could muster right now.

It was silent when I stepped outside. Even though curfew lifted at six in the morning, there were no cars on the interstate. It was oddly quiet, even for this time of day.

Slipping into my vehicle, I pulled a water bottle and energy bar from the backseat while I let the heater run. The energy bar was homemade, by me. In other words, it tasted like bark and smelled a bit like it too. However, it was packed with calories and nutrients, which at the end of the day, was all that mattered.

Since I'd memorized the map I'd bought last night, I didn't need to pull it out as I drove.

When I pulled onto Franklin Street, towering trees lined the boulevards and covered the single level houses like large umbrellas. The houses were similar. Old, a bit rundown, but cared for as best as possible. Most of them had peeling paint and decaying looking porches, but the homes appeared occupied.

Bits of cheer were evident. A wreath on a door. Pots of

artistically displayed evergreen branches on a porch. If this was where Davin had grown up, it had been a simple yet loved neighborhood. I felt a little better knowing that, considering what his life was like now.

Sharon's house was a small bungalow that sat midway down the street. Blue shakes and shutters, that had probably once been white, stared back at me when I parked. It was still early, not even eight. Cutting the motor, I stayed in the car.

I didn't see a light on in any of the windows, so I decided to wait until signs of life appeared. If she was home at all. It could be a long wait, but if she was sleeping, I didn't want to wake her just yet. I'd give her till nine.

It felt a bit weird, munching on another energy bar while staring at a stranger's home. The word *stalker* came to mind. *Is that what I'm doing?* My stomach twisted.

It was definitely weird that I'd packed up in the middle of the afternoon yesterday, drove as fast as my small car could manage on a pot-holed filled interstate, and woke first thing the next morning to track down Davin's mother. *Is it a testament to how much I want to help Davin, or is my interest in him going too far?*

I pictured his fierce blue eyes and aloof demeanor. My stomach flipped at just the thought of him. I shook myself. Perhaps it was best I didn't put any more thought into *that* department.

Taking another bite from the energy bar, I started to wonder if anyone was home, but just as I took another drink of icy cold water, Sharon's porch light turned on.

I almost choked.

The front door opened. A woman's head appeared around it. She bent over and picked something up. It took me a minute to understand what it was.

A newspaper.

She was picking up a *newspaper*.

It had been so long since I'd seen anyone do that, it took me a second to process it. Some long-ago, distant memory stirred. Sitting around the kitchen table at home, legs dangling from the chair, eating Cheerios with Jeremy while our father sat beside us reading the local newspaper he'd collected from the front porch.

Sioux Falls didn't deliver newspapers anymore. That had stopped years ago. Now, they were only available for purchase at the South Dakota Food Distribution Center. Apparently, Rapid City refused to give up the tradition of delivering papers.

The woman retreated inside. I hastily wiped any crumbs from my mouth and took one last drink.

It was now or never.

I tried to shut my car door quietly, but the bang seemed to echo down the street. I glanced over my shoulder several times as I hurried across the road and cut through Sharon's lawn. Against all logic, I half-expected someone to stop me, grab me by the shoulder, and demand to know what I was doing. Funny how when you were doing something wrong, you assumed everyone else knew too.

Of course, there was no one around to even care.

Once on Sharon's small porch, I took a deep breath and knocked. *Will she even answer?* Maybe the woman I'd seen wasn't Sharon. Maybe this wasn't her house. Maybe the search I'd done on the internet was wrong. For all I knew, Davin's mother was working, or had moved, or had never lived here in the first place. I balled my hands into fists in my pockets. I was still wondering if anything good would come from this trip when the door opened.

"Yes?" The woman I'd seen earlier peered through the door. She only cracked the door a few inches. I could barely see her face in the shadows.

"Sharon Kinder?"

"Yes?" she repeated.

I sighed in relief. "My name's Dr. Meghan Forester. I work at Compound 26 in Sioux Falls, with your son, Davin. May I come in?" I'd never used my full title before, but I hoped it would make me sound more legitimate.

Unfortunately, that was exactly what happened.

Sharon's mouth dropped and she stepped back. I heard a strangled, "No!" before her eyes rolled back in her head.

I pushed the door open just as she hit the floor.

17 - SHOCK

I didn't catch her, but I managed to break her fall. My heart beat painfully in my chest as I crouched beside her. My first thought was that I'd given her a heart attack.

I felt her neck for a pulse. It was strong and steady.

"Sharon? Sharon?" I gripped her wrist and shook. When that did nothing to rouse her, I grabbed her by the shoulders. "Sharon! Wake up!"

Her eyes fluttered open. She looked around, squinting.

"Are you okay? Are you hurt?"

Her eyes snapped to mine. *Davin's eyes.* They were the same electric blue. My breath caught in my throat.

Seeing me, she scrambled back as quickly as she could. Any concerns I had about her health, vanished.

"No!" She shook her head vigorously. "No, no, no! I don't want to know! Please don't tell me! I couldn't bear it!"

I held up my hands, not entirely sure what she was talking about. "I'm sorry if I've frightened you. Please, let me explain why I'm here."

"Oh, I know why you're here." Tears filled her eyes. "Just

please, don't say it. I couldn't bear it if I lost him too."

Everything clicked.

I sank to the floor but kept my distance. "Davin's fine. Davin's *not* dead. He's just fine. I'm so sorry that's why you thought I'd come."

Her mouth opened, then closed, then opened. "But… if he's not…" She frowned. "I don't understand. If he's not dead, why are you here?"

I slowly stood but still kept space between us. "I'm hoping you can help me with something. I work directly with your son, but I think I need *your* help to help him."

She just stared at me.

I could tell this was too much information, too soon in the morning, and too much of a surprise. "I'm sorry." I held my hand out to help her up. "Is there somewhere quiet we could talk?"

She let me help her stand but her frown remained in place. "Yes, yes of course. Come in. I'll make some tea."

SHARON LED ME to a small, round table in her kitchen and told me to sit. The house was old and dated. Everything in it appeared to be from the last century. The faded linoleum floor peeled in the corners. Wallpaper covered every vertical surface. Its floral patterns reminded me of the nursing homes my mother visited for her charity work.

The house smelled clean, though, and there were touches scattered throughout that hinted at effort. Clean, pressed towels hung from the stove's handles. Not a hint of dust on the worn cabinets. A freshly laundered, wrinkle-free tablecloth covered an old, scarred table.

"I hope you like your tea plain." Sharon approached the table, balancing a tray with a porcelain teapot and two matching cups with saucers. "I'm out of milk and sugar."

The tea set was old, probably antique, but immaculately cared for. Not a chip to be seen anywhere, and the fine bone china gleamed.

"Black tea is fine. Thank you."

She set the tray down and poured us each a cup, her hands trembling. A little tea dripped over the side onto her saucer. "Shoot," she whispered.

I felt the urge to reassure her, but I had no idea what to say. During the long drive yesterday, when I pictured all of the different scenarios for how today could play out, this was *not* it. I thought for sure I'd be the anxious, tongue-tied mess, unsure of myself while twisting my hands. In reality, I was the calm one. Sheer panic gleamed in Sharon's eyes.

When she finally settled beside me, she took a few more minutes to drape a cloth napkin in her lap. Her eyes never met mine as she straightened and smoothed the clean linen more than once. I placed my napkin on my thighs as well but didn't fuss. I waited for her to start drinking her tea before I did. The manners my mother instilled in me would probably be with me until I died.

"You probably want to know why I'm here." I set my teacup down. The brew was deliciously hot.

Sharon tried to smile as she smoothed hair behind her ears. "Yes." Her voice shook.

I took a deep breath, studying her for a minute, trying to figure out how to begin. I couldn't get over how identical her eyes were to Davin's. Beautiful, large, and so very blue. Other than that, they didn't resemble each other that closely.

Where Davin's skin was a dark golden, fiery hue, Sharon's was a pale ivory. Where Davin had thick, black hair, Sharon had fine, wavy auburn. Where Davin was muscled and lean,

Sharon was petite and curvy.

She was a beautiful woman who looked younger than she had to be. Davin was twenty-four, so even if she'd had him young, she'd still be in her forties. Most likely late forties to early fifties, but other than a few lines around her eyes, she didn't look her age at all.

Taking another deep breath, I said, "I need to tell you that nobody at the Compound knows I'm here."

"Oh?" Her hand paused midair, still holding her cup.

"If anyone were to find out, I could be fired."

"Okay…" She carefully set her cup back down.

"I know it's asking a lot, and it's not appropriate, but could you keep this meeting and everything we discuss a secret? I'm trying to help your son, but if anyone finds out I came to you, I wouldn't be allowed to work with him anymore. I'd most likely be fired and arrested."

Sharon frowned. "Did something bad happen to him? Is that why you're here?"

I didn't know how to answer that. Technically, nothing had happened to Davin that was against Compound 26's rules, but what had been done to him violated every moral code imaginable.

"No, not exactly," I said tentatively.

Sharon's eyes narrowed. "How do I know I can trust you? How do I know you're telling me the truth?"

I pulled out my access badge, to prove that I really was who I claimed to be. She studied it for a moment and handed it back, seemingly satisfied.

"As for your other concern," I replied with a shrug, "I can't prove to you that what I'm saying is true. You'll just have to trust me. That is, if you're willing to listen."

She bit her lip, her blue eyes never leaving mine. "Okay,"

she finally said. "I won't say anything about this meeting to anyone, but please, don't deceive me."

"I won't."

She must have believed me because her tensed shoulders relaxed. She took another sip of tea and then smiled tentatively. "All right, tell me what's going on with my son."

I HATED TO quench the hope in her tone, but as I described what had been done to Davin over the past few months: the Chair, the isolation, the psychological trauma, her face fell more and more. I promised to be honest, though, so I was.

"But now, we're trying to change." I put my hand over hers. It was so unlike me, to initiate contact with another person whom I barely knew, but silent tears poured down her face, and I had to do *something*. "I've been assigned to work with Davin every day, doing the new practices that Compounds 10 and 11 are initiating, but I can't get through to him. He won't talk to me, or even look at me, and if this continues, he'll be assigned to someone else. If no one can get through to him, I hate to think what Dr. Roberts will do."

With her free hand, Sharon dabbed the corners of her eyes with a napkin. "I had no idea it had gotten that bad. I knew when they cut off our communication that something must have changed, but Davin never alluded to being treated unfairly. It must have only just begun."

I didn't correct her, even though I felt dishonest doing that. Davin had been mistreated for months if not years. I had no idea what the previous MSRG Director was like, but from what I'd gathered, he'd also sanctioned samples taken from the Kazzies without consent. Davin had obviously kept everything negative from his mother. Either that or the social worker had censored it out. Regardless, I guessed it wasn't something Davin wanted his mother knowing, so I wasn't going to enlighten her.

"Can you help me?" I asked gently. "Is there anything I could do that will help me get through to him?"

She pulled her hand free from mine, grabbed a tissue, and blew her nose discreetly. She shrugged. "I'm not sure if there is. Davin was always a headstrong, stubborn little boy, who turned into an even bigger headstrong, stubborn adult. Once he sets his mind to something, it won't change."

If there was one thing I already knew about Davin, that was it. "I learned that pretty quickly."

She laughed humorlessly, wiping her eyes again.

"Maybe you can tell me more about him," I suggested. "Perhaps something you say will trigger an idea to convince him to talk to me."

"Okay." She chewed her lip and then stood. "I have an idea. All of the family albums are in the living room. We can start by looking through those."

SHARON'S LIVING ROOM was like the rest of the house. Dated, worn furniture, but clean. I settled on a pale, green couch that was surprisingly comfortable.

"Did Davin grow up here?" I asked as Sharon dug through a cabinet by the wall. My heart pounded again. I pictured Davin standing in this very room. *What if this very sofa is where he once lounged while watching TV? What if the carpet my feet are touching was once touched by him?* As soon as those thoughts entered my mind, I wanted to kick myself.

Seriously, what's wrong with me?

Sharon finally stood with an armload of photo albums. She sat beside me on the sofa. "Yes, Davin grew up here. We bought this house thirty years ago. Davin and all of his brothers and sisters…" Pain entered her eyes again. "They all grew up here." She busied herself with the albums.

"I'm sorry. I know they all died."

She nodded. Tears filled her eyes again. "I'll never forget that time. All of my babies were up on the reservation. Every single one of them. I knew the instant I heard what happened I'd never see any of them again. I didn't think I could bear it."

I sat silently, feeling the weight of her sadness. It was like being at the bottom of the ocean, the pressure so immense it threatened to crush the life right out of me. *What can I possibly say to that?* Sharon had birthed five children. Five. And not one had escaped *Makanza.*

No wonder she'd collapsed when she thought I'd turned up to announce Davin's death. Her last child, while lost from her life, was at least still alive, somewhere. Perhaps knowing that Davin was still alive was the only thing that kept her going.

"We'll start with this one." Sharon wiped her eyes and opened an album.

The first picture showed a much younger version of Sharon in front of this very house. The exterior was almost the same as it was today, but newer and fresher looking. A man stood beside her, his arm around her shoulders.

I knew immediately it was Davin's father. He was tall, Native American and had the same coppery skin as Davin, albeit a slightly darker shade. Also, like his son, he was lean yet muscled, and had chiseled features and midnight hair. However, unlike Davin's, his hair was ramrod straight, not wavy.

"Is that Davin's father?" I pointed to the man.

"Yes, we were married only a few months before this picture. I was so young at the time and so naïve. I thought we had our whole lives in front of us and would be in love forever." She smiled wistfully. "Even though that's not exactly how it turned out, it was still one of the happiest times in my life." She fingered the picture.

"What was his name?"

"Chayton. His mother gave him a traditional Lakota name. It means Falcon."

Sharon stared at the picture, still fingering it. "He completely whisked me off my feet. I was only twenty at the time and new to South Dakota. I'd grown up in Wyoming, but my family…" Tiny wrinkles appeared around her eyes when she frowned. "We weren't exactly close. I came here to get a fresh start. I hadn't been here even a month when I met him. Chayton was a student at BHSU, like me. We were both studying Sociology so we had a lot of classes together. Also like me, he started a few years after most of the other freshmen. He was twenty-two our freshman year."

She trailed on, telling me how they'd fallen in love fast and hard. After six months, they were living together, a year later, married.

"It seemed perfect," she said. "We bought this house while still in school, knowing we wanted to stay in South Dakota. Times were tough. We both worked full time while studying to meet the bills, but Chayton had scholarships, so that helped."

That wistful smile appeared on her face again. "Davin arrived a year after we married. Having him was one of the best things that ever happened to me, but it did derail my career plans. I dropped out in my junior year to care for him. I tried going to school full-time at first, but it was too hard. It broke my heart every time the babysitter showed up to take care of him, like someone else was raising my child."

I nodded encouragingly so she'd keep going.

"Mina was born two years after Davin. Lars followed and then Elliot and Aurora." Sharon flipped through the album. "They were my whole life."

I followed her fingers as she moved from picture to picture, telling me about her children in each photo. What they'd been doing or where they'd been. It was like most family photo books, pictures of the kids playing, or goofing around, or having some milestone documented.

Each of Davin's siblings looked similar to him. They all had dark hair, although they didn't all inherit Sharon's eye color. Lars and Elliot both had brown eyes.

"Who's this?" I asked when she turned the page. It showed a close-up of a little girl, probably no older than four, with blue eyes and lighter-colored skin than all the rest.

Sharon smiled tenderly. "My youngest baby. Aurora. She looked the most like me, but her personality was most like Davin's. They were very close, even though they were eight years apart. Davin always talked to her like an adult. He was never condescending, and he always had time for her. She loved that about him."

She pointed to a few more pictures, showing Aurora as she got older. "After Davin turned eighteen and moved out, Aurora would sit at the window, waiting for him if she knew he was coming home. Little did I know the Second Wave was coming." She bit her lip and fingered the photo. "I never told him that. How she'd wait for him. He felt guilty enough as it was, not being around for her all the time. And with Chayton's and my divorce, things were already hard on the kids."

She shook herself. "We'd only been divorced for a year. Chayton had been drinking a lot before we split up. I knew he had an alcohol problem when we first met, but he didn't drink every day. Just every now and then, but when he did, he'd get so drunk he couldn't stand for days. I thought it was a phase he'd get over. So many guys did stuff like that in college, and we were both so young. I figured it would eventually pass. But that never happened. As we got older and our family grew, things got harder, money grew tighter, and Chayton drank more and more."

Sharon stopped flipping pages. "He was never abusive, and he loved the kids, but he just couldn't handle it. The stress, the pressure. It got too hard for me. After twenty years of marriage, we divorced. Things got better when he left and moved back to the rez. The kids would visit him two weekends a month. Being on his own was good for Chayton. He never got sober, but from what Davin told me, he wasn't drunk all the time. Most weekends they visited, Chayton stayed sober the entire time they were there. At least, he tried."

She wiped her eyes.

"When the Second Wave hit… it was on one of the weekends they were all there. I knew as soon as I heard the news that they'd all get it. It was so contagious. So deadly. But still, I prayed and prayed and prayed. Just prayed to let them be safe. Maybe they'd be off on an outing for the day and were far away from the rez. Or maybe they'd decided to go camping and Chayton had been on a bender, locked away in his house, not having contact with anyone while he drank for the few weeks prior. Would you believe that was the one and only time I ever prayed that he'd been so drunk he wouldn't have left his house?" She gripped my hand, her fingers surprisingly strong.

I clasped her tightly.

Tears poured down her cheeks. "But of course, Chayton had done everything he could to sober up for their visit. He hadn't drunk for two days. He'd gone to all the stores to get the things they liked, rented movies, bought Elliot a woodworking tool he'd been asking for. It was probably on one of those outings that he came in contact with someone infected. And then all my babies arrived, and they all became infected too. I'm sure Chayton hadn't known he was sick. He would have never knowingly given them anything."

Sharon grew silent, her eyes going blank. Memories of that time would no doubt haunt her for the rest of her life. Everything she described brought back painful memories of my own, only my pain was different from hers.

"I'm not sure if any of this helps. Perhaps talking to Davin about Aurora would at least get his attention." She closed the album. "They were so close, and he loved her so much."

"I'll try that."

"Well." She stood. "I could really use another cup of tea. You?"

Before I could respond, she left the room. I heard a few rustles of movement from the kitchen and Sharon softly blowing her nose. A few minutes later, she returned, carrying something. She held it out to me. "Here. I want you to take this to Davin. Give it to him if you can."

I took what she held in her outstretched hand. It was cool, metal, circular in shape, and small. It easily fit in the palm of my hand. I turned it over. It was a miniature picture frame holding a photo of Davin when he was younger with his sister, Aurora, beside him.

"I've wanted to give that to him for years. I think her death was the hardest for him, but I also know he never wants to forget her."

I fingered the photo. I knew exactly what it was like, to love a sibling more than yourself. "I'll find a way to get it to him." I put the photo in my pocket. "I promise."

WE SAID OUR goodbyes an hour later. Sharon insisted on making me lunch before I left, but she didn't seem to have the energy to talk about Davin or any of her kids anymore. I didn't press her. She looked exhausted.

When I stood at the door to leave, she abruptly pulled me into a hug. "Thank you," she whispered. "You have no idea how much it means to me that someone else cares for him too."

I stood stiffly as her soft form embraced me. She didn't seem to notice. Surprisingly, as the seconds passed, I felt myself relaxing against her before I tentatively hugged her in return. "I'll do everything I can."

She pulled back and smiled, her blue eyes so bright and so familiar, I felt like I was looking right at Davin. "I know you will. I can tell you're the type who doesn't give up easily."

I smiled and pulled my hat on as I left.

When I slid into my car, I fastened the seatbelt but didn't move. Meeting Sharon and seeing all of those photos made me feel even more strongly about not failing Davin. I had to get through to him. I had to. Now, it was just a matter of figuring out *how*.

18 – PICTURE

I brought the photo with me when I drove into work the next morning. It was so small it easily fit into my jean pocket, but it was still against the rules to bring anything from the outside in. With every step, it seemed to burn a hole in my leg.

There would be so many questions if I got caught. *Where did you get this? Why did you visit his mother? What else have you done?* The interrogation would be the first step. After that, it would be arrest and prosecution. The state took public health very seriously, and this could be seen as a violation of the Public Health Protection Act.

I took a deep breath when I pulled into my parking spot. I hadn't bothered waking at four, mostly because I knew it was useless. Davin was definitely not impressed with my morning wake-up greetings. Besides, my lab group knew I was meeting Davin, so I didn't need to hide it anymore.

Once again, since I knew I was doing something wrong, I thought everyone else knew it too. I expected Private Williams to pat me down when I entered the Compound, even though he'd never done that before. I waited for the glowering and suspicious glances from Carol, but she hadn't arrived yet. Even though it felt like guilt glowed on my face like a shining beacon, apparently, it didn't.

Nobody looked at me twice.

I did my usual routine when I sailed past the lobby. Stop at my office to drop off my bag. Check my email to see if anything had happened over the weekend. Glance into the lab to see if anyone was working. Leave my office and hurry to the Inner Sanctum.

I'd become used to seeing the Kazzies over the past week since I passed them daily. They'd all been asleep last week when I'd sped down these halls at five in the morning, but today, some lights were on.

Garrett watched me when I walked by. He looked like he'd just woken up. I tentatively waved.

His eyes narrowed, making his egg-like orbs look less like golf balls and more like flying saucers. I wondered sometimes if he felt uncomfortable having eyes that big. *Do they hurt? Ache? Bother him in any way?*

None of us knew since he wouldn't tell his researchers.

The Sisters were up when I entered their hall, both still in their pajamas. That was a surprise. It was barely six. They usually slept later.

Sara grinned when she saw me and walked to the window so she could hold her hand up to the glass. Once again, her actions baffled me. *Why is she so taken with me?*

I placed my hand over hers, the glass the only thing separating us from touching. Her smile bloomed, and again, that strange ache began in my head. It was something I regularly felt when I stood beside her now. It was only last week that I'd put two and two together.

See Sara. Feel the beginnings of a headache.

Coincidence? I think not.

However, I had no idea what that meant. I fingered the picture with my other hand. Sara's eyes dropped to my pocket. Stepping back, I waved goodbye.

In the next hall, Dorothy was still in her coma, and Sage and Victor were both asleep. I hurried to Davin's cell.

When I stepped into Davin's watch room, Sergeant Rose greeted me with a warm smile. Scents of coffee, as usual, filled the air. Since it was after six, Davin was up.

"Morning," Sergeant Rose said when I sat beside him.

"Good morning."

"Have a nice weekend?"

Was there an edge to his tone? I shook myself. *You're just being paranoid.* "Um, yes. You?"

"Yeah, we went to that community event at the park on Saturday. Did you go?"

I shook my head.

"That's too bad. You missed a good time. It wasn't too cold, and there was a local acoustic band playing. The kids liked it, my wife did too. They even served hot apple cider at no charge."

"Really? Who funded it?"

"The city. The mayor said something about having enough apples this fall to do something for the community. It was great. Different for a change."

I knew what he meant. While most communities in South Dakota did their best to have gatherings, funds were slim. That usually equated to people meeting at a common ground and hanging out. And that was it. Normally, everyone had to bring their own beverages, food, and seating. It was really more of a glorified park outing than anything, but people enjoyed it, and it helped. Anything to distract everyone from how much we'd lost in the entertainment world.

"What'd you get up to this weekend?" Sergeant Rose sipped his coffee.

I averted my gaze. "Ah… nothing really. Just kept trying to figure out how to get through to him." I nodded toward Davin. He ate breakfast at his desk. At least, it wasn't a total lie.

"Come up with anything?"

I thought of the picture in my pocket. "Maybe."

"Well, I hope so. The guy deserves a break." Sergeant Rose tipped his coffee back and drained the last drop.

"Want another?" I pointed at his empty mug.

"Sure, if you're going to get yourself one?"

Nodding, I took his cup. Sergeant Rose couldn't have any idea what I'd done, but I hated lying. I figured it was best to get out of here instead of continually fabricating the truth.

I returned five minutes later with cups for both of us. Davin's lights were on when I walked into the hall. I expected him to be in his usual state, either with his back to us or reading the paper. But when I rounded the corner and stepped into the watch room, I stopped short.

Davin sat on the edge of his bed, except this time he faced us, and he looked directly at me.

My breath caught in my chest.

He was looking at me. More than just that, he was *staring* at me. I kept waiting for him to avert his gaze.

He didn't.

His eyes held mine, his expression blank. I stared back, captivated by the beautiful shade of his irises. *Why the heck is he holding eye contact?*

He had *never* done that before.

"He doesn't seem too grumpy this morning." Sergeant Rose reached for his cup. It wasn't until he pried it from my hands that I realized I stood rooted to the spot.

I shook myself, breaking eye contact with Davin. "Um, yeah."

When I glanced back up, Davin was in his bathroom. He must have moved at his speed.

Sitting down beside the guard, my fingers shook when I brought the coffee to my lips. The picture Sharon gave me pressed into my thigh and reminded me of what I promised to do. Not only did that give me anxiety, but Davin's strange behavior did too.

I tried to shrug off both worries, but all I did was spill more coffee on my pants when my hands continued to shake.

"Are you going to try talking again today?" Sergeant Rose asked.

I drained my cup. "Yes, after he's done in the bathroom." *Which means I have time to sweat while I work on a plan to get Sharon's gift to Davin.*

Thankfully, Sergeant Rose was oblivious to my inner turmoil. He filled the silent void with steady conversation. I didn't have to contribute anything past *Hmm* and *Oh*.

When Davin appeared in his cell again, I stood. The time had come. "I'm going in today," I announced.

Sergeant Rose cocked his head. "You are?"

"Yes." Going in was the only way I could deliver the picture, so I had to, whether Davin liked it or not.

Sergeant Rose stood, his relaxed demeanor gone. He was suddenly completely professional and serious. That switch made me feel better. *No dying today.*

"I'll get him in the Chair after you're ready to go in."

Right. The Chair. I'd forgotten about that.

In the containment room, Sergeant Rose helped me into the suit. When I turned my back so he could hook up the respirator, I hurriedly fished the picture out of my pocket. Breathing hard, I pushed it into the suit's belt and stuffed my arms in the jacket. Sergeant Rose didn't seem to notice, which was good, since as much as he and I were becoming comfortable working with each other, I knew he wouldn't compromise his position to help me. Luckily, the photo didn't budge as we finished all the safety checks.

Giving me the thumbs up, Sergeant Rose returned to the watch room, sealing me inside the containment room. Only a few minutes passed before the guard's voice sounded in my earbud. "Ready?"

I cocked my head. *It only took a few minutes to get Davin in the Chair?* Just to get the Chair into position took almost a minute. *Does that mean…*

"Yes, he went willingly into the Chair when I told him you were coming in. No fight at all," Sergeant Rose said, as if reading my mind.

I breathed a sigh of relief. At least I wouldn't have to feel guilty about Davin being in the Chair, but I wondered *why* Davin had willingly sat in it. He'd never been compliant about anything. Ever. I wasn't stupid enough to think he suddenly wanted to be my friend and everything would be roses. *So why did he do it?*

"Are you ready?" Sergeant Rose asked again. I still hadn't said anything.

"Oh. Yes."

The dials in front of me spun and the light above flashed red. With a hiss, the door opened. I stepped forward, my thumb going to the picture in my belt.

19 – TEST

Davin sat calmly in the Chair. He watched me lumber slowly into the room, his expression blank. For once, rage didn't coat his chiseled features. That angry, ugly expression was gone.

When I pulled his desk chair over and sat, Davin's eyes stayed glued to mine. I faltered. *Why does he keep looking at me?* I had no idea what was going on. The aloof, cold Davin that ignored my every move seemed to have evaporated, and I had no idea why. It wasn't like anything had changed between us.

Regardless of his one-eighty shift, a part of me wanted to stare. He was so strikingly handsome. There was a steely beauty to him that reminded me of the proud Sioux warriors he'd descended from.

As we sat there, I discreetly gripped the suit's belt, to make sure the picture hadn't fallen. His eyes followed the movement.

"How are you today?" I asked.

His brow furrowed slightly. "Fine."

My eyes widened. *Did he just speak to me? He's never willingly spoken to me.* My heart rate sped up as my confusion grew. *What the hell is going on?*

I knew if I dwelled on it I'd lose all train of thought. And right now, I *needed* to stay focused.

Taking a deep breath, I stammered, "Ah… that's good. I… ah…" I glanced awkwardly over my shoulder. Sergeant Rose watched us while sipping his coffee. "Um, Sergeant Rose?"

"Yes?" His voice sounded through the hood and cell's speakers. I knew Davin could hear him too.

"Would you mind turning off the speaker system in the watch room? I'd like to speak to Davin privately."

The guard frowned.

"You'll still see everything that goes on. I'm not asking you to step out. You're still following policy." I pleaded with my eyes. I knew Sergeant Rose was a good man. He knew I wanted to help Davin. Now it was just a matter of how much *he* was willing to help too.

He sighed audibly. "All right. I suppose I could. Switching off." A click sounded in my earbud.

I turned back to Davin, but before I could say anything, his gaze narrowed. "What's in your belt?"

My eyes bulged. *He noticed? But how did he see it?* I glanced at my belt. Only a tiny corner of the picture poked out. *He must have really good eyesight.*

"Um, it's…" *Meghan, pull it together!*

Taking a deep breath, I made a motion, trying to make it look like I was adjusting something on the suit for Sergeant Rose's benefit, but instead, I carefully extracted the photo. Luckily, my gloves were made of thick rubber that offered protection without sacrificing dexterity.

I showed him the picture, making sure to keep it out of Sergeant Rose's sight. "I brought this for you."

Davin's face tightened. "Where did you get that?"

I took a deep breath. I'd had a gut feeling since meeting Davin that I needed to be one hundred percent honest with him about everything. That meant being completely honest now.

"Your mother."

His nostrils flared. A stretch of silence fell between us, yet I could practically feel its weight.

Keep it together, Meghan. He's actually talking to you.

"When…" He cleared his throat. "When did you get it from her?"

"This weekend."

"Did she find you? Track you down somehow?"

"No. I went to her."

"In Rapid City?"

"Yes."

The silenced stretched again. "Why?" he finally said, his voice hoarse.

"I needed to get through to you. I was hoping she'd have an idea. And she did, she gave me this." I indicated the photo discreetly.

Pain flashed through his eyes. "Did she tell you who that is?"

I nodded.

"And did she tell you she's dead?"

"I already knew that," I replied quietly.

"She was only ten-years-old when she died."

"I know."

"What else did my mom say?"

"About Aurora?"

He flinched when I said her name. "About anything."

I shrugged. "She told me about your childhood, your brothers and sisters. We went through some family photo albums. When I showed up at her doorstep, she thought I'd come to announce your death. She fainted."

Davin's eyebrows rose. They were dark, midnight lines, perfectly shaped. "She's never fainted before."

"She thought she'd lost you. She loves you very much."

The silence stretched again. My heart beat frantically. I'd never dreamed we'd talk as candidly as we were now.

"How is she?" There was a catch in his voice.

"Good. I think. She served me tea and lunch. I was there for half the day."

A small smile tugged his lips up. "Did she use her good china?"

I thought of the pristine tea set. "The ones with the pink roses and cherry buds?"

He nodded or tried to, but the Chair's restraints halted the movement.

"Yes," I replied.

He smiled this time, a real smile. It transformed his face. My heart rate increased as his straight white teeth flashed. His eyes lit up as his proud expression softened and warmed. The hard, intimidating edge left.

My mouth went dry. I averted my gaze. I needed to *not* notice things like that.

"She loves that tea set," Davin said. "She only uses it for guests." A faraway look entered his eyes.

I wondered if he was remembering happier times. I tried to look at him objectively, to stop these ridiculous feelings I was having. In doing that, I noticed something else: how bizarre this situation was. Here Davin sat in front of me, metal bands holding all of his limbs and head in place, yet he looked comfortable. Serene almost. And here I was, in a suit that made me look like a marshmallow.

What an odd way for two people to truly meet for the first time.

"Has she lost weight?"

I snapped myself out of my reverie, but Davin immediately shook his head. "No, of course, you couldn't know that. You've never met her before."

I cleared my throat and tried to force my feelings under control. "Are you worried about her? Worried that she's lost weight?"

He stiffened. It was like he suddenly realized who he was talking to and what he was saying. "A little," he said tentatively.

"I could visit her again, check up on her to make sure she's okay, or relay a message to her if you'd like." The sentence popped out of me before I knew what I was saying. Then my brain kicked in. *Go back to Rapid City? Meet with Sharon again?* There was no way I could keep that kind of deception from the Compound forever.

"You would really do that?" Surprise was evident in Davin's tone.

I bit my lip. "Yes."

He frowned again, studying me. "Why are you helping me?"

I paused. "I don't really know. I just… I think it's wrong, what we've done to you. I know I can't fix it, not yet at least, but maybe I can make it better, for the time being."

He gazed at me intently. "Won't you lose your job for visiting my mom? Dr. Roberts forbid any contact with our families a few months ago. He personally delivered that message to me."

Why isn't that surprising? "I would lose more than my job."

He frowned. Once more, he studied me, as if trying to see into me. "How old are you?"

"Twenty-three."

He frowned further. "Isn't that pretty young to be working here?"

"Yes."

I could tell he wanted to ask more, a flash of curiosity flittered across his face, but he didn't say anything else.

"Is there something you'd like me to tell your mom?" I asked.

He cocked an eyebrow. "Tell her I love her and tell her… the thunderbird sings in Sweden."

The thunderbird sings in Sweden? "Okay, I will."

SERGEANT ROSE INTERRUPTED. I heard the click in my earbud as my speaker turned back on. "Dr. Roberts and Dr. Sadowsky will be in soon. Just wanted to give you a heads up." The speaker clicked off again.

My stomach dropped. *The Director and my boss are coming here?* That could only mean one thing.

They heard me. They heard everything we said.

Panic kicked in as my heart began to pound. I was a fool to think the Compound would ever let me speak privately to a Kazzie. There must be another sound system in here, a secret one, maybe wired to the Director's office?

My eyes darted around the room, searching for it. I didn't see anything. *Of course, you don't see anything! Would they really hide a secret communication system in plain sight?*

I wondered if Sergeant Rose heard us too, but I was sure I heard his speaker system switch off.

"What is it?" Davin asked.

I met his gaze, my eyes large with panic. From the surprised expression on Davin's face, I guessed Sergeant Rose hadn't turned on Davin's speakers when he relayed the message. Only I knew who was coming.

"Dr. Roberts and the Compound's Director will be here any minute."

An icy chill settled over his features. "Why?"

"I don't know."

"Did they hear what I told you?"

"I don't know. Maybe."

"Is this some kind of game you're playing?" His voice turned glacial.

I couldn't help my irritated glare. "No, Davin. This isn't a game. If they really heard us talking, I'll get fired for bringing you that photo. Does that seem like a game I would play?"

His tense expression relaxed. For a mere second, he actually looked contrite. "Sorry."

I offered a small smile. "It's okay."

"You better get out of here. You shouldn't be in here when they arrive."

I stood and almost turned before I realized I hadn't given him the photo. Stepping closer, I discreetly pushed the small picture into his palm, keeping my back to Sergeant Rose. Davin's fingers closed over mine.

My breath stopped.

I could feel his heat through the glove. More than that, I felt his power. I'd seen firsthand what he was capable of. If he wanted to right now, he could rip my fingers off.

I stood frozen, waiting to see what he would do. At the moment, I was helpless.

All Davin did was squeeze me gently. "Thank you," he whispered.

I let out a sigh of relief. "Just hide the photo. Don't let them find it."

I knew that wouldn't be possible, not if the Compound did

a search, but still, I could hope.

Davin nodded and released my fingers. I looked at his hand before leaving. His palm was large, strong. Just like the rest of him.

THE DECONTAMINATION PROCESS seemed to take forever. Sergeant Rose smiled when I returned to the watch room. "Did it go okay? It seemed to. You two spoke for a while."

He looked happy, completely guileless. I knew he'd told the truth when he said the speaker system was off. *Sergeant Rose didn't eavesdrop on us, but did my boss and the Director?*

"You said Dr. Roberts and Dr. Sadowsky are coming here?"

"Yeah, they called about fifteen minutes ago. They're doing rounds right now to see how the new procedure's going. They should be here any minute."

Rounds?

The access door to Davin's hall opened. Dr. Roberts wore his usual military attire, his stomps loud and marching. Dr. Sadowsky, however, wore a crisp business suit and silk tie. He was an older gentleman, with gray hair and a sharp gaze. I'd never met the Director before, and it now seemed I would, as I possibly got arrested.

"Dr. Forester." My boss stepped into the watch room. He glanced over my shoulder. Davin was still in the Chair. I didn't dare look at our Kazzie, for fear my face would give away the unease I felt.

"Hello, Dr. Roberts," I said, as evenly as I could.

"Have you met the Director?"

I shook my head.

"Dr. Forester, this is the Compound's Director. Dr. Ethan

Sadowsky."

The Director held out his hand, smiling warmly. "I've heard a lot of promising things about you."

I shook his hand, my heart rate increasing as my ever-present anxiety cranked up. "Thank you."

"How is everything going with Davin? You must have just been in his cell?"

"Yes."

"Any progress?" The Director's eyes flickered to the Kazzie.

Sergeant Rose grinned. "Davin spoke to her for over fifteen minutes."

Dr. Sadowsky's eyebrows rose. "Is that right? The Kazzie who never speaks to anyone, spoke to you for fifteen minutes?"

I nodded hesitantly.

"What did you two speak about?" he asked.

I swallowed and glanced at Dr. Roberts. He was watching me, his face unreadable. *Are they toying with me? Trying to get me comfortable? Or did they not hear me?*

Sergeant Rose said they were doing rounds. Perhaps the timing was all a coincidence.

"Not much," I finally replied. "We're just getting to know each other."

Dr. Sadowsky nodded. "I'm pleased to hear it. From what Timothy's told me, Davin can be difficult to work with." He glanced through the watch room window again. "I see he's in the Chair," he said grimly.

Dr. Roberts' gaze hardened. "That's necessary for most of what we do with him."

"Is it?" the Director responded.

Before I had time to process that response, Dr. Sadowsky

turned to leave. "Keep up the good work, Meghan. I'll be interested to hear what Davin's samples reveal after you collect them."

"Um… right… of course," I stammered.

When both men exited the watch room, I slumped against the wall. *So they didn't hear me?*

Surely if they had, I'd be walking out of here in handcuffs right now. I bit my lip, my mind racing over the short conversation. *And what about the Director's comments on the Chair? Does he oppose using it?*

I thought again of the conversation Amy and I had in Sean's Pub. About going to the Director with our concerns. I hadn't yet, only because I didn't know how he'd react. I couldn't risk that right now, but maybe he would listen. Maybe I *wouldn't* be demoted for voicing my concerns.

I chewed my lip as I considered that possibility but eventually concluded that I needed to learn more about the Director first. I couldn't risk losing my position right now.

"Are you okay?" Sergeant Rose asked.

I straightened, wondering how long I'd been lost in thought. "Yeah, of course."

Davin was still in the Chair. His fingers were still curled around the picture. I hoped he'd find a place to hide it.

"You can release him now," I said. "I'm not going back in today."

I waved goodbye to Davin. He acknowledged me with the barest hint of a nod. I let out a breath and walked out of the watch room.

There were two more things I had to do today. One, figure out how the heck I'd get Davin's coded message to his mother. And two, devise a plan to carry out what I'd started with Davin without getting caught by the Compound.

If that was even possible.

20 - GERRY

As I headed out of the Sanctum, I passed all of the Kazzies' cells.

My eyes widened more and more. All of the Kazzies had researchers in their cells. It was the first time I'd seen so many of my colleagues actively engaged in working toward our common goal.

Both Sage and Victor were talking with scientists. Even Dorothy was. My mouth dropped when I passed her. I'd never seen her awake. She sat on the edge of the hospital bed, still hooked up to the monitoring equipment. A researcher kneeled awkwardly in her suit beside her.

Dorothy wore a confused expression and cradled her head in her hands. I wondered how long she'd been awake. From her constant squinting and temple rubbing, I guessed she had a pounding headache. She'd lost weight too, no doubt from being starved, but she wasn't thin.

Amy was probably right – the way *Makanza* affected her would never allow her to achieve a normal weight.

As I stepped into the Sisters' watch room, any earlier fears of being discovered evaporated. All of the researchers were with their Kazzies right now. Dr. Roberts and the Director really *had* been doing rounds.

I let out a sigh of relief and peered into the twins' cell.

Gerry sat in a chair beside Sara and Sophie. Her large biohazard suit looked awkward and formidable. *Is that how I appear to Davin?* I almost snorted. I was fairly certain Davin would *never* find me formidable.

The Sisters sat curled up on one twin bed. Neither of them seemed very engaged in the conversation. From the words flowing into the watch room through the speakers, Gerry was asking the twins about their parents, but when she asked a question, the twins would look away, clearly uncomfortable with the subject.

The guard glanced over his shoulder. He did a double take. "Good afternoon, Dr. Forester."

I managed a smile. "Sorry to sneak up on you. How long has Gerry been in there?"

"Over two hours."

Crossing my arms, I watched as Gerry tried to engage the twins.

Neither seemed interested.

Instead, Sara stood and strode to the watch room's window. It was only then I realized that none of the Kazzies were in their Chairs. All of them were freely wandering around their cells with their researchers.

I stepped back when Sara raised her hand to the glass, her eyes on me. She smiled.

I sheepishly smiled back, feeling guilty for interrupting whatever Gerry was in the midst of doing.

Gerry frowned when she saw me.

"I better be on my way," I told the guard. "Can you tell

Gerry I said hello?"

I nodded goodbye to Sara before leaving.

I DECIDED TO double back to the breakroom to grab a cup of coffee before leaving the Sanctum. Considering it could be a long night, I needed all the caffeine I could get.

I was in the midst of pouring a cup when Gerry strode into the room. From her heavy frown, she didn't look happy. I just hoped I wasn't the reason.

"Meghan, how are you?" Before I could reply, she moved to the counter and poured a cup of coffee.

"I'm fine. How are you?" It was hard to meet her gaze. I tried not to be intimidated by Gerry, but she carried such a boldness about her. The woman commanded attention as if by genetic right. Her height, level stare, and confident aura projected throughout the small room.

"I've been better." She sighed. "Neither Sister will talk to me about anything other than frivolous things. Every time I try to get to know them better, they clam up like an oyster that's about to be bait. And then the Director decided to do his rounds, so he witnessed the entire thing. That didn't help."

Her words confirmed that they really were on rounds. I slumped in relief. "Is this the first time you've tried to talk to the Sisters?"

"About serious stuff? No. Sometimes they'll relax around me, and I'll attempt to create a deeper relationship, but every time I've tried that, they close down. They don't trust me or any of the other researchers."

"Do *any* of the Kazzies trust their researchers?"

Gerry frowned. "No, I don't think so. Dr. Roberts has done a good job of making us the bad guys."

I frowned. Sara and Sophie had been here for eight years.

They'd come to Compound 26 right after it opened. As kids, their entire family died in the Manhattan Disaster which meant they'd spent the first two years following the First Wave in MRRA makeshift quarantine facilities.

Does that mean, in all that time, they haven't talked about how they're doing? For a kid to lose their entire family in the First Wave, and also turn into a Kazzie, seemed doubly traumatic.

"So, they've never spoken about what happened to anybody?" I set my cup down.

Gerry shook her head. "No, they have. When they first arrived, Dr. Sadowsky had a psychologist visit with them. I don't know how long their therapy lasted, but they've never spoken about their parents to anyone else, as far as I know at least."

A thought struck me, causing my insides to turn. The twins had been children for the first five years they'd been at the Compound. Had research been done on them during that time? When they were *kids*? I almost didn't want to know, but I had to.

"When did you guys start studying them?"

Gerry stared at me for a minute, as if trying to figure out where I was going with this. "I've been here four years, and we've studied them the entire time I've been at this Compound. I believe we've studied them since day one, but I'd have to check."

Bile rose in my throat. "But they were only kids."

"Yeah, I know. No wonder they hate us, right? That made me mad too when I first found out, but that was until I learned nothing invasive was ever done on them until they were older. Mostly, it was benign tests. Kyle said they always tried to make it a game. Sometimes Sara and Sophie even enjoyed it, according to him at least. He said it broke up the day to day monotony."

I felt a little better knowing that and reminded myself most of my co-workers were good people. We were just in a facility that sometimes did bad things.

"So what's up with you and Sara by the way?" Gerry's curious eyes met mine.

"What do you mean?"

She leaned against the counter and sipped her coffee. "You know, how she's always seeking you out? Holding her hand up to you? I've had a few people tell me she's always happy to see you and seems to be constantly searching for you when a group of researchers shows up."

I swallowed uneasily and debated telling Gerry about the strange headache feeling I got off Sara. But nobody else had mentioned anything like that. *I better keep that one to myself.*

"I don't know." I shrugged. "Mitch and Amy told me it's really unusual behavior for her."

"It is." Gerry studied me again. I tried not to fidget under her gaze. "I wonder if you should try speaking to her instead of me."

"Me?"

Gerry nodded. "She seems to prefer you."

"Isn't that against the rules?"

A disgusted sound emitted from her throat. "Only since Roberts took over."

"Should we ask him?"

She sighed heavily. "I already know what the answer will be, but yes, I'll ask him."

We talked for a few more minutes before I left. Sara approached the window again when I passed her cell. I got the feeling she wanted something from me, that she hoped I would do something, but for the life of me, I didn't know what.

MY NEXT STOP was at my office. I needed somewhere private to think about how I'd get Davin's message to his mother. *The thunderbird sings in Sweden.* I briefly shook my head over the absurdity of it. I'd seen enough James Bond movies to know that equated to code talk. No wonder Sergeant Rose said they hadn't been able to understand anything Davin and his mother were saying in their letters. I sat in my chair, my forearms falling on my desk, my head collapsing onto them.

What am I doing? Pretending to be a spy? A secret messenger? I almost laughed. Jeremy's response would be a roar of laughter. It was so out of character for me. Exactly something I'd *never* do.

The seriousness of what I contemplated deflated any humor in the matter. If I got caught even talking to Sharon without Dr. Roberts' permission, much less passing secret messages between her and Davin, I'd be fired and possibly arrested.

I'd never broken the law before working here. I wasn't going to pretend I felt comfortable doing that, but I promised Davin I'd pass along the message, and I needed to keep my promise.

I took a deep breath and pulled my head up, sitting back in the chair. *What's the best way to tell Sharon? Phone call? Email? Letter?* I knew before I thought it, that the first two options were out. Phone and email records could be traced. With the tracking the MRRA did on cell phones and email to help prevent human movement across state lines, I wasn't willing to take that chance.

A letter would be better, but again, a letter was evidence. *I know Sharon will never turn me in, but what if someone else finds it? What if a visitor reads it, happens to be a diligent citizen, and reports it?* I'd hate to wake up one Saturday morning to a police officer greeting me with a knock on the door. I sighed. That only left one option.

I'd have to deliver the message in person.

It was the only way.

I EVENTUALLY LEFT my office and went to the lab. Amy and I spent the afternoon working beside one another. She kept giving me sideways glances. It only made me sweat more.

"Something you'd like to ask?" I finally said.

Her curls swished against her shoulders when she turned. "Did you speak with Davin today?"

"Yes."

"And?"

"And what?"

I felt, more than saw, her roll her eyes. It was hard to see her clearly through the side panel of my goggles.

"Meghan, seriously, you know what. Just two days ago you're telling me you couldn't get through to him, and I gave you all those ideas on what you could try, but now you won't tell me a thing? You've got to know I'm curious. Did you get him to talk to you or not?"

"Yes. I did."

She grinned. "Well? What did he say?"

The thunderbird sings in Sweden. "Not much."

"That's it? *Not much*?"

I shrugged. "He really didn't say much, but I'll keep trying."

"You're really not going to tell me?"

"It was only small talk. You know the usual, 'how are you doing,' and whatever. Not much beyond that, I swear."

She frowned and turned back to the bench. "Well, at least

he spoke to you."

"Yeah." I bit my lip and kept working.

Lying to Amy didn't feel right. I knew I could trust her, but I couldn't bring her into what I started. She didn't deserve to be punished if I got caught. My anxiety returned full force at the thought of Amy getting fired too. Sweat popped up on my brow, and my heart hammered in my chest.

With shaking hands, I snapped my gloves off. "I think that's all I'm going to do today." I stepped back from the bench, shrugging my lab coat off. "See you tomorrow?"

Amy glanced at the clock. It was only five, earlier than I'd ever left. "Got plans tonight?"

"No, just tired."

She gave me a concerned look. "Okay, see you tomorrow."

JEREMY WAS AT my apartment when I got home. I was so relieved to see him that I almost burst into tears. Ever since talking with Amy, it felt like a fire of deception burned in my gut, its flames licking and singeing my nerves to the point of combustion.

"You look like you've had a good day." Jeremy sat at the kitchen table, his legs propped up on the table, a book in his lap.

I laughed shrilly.

"I'd ask you what happened, but I know better," he added.

I plopped down on the chair beside him. "What am I doing?" I mumbled, more to myself than to him.

"You're currently sitting at your table, looking like you haven't slept in a few weeks."

I almost stuck my tongue out at him.

He put his book down, pulled his legs off the table, and sat up. "Seriously, do you want to talk about it?"

I bit my lip. I knew I shouldn't.

"Come on, Meg, what's going on?"

I met his gaze, his coffee brown eyes open and serious, all joking gone. I swallowed. "I'm breaking the rules at the Compound."

He laughed. "And here I thought it was something serious, like you killed someone or poisoned a co-worker with your cooking."

"It *is* serious, Jer. Do you know what happens to MRI workers that break Compound policy? We get arrested and face prosecution."

He sat back, crossing his arms. "Are you talking about the Public Health Protection Act?"

"Yes."

"Are you doing something that would jeopardize public safety?"

I thought about visiting Sharon, giving the picture to Davin, and agreeing to pass a secret message between him and his mother. *Will any of that jeopardize public safety?* "No, probably not. But what I've done is strictly against MRI policy."

"What did you do?"

"I can't tell you."

He sighed. "Okay, but will it hurt anyone in the public?"

"No, I guess not."

"Will it hurt anyone within the Compound?"

I thought again before answering. "I don't think so."

"Then what are you so worried about?"

"I could still get arrested!"

"And what, get dragged down to the local police station for a couple hours of interrogation only to learn you haven't actually broken any laws, you've just broken MRI policy? Last time I checked, that wasn't illegal. Yes, you'd lose your job and any chance at working for the Compounds again, but you wouldn't go to jail."

"Hmm." I frowned.

"See, I told you I should be a lawyer."

"Yeah, but are you *sure* I wouldn't go to jail?"

"Yes."

"How do you know that for a fact?"

"Because I've read the Act. All of it. The Public Health Protection Act was created to keep the public safe. That's it. It doesn't mean your employer has absolute control over you and can prosecute you for breaking their rules. The government will only prosecute a MRI researcher or MRRA soldier if, by breaking MRI or MRRA policies, he or she puts the public at risk. As much as it feels like it, Big Brother is not watching."

It felt like an ocean of weight lifted off my shoulders. "Thanks, Jer, that really helps."

"Always happy to be of service. Keep in mind, though, if I ever become a lawyer I'll be charging you for these sessions."

21 – REVELATION

After Jer left, I fell asleep on the couch and only woke the next day because of the singing birds outside my living room window. The clock read almost seven in the morning.

Crap!

When I arrived at the Compound, I hurried to the Inner Sanctum, bypassing my usual routine. Sergeant Rose helped me into the biohazard suit. We hooked up cuffs, clicked gloves into place, twisted on the hood, and activated the respirator and electronics. When I was fully encased, we went through the final checks. He gave me the thumbs up and exited the chamber.

A few minutes later, his voice sounded in my earbud. "He's in the Chair. Ready?"

"Yes."

The familiar hiss of the door opening into Davin's cell no longer made me fearful. Since Davin had willingly sat in the Chair, I anticipated we'd have another good session. Consequently, I should have felt calm and purposeful, especially since I didn't have to worry about him ripping my head off. As for why my heart suddenly pounded, or why my breath caught when Davin's eyes met mine, I had no rational explanation.

In my lumbering suit, I walked carefully toward his desk chair and pulled it over. I felt him watching me. Thankfully, the hood blocked most of my face, and there was no way he'd hear my heart galloping in my chest. I took a deep breath.

Seriously, this is ridiculous! So what that he's attractive. So what that, for whatever reason, his very presence gets my pulse racing.

It was obviously just the adrenaline of what we were doing, conspiring to establish communication with his mother, that caused these feelings. There was no way I could explain it other than that. I couldn't have feelings for someone I barely knew. And I certainly couldn't have feelings for someone, who just two days ago, would have rather seen me nailed to a stake than seated in front of him.

I sat and met his gaze. "Good morning, Davin."

"Morning."

I turned slightly, making eye contact with Sergeant Rose. "Do you mind turning off the speakers?"

"Shutting off now." A click sounded in my earbud.

Thankfully, Sergeant Rose seemed to be under the impression that it was privacy that made Davin talk. Not the fact that I'd given him something from the outside world, something that would guarantee my termination from the MRI.

"The speakers are off," I told Davin.

"Did you give the message to my mother?"

I tried to stop the flip in my stomach. His voice was so deep and rich. "Not yet, but only because I have to tell her in person."

The hopeful look in his eyes vanished.

I rushed to explain. "I have to tell her in person, Davin. I can't email or call her. If there's any trace of me contacting her, and if Dr. Roberts found out, I'd be fired."

He studied me, his dark eyebrows knitting together. Finally, he nodded. "Okay, but how are you going to tell her?"

"I'll drive to Rapid again this weekend."

His eyes widened just as a lock of hair fell across his forehead. Since his arms were tied down, he couldn't move it. "So you're going to drive out there again this coming weekend?"

"Well, yes. It's the only way I can get her your message."

He just stared at me.

"If you'd rather I not see her in person again so soon, I don't have to. I could–"

"No," he interrupted. "It's not that…" A contemplative expression crossed his features. "I guess I didn't expect you to go to such lengths, but what you're saying makes sense. I'm, ah…" He cleared his throat. "I'm sorry you have to do that."

I'd never seen him apologetic before. Angry, yes. Full of hate, yes. But sorry? No.

"It's fine, really, it is. I like your mom, and besides, it'll give me something to do on the weekends."

His eyebrows shot up. "Week*ends*?"

"I'm assuming you're going to have more than one message for her, so I'll have to go there multiple times."

"That'd be nice, but…"

"But what?"

He shrugged. "You probably don't want to spend every weekend doing that."

"Oh." My cheeks grew red. Davin obviously thought I was like any normal twenty-three year old. One with friends who spent her free time going to movies, hanging out at other's homes, or doing whatever normal people my age did. Not conspiring with a Kazzie's mother because she didn't actually have any friends to hang out with. "It's not a big deal, really."

"It is." His eyes were bright.

I wanted to sink right into them.

"Actually," I said, clearing my throat. "Driving to Rapid to see your mom will be much more interesting than what I normally do."

He cocked his head, or tried to, but the Chair stopped him. "What do you normally do?"

"Well…" I stopped. What could I say? *I don't have any friends. I basically hang out by myself in my apartment, reading research papers, and if I talk to anyone, it's only my brother.* "Um, I just work a lot on the weekends."

"Oh. Since I've never seen you here on weekends, I assumed you were off."

Does that mean he thinks about me? I shook that thought off. That was obviously *not* what he meant. "I do have Saturday and Sunday off, but I still do work, at home."

"I see."

Hopefully, he didn't see. I couldn't think of anything more humiliating than Davin learning I had no life outside of work. But I promised myself I'd be honest with him. "Actually, I usually spend my weekends working because I don't have anything else to do."

He raised his eyebrows. "Really? What about seeing your friends? Or family?"

I thought of my parents. That was *not* my idea of a fun weekend. I looked down so I wouldn't have to see his reaction when he found out about the other.

"I don't really have many friends, and my parents live in Vermillion, so I don't see them much."

I stared at my boots, waiting for him to say something.

When he didn't, I glanced back up.

"I never had many friends either."

My mouth dropped. He was so ridiculously attractive I had a hard time believing that. "Really?"

"Being Native American put a stigma on me. It didn't help that my dad drank. It fit perfectly into the stereotype of Indians, so it just added fuel to the fire when kids saw him drunk, stumbling around our lawn. All of that meant that I wasn't cool. Usually, I hung out with my brothers and sisters. We kept to ourselves for the most part."

His expression didn't change, but a part of me awakened, feeling the flutter of a connection that bypassed all flippancy and trivialness. Davin also knew a childhood of loneliness.

I shifted in my seat. "I never had friends in school either. We moved around a lot when I was a kid. My only friend was my brother, and then when *Makanza* hit, I never saw anyone since we were locked in our home."

He gazed at me so intently, my breath stopped. "Yeah, it didn't make growing up the easiest."

"No, it didn't."

"So you must be pretty smart then, if you got hired here and you're only twenty-three?"

"Um, yeah, I guess." Normally, I hated when people brought that subject up. It was definitely not normal to be my age and have all my degrees. Most people my age were still trying to figure out what they were doing with their lives, but with Davin it felt more like simple curiosity, rather than him pointing out I was different.

"You must be. Do you have an advanced degree? Like everyone else working here?" he asked.

"I finished my Ph.D.'s last Spring."

"Ph.D.'*s*?"

"Yes, I have two."

"Wow, that's impressive."

I smiled as my nerves slowly evaporated. It was weird how quickly I had grown comfortable with him. That had never happened with anyone before.

WE TALKED FOR another hour. I was surprised at how easily I opened up. For the most part, he wanted to know the usual things when getting to know a person. What cities had I lived in? What were my hobbies? What did I study in school? Where had I gone to school? He seemed genuinely interested.

A part of me knew that was most likely due to the boredom of his daily life, not because he found me so fascinating. When was the last time he'd met somebody who wasn't another Kazzie? Or a researcher who wasn't talking to him to get something? Granted, sooner or later, I'd need to obtain his sample, but that wasn't why I was doing this, not really.

"What kind of books do you like?" he asked.

"Do you mean fiction books?"

"Or any books. I'm guessing you read a lot of science stuff?"

I smiled. "I do. Most of my reading is related to work, but when I can pry myself away from it, I usually read dramas or romance."

He raised his eyebrows. "Romance, eh?"

I blushed. "There's nothing better than a romance if you truly want to escape the world."

"I'll have to try one of those."

"So you're not a romance fan?"

He chuckled. "Usually crime, thrillers, or science fiction, but I read non-fiction too."

"Like what?"

"Medical stuff, mostly."

"Oh. Were you trying to learn more about *Makanza*?"

"Trying. As you know, when the virus first hit, there was no literature on it. If nothing else, I've learned a lot about viruses."

"That makes two of us."

He chuckled again. "What about your parents? Where do they live?"

"Vermillion. They've been there since the First Wave."

"And you said your best friend growing up was your brother? Do you only have one sibling?"

"Um…" I hesitated. "Yes."

"What's he like? Does he live here?"

Those questions stopped my breath. I looked down and fidgeted with the belt on my suit. *Do I have to answer that?*

"Meghan?"

I kept fiddling with it.

"Meghan?" he said again, more warily this time.

I couldn't meet his gaze. Tears sprang into my eyes. I blinked them back as best I could and looked up, trying to smile.

"Whoa, Meghan, I'm sorry. Hey, I didn't mean to upset you. You don't have to answer that if you don't want to." Genuine concern filled his eyes.

I shook my head, telling myself I was being overly emotional. "It's okay, it's just…"

"He's dead?" he finished for me.

I looked away and thought about Jeremy, about that day. That horrible, awful day, six years ago.

The day my life stopped and time stood still.

My heart felt like it was breaking all over again.

"Yes."

Davin nodded.

I stared at my hands. A part of me wanted to keep all of these emotions buried away. They hurt. They hurt so damned much! I hated feeling them. But the other part of me, the part I'd buried away and refused to acknowledge for the past six years, ached so much to talk about it. I'd never spoken about Jeremy with anyone.

Maybe Davin will understand. He lost his little sister, and he loved her as much as I loved Jeremy. Maybe, just maybe, he'll understand why I pretend my brother's still here.

I took a deep breath. I was about to tell him something that I'd never told anyone. Not a single soul.

"He died six years ago, in the Second Wave, but I still talk to him sometimes. I pretend that he's here."

I felt Davin listening even though he didn't say anything.

"Sometimes when I've had a bad day, or when I really wish, more than anything that I could talk to my brother, I pretend that he's in my kitchen, sitting at my table, talking to me, just like we used to."

I couldn't meet his gaze after I said that. It was embarrassing, and I was afraid of what I'd see in his eyes. *What if he doesn't understand? What if I just made the biggest and most embarrassing declaration in my life?*

"Meghan," Davin said quietly. "Look at me."

I slowly looked up. Pain rimmed his eyes. Pain only someone who'd gone through the exact same thing could feel. "I understand, okay? I really understand."

"You do?"

"Yeah. I really, really do."

My shoulders shook as more tears streamed down my face.

From what Sharon told me, Davin had been as close to

Aurora as I'd been to Jeremy. It was the only reason I'd told him, and because I'd promised myself I wouldn't lie to him. Still, for me to admit that I pretended my dead brother was actually alive was huge. I'd never told anyone how much Jeremy's death affected me. It had been six years since it happened, yet each year on the Second Wave's anniversary, I cried and cried and cried. I didn't think I'd ever get over the pain of losing my only brother, and the only true friend I'd ever had.

"How did he die?" Davin asked quietly.

I sniffed, wishing I could wipe my nose with a tissue and cursing the large hood which made that impossible. "One of his friends called him. He thought it'd be fun to get a group together to sneak out one night during the Second Wave when martial law was in effect and no one was allowed to leave their homes. They didn't think anything would come of it of course, and they were sick of being cooped up after the Second Wave hit." I paused. I hated remembering that night. It was the last time I'd seen my brother at home. The last time I'd hugged him. The last time I'd seen him healthy and whole.

"They'd gone down to the skateboarding rink to get outside and do something. Who would have thought they could contract it there? But they did. After they'd been out for a few hours, they got picked up by the MRRA and put into mandatory quarantine for breaking the law. I'm sure those officers thought it was all for nothing, after all, they'd been *outside*. How could they possibly have contracted it? Imagine everyone's surprise, when they all started showing symptoms three weeks later. The MRRA later found a homeless man dead in the woods. He'd died from *Makanza*. I guess he frequented that park and constantly touched the railings when he walked back and forth. That was how they figured Jeremy and his friends got it. If they'd only gone to a different park, or if that guy hadn't been there just minutes before they'd arrived – it was absolutely the worst luck ever."

I stopped. My brother, my only friend and my only family who actually *felt* like family, was gone and was never coming back.

I played with my fingers. "It's why I wanted to work with the virus. I made a promise to myself, when he died, that I'd do whatever was needed to find a vaccine or cure for *Makanza*. I owed Jeremy that much, so his death wouldn't be in vain. I've dedicated the last six years of my life to that. It's why I'm so young and working here. Six years of studying around the clock, barely sleeping, never taking any time off…" I bit my lip. "It's another reason why I don't have any friends, but it's what I needed to do, so I could work for the MRI. It was the only way I could make some kind of sense out of Jeremy's death."

I stopped. The silence stretched.

"I'm sorry," Davin finally whispered. "I know that doesn't help, but I'm sorry you lost him."

I shrugged. "I'm sorry you lost Aurora."

He smiled sadly. I could tell he wanted to hang his head, or look away, but the Chair stopped him.

A flash of anger, so intense it took my breath away, coursed through me. All Davin wanted was to move his head, and he couldn't. Because of the Chair. Because of the damned Compound.

I dropped my chin, forcing myself to calm down and take a deep breath. As angry as the Compound made me, this anger wouldn't help. I needed to focus and rationally devise a plan to help Davin and the Kazzies.

"Do you miss him?" Davin asked.

"Every day. Do you miss Aurora?"

"Yeah, every day."

We fell silent. It was strange. It should have been an awkward silence, or a moment when we both looked anywhere but at each other, but instead, it was the opposite. We both stared into each other's eyes, the silent exchange saying more than any words could. I'd never felt more close to another human being. I wanted to cry at the irony of it all.

The only person I've ever been able to relate to about my lonely childhood and suffocating pain that plagued me every day since the death of my brother, was the only person I could never truly have in my life. He'd forever be in here, locked away.

At that moment, I hated the virus more than anything.

22 - TELEPATHY

After our raw, openly honest conversation on Tuesday, Davin and I spent the rest of the week talking. Each day we found more to say. It was like the dam had broken.

By Friday, I was spending hours at a time in Davin's cell. Luckily, Sergeant Rose didn't frown upon the longer and longer periods. Instead, he seemed to support them.

I wasn't entirely sure what to make of everything. Davin confused and intrigued me. He was an enigmatic puzzle. One minute, he was smiling and laughing, but the next he was angry and withdrawn. I'd learned what triggered the latter: the Compound and Dr. Roberts. As for what made him smile, talking about his family, his time on the reservation, and the hobbies he'd enjoyed before *Makanza.*

He was a loner, like me. One of his favorite things had been walking along the Missouri River with nothing but the sky and hills for company. He had an affinity for nature, something his mother and father instilled in him. That was one of the hardest things for him about living within the Compound, the fact that he never got outside. At times, he said it was suffocating.

As for how Davin felt about me, I had no idea. I knew he enjoyed my company, but then again, I was the only person he'd really spoken to in six years. And while he was friendly, he was by no means flirtatious. I knew he was grateful I contacted his mother, and I knew he enjoyed how our conversations broke up his day, but beyond that, I had no idea how he felt.

Regardless of whatever Davin was thinking, I never thought it would be possible for *me* to spend so much time talking to someone. Normally, it took me months, sometimes years, to really feel comfortable with another person. Even the tentative friendship I'd formed with Amy was unusual.

Being with Davin, however, had begun to feel like breathing. Natural. Normal. He understood more than anyone what I went through losing my brother, and he gave me hope that someday I'd be completely whole again.

"ARE YOU READY?" Sergeant Rose asked.

His question shook me from my thoughts. We snapped my hood into place and finished the last safety check. The green light shone on my wrist. I was ready to enter Davin's cell. It was my fifth time visiting him this week.

Tomorrow I'd drive to Rapid City to see his mother. However, this time my trip wouldn't be impulsive. I'd leave early, which would give me plenty of time to arrive. Since I'd already met Sharon, I'd go straight to her house, even if it was unannounced. Davin told me she was a homebody and usually spent her free time indoors. He felt fairly certain she'd be there when I arrived.

Sergeant Rose did the final check on my respirator. "I'm sure he'll get in the Chair right away. It shouldn't take long."

Just as he was about to exit, I flipped the switch on my

wrist, activating the external speaker. "Wait. Does he have to be in the Chair?"

Sergeant Rose frowned. "Well…" He truly looked at loss for what *that* policy was.

"None of the other Kazzies are restrained when their researchers are in their cells, so why does Davin have to be? He won't hurt me."

Sergeant Rose sighed. "No. No, I don't think he would."

"So you won't restrain him?"

Again, Sergeant Rose didn't look entirely sure what to do. In the six years Davin had been at the Compound, I felt fairly certain he'd *always* been restrained.

"I'll take full responsibility for whatever happens because I'm sure *nothing* will happen."

Eventually, he nodded. "Okay, but only because I agree with you."

Sergeant Rose returned to the watch room, sealing me inside the containment area. Soon, the dials turned, the red warning light flashed, and the hiss alerted me to the door opening.

Davin's head snapped up as soon as I walked in. I could only imagine what I looked like, lumbering toward him like an astronaut on a mission to Mars. He was sitting on his bed, as if waiting for Sergeant Rose to activate the Chair. When our eyes connected, he smiled.

He was so beautiful, it took my breath away.

"Turning off the speakers," Sergeant Rose stated. The familiar click sounded in my earbud.

"Hi," I said. "We're alone," I added, with a wave toward the speakers.

Davin continued smiling.

Just a week ago, I would have felt paralyzing fear in the

situation I was currently in. Last Friday, Davin might have lunged at me, ripped my hood off, and exposed me to *Makanza*. Now, I knew he'd never do that. He may not have feelings for me, but I knew he may consider me a friend. How much had changed in such little time.

"No Chair today, huh?" he said.

"Not today and not anymore if I have any say in it."

He kept smiling. "I almost don't know what to do." He reached up, stretching his arms, showing off the freedom he had.

I laughed. "Neither do I. It was awkward enough trying to sit on your desk chair in this thing." I indicated my suit. "But if I were to sit beside you on your bed, I'd probably fall off."

He chuckled. "I'll get the chair for you."

In one of his lightning-fast moves, he had the chair at my side.

"Whoa." I'd only seen him move like that while I was in the watch room, never this close.

"Sorry," he murmured.

"Don't be." I sat.

He returned to the bed, leaning back on his elbows. I tried not to notice how his t-shirt spread across his chest, revealing strong pectorals underneath. I cleared my throat. "So, did you do anything fun last night?"

He snickered. "You mean besides watching TV, reading another book, and doing jumping jacks and push-ups?"

I rolled my eyes, smiling. "Yeah, besides that."

"That would pretty much sum up my night. What about you? What did you get up to?"

"I went grocery shopping. Exciting life I lead, isn't it?"

He leaned forward and rested his elbows on his knees. I tried to ignore his bulging biceps. "What's grocery shopping like nowadays?"

And just like that, we fell into easy conversation again. I told him about the South Dakota Food Distribution Centers and was shocked to learn he'd never heard of them. After that, he wanted to know more about my apartment and what life was like on the outside. His interest warmed me, but again, reminded me I was his only connection to the outside world.

While my heart fluttered at the sound of his voice, his was most likely beating steadily as if I was just another person who could break up his boring, routine.

"So, about tomorrow." I changed subjects. "I'll leave first thing in the morning, so I get to your mom's with plenty of time to spare before curfew. Hopefully, on Monday I'll have a few messages for you from her."

He sat up straighter. "About that…" He glanced at the watch room before looking back at me. "You're sure the speakers are off?"

"Yes."

His gaze again went to the speakers. "You're absolutely sure they're off?"

"Yes, I'm sure."

He swallowed. He looked visibly nervous. I'd never seen him like that before. He licked his lips. "There's something I'm going to tell you, but you have to promise not to tell anyone. Not a living soul. Do you understand?"

I swallowed uncomfortably. "Um… okay."

"I mean it, Meghan. Not a soul. Can you do that?"

Keeping secrets was one thing I was very good at. I met his gaze steadily. "Yes. I promise. I won't tell anyone. Not a single soul."

He took a deep breath. "Okay, so there's one other thing I'd like you to do before you go, if you're willing."

My heart rate picked up. "Yes?"

He frowned, his eyebrows drawing together. "You know Sara? The Kazzie with her twin in the other cell? Do you know how she and her sister share a link? A… mental link?"

"Yes, telepathy. Or at least, that's what we think they share."

"They are telepathic, but there's something else Sara can do, that the researchers don't know about. She can communicate with other people, telepathically, if they're open to the communication."

"*What?*"

He nodded. "All of us can communicate with each other through Sara, but it's imperative nobody in here finds that out."

My mouth dropped. I sat dumbfounded for a moment as I processed what he said. "You mean, you can *talk* to Sara? And she can talk to you?"

"Yeah."

"And she can talk to all the other Kazzies too? Dorothy, Garrett, Sage, and Victor?"

"Yep."

I sat for a minute. Finally, I replied, "I had no idea. Nobody has any idea you can all do that."

"Good. We don't want Dr. Roberts knowing."

"Because you're afraid of what he'd do to her? That's why you want me to keep it a secret?" I shook my head, suddenly realizing something. "So you really haven't been alone in here, mentally I mean, with no one to talk to, for the last four months?"

"No."

"That's a relief."

"There's more, though," Davin continued. "I was

wondering if you'd…" He once again looked unsure. A very un-Davin-like trait.

"What? Tell me."

"Would you make a link with Sara? I know you don't work with her, but she doesn't know how far her range can go, and she wants to test it. She's been trying to make a connection with you since you started, but unless you're willing, she can't."

It suddenly clicked.

Everything made sense now.

Those strange headaches I got around Sara. The way I felt like she wanted something from me. All of the times she held her hand up to the windowed hall, smiling, trying to engage me. *All of that was her trying to get through to me? To make a mental link?*

"So that's why she's always happy to see me," I breathed. "Everyone's been wondering why she's so interested in me. But why would she want to form a link with me? What if I told Dr. Roberts about it? Couldn't that backfire?"

"That's what I tried to tell her," Davin said, "But she said you have such a receptive mind, that she saw glimpses of you, on the inside. She knew you were good and wouldn't hurt us. She's been trying for over a month to get me to trust you."

"But you wouldn't listen."

"No, I wouldn't," he replied sheepishly. "I told her she was a fool to think she could trust you, but then she told me about the picture, of me and Aurora–"

"*What*? How did she know about that?"

"Apparently, you give out mental images when you're stressed. She told me on Monday there was something in your pocket, before you entered my cell, and that it was from my mother."

I remembered how Davin had talked to me right away on

Monday, and how he'd stared at my belt when I sat in front of him. It all made sense now. He'd known it was there.

"Wow. Could she see anything else in my mind?"

"No. Like I said, she just gets feelings and glimpses into you, but that's it."

I bit my lip, trying to wrap my head around everything. "So, what would I need to do? To make this connection with Sara?"

He frowned. "It's not easy. You'll have to stop thinking about everything, and it'll help if you're close in proximity. Most of us had to be in the same room to make that first connection, but now that it's there, we can talk to her even though walls surround us."

"So you can never get away from her? She's always in your head?"

"No, it's nothing like that. She can only talk to me if I'm open to it, and I can only talk to her if she's open to it. If I don't want to talk, I shut her out, but since we established the link, it's easy to get back in touch."

I tried to imagine it. I couldn't. "What's it like?"

Davin leaned back on his elbows again, looking thoughtful. "Strange at first. You literally have a voice in your head, but it's just Sara."

"So you *hear* her talking?"

"Yeah."

"How do you know when she wants to talk again, if you've shut her out?"

He cocked his head as if trying to find the words. "It's hard to explain, but when she wants to enter my mind, I feel a scratchy, fuzzy feeling. You'll know what I mean if you make the link. So when I feel her, I stop thinking about everything and open my mind. Then, she's there again. You'll get used to it after a while, and it gets easier with practice."

I thought about it for a minute. *Am I willing to do that? Open myself up to Sara completely?* I was such a private person. I didn't feel entirely comfortable with it, but if what Davin said was true, I could shut her out anytime I wanted.

"Would she read my thoughts or see my memories?"

"No. She's in your mind, but she can't see anything, at least not from me. Since she got that mental image from you, she may see more from you. I don't know."

I bit my lip. "And once the link is established, it can never go away?"

"I honestly don't know. None of us have tried to break it."

"No, of course not."

I thought for another minute, about what that link would mean. Not only would I be conspiring with Davin, but I'd be conspiring with Sara and the Kazzies since that would open secret communication between me and all of them through Sara. *Am I ready to do that?*

I already knew the answer. The whole reason I'd decided to stay at the Compound was to help them. All of them. Not just Davin.

"Okay, I'll stop by her cell on my way out and see if I can make it work."

"Really?" Davin's eyebrows rose. He looked surprised, and then murmured, "Sara was right about you all along."

"What?"

His head snapped up. "I mean, Sara tried to tell me you were different. She seemed to know right away, from the first time she saw you and got that feeling off you."

Different. I paused as that word sank in.

I didn't know if he meant that I was different because I was receptive or different because he thought I was a freak or something like that.

I swallowed tightly. "And you think that now? That I'm different?"

"Yeah, I do."

It felt like the wind got knocked out of me even though I knew he probably didn't mean it in a negative way. But still, the age-old response I had when someone pointed it out, stung.

A lot.

"Meghan? Is something wrong?"

I cleared my throat. I couldn't meet his gaze.

For just once in my life, I wanted to be like everyone else. Not different, not an outsider, just normal, but apparently, even with Davin and the Kazzies, I wasn't.

"Meghan?" His tone grew more worried.

I forced a wooden smile. "No. I'm fine, but I should go."

He frowned, his eyes searching mine. "Are you sure you're okay? You don't have to make that connection with Sara. I just wanted you to know you could, and then we could all talk to you, even when you're not here."

"I know, I know. I get it." I stood. "I'll see you Monday?"

A blur to my right and he was in front of me, towering over me. His worried gaze searched my face as he stood directly in my path, blocking me from the containment room. He'd moved so fast.

For the first time, I realized how vulnerable my position was. Davin was incredibly powerful and without the Chair, I was pathetically defenseless against him. And he currently blocked my one and only exit out of this room.

My breath rushed out.

"Meghan, are you sure everything's okay?" His bright blue eyes traveled over my face.

His words rolled right over me. All I could think about

was that if he wanted to, he could kill me. My heart was beating so hard I felt lightheaded.

I took a fearful step back.

Davin's demeanor instantly changed.

He stiffly stepped aside. "Sorry. I didn't mean to frighten you."

I couldn't reply. Too many emotions were swirling around inside me. It still hurt that he thought I was different, and then his abrupt movement had taken me completely by surprise.

I finally mumbled, "That's okay. I'll see you Monday."

Davin stared over my head as I brushed past him, his body as stiff and hard as steel.

As I walked by the watch room, Sergeant Rose stood on high alert, the plastic lid raised over the button that would release the tranquilizing gas. He'd no doubt seen Davin's sudden movement, even if our Kazzie hadn't laid a finger on me.

I mouthed that I was okay and entered the containment room.

I TRIED TO shake off my reaction to everything that had just happened in Davin's cell as I walked to Sara's. I didn't actually think Davin would hurt me. I knew he never would, but he'd moved so fast and that angry expression had taken me completely by surprise.

For a minute, I'd been sucked back into my first day, when I'd watched his rage in action.

But my first day at the Compound was a long time ago and so much had changed since then. If there was one thing I was sure of now, it was that Davin would *never* hurt me.

But as for my emotional reaction to him pointing out I was different… That was a different story. When I was younger, if someone pointed out I was different it was only for two reasons: I wasn't one of them, and I didn't belong.

A freak.

I sighed in disgust. *Meghan, stop. He didn't say anything like that. You're overreacting.*

I sighed as some reasonable thoughts prevailed. Luckily, those reasonable thoughts continued. By the time I approached the twins' access door, I was feeling more and more embarrassed at my heightened response to Davin's words.

I sailed through the access door into Sara and Sophie's hall and did my best to forget about what just happened.

Sara already stood by the window, like she'd been waiting for me. I took a deep breath, trying to prepare myself for whatever was to come. Once I was connected to her, I may never be alone in my head again.

I approached the window until Sara and I stood facing one another. She grinned. Her white teeth flashed brightly against her blue face.

A slight throb started in the base of my skull. It was the same feeling I'd had the other times around her, except now, I knew what it was.

All right, Meghan, here it is. If you want to establish this connection, you're going to have to do it now. Taking a deep breath, I let my arms fall to my sides and opened myself up completely, trying to do as Davin instructed.

Sara grinned.

Something strange started in the base of my skull. Like warmth and pressure building at once. My breath stopped as a moment of panic filled me, but then the pressure expanded until the crushing force disappeared.

Meghan?

My eyes widened. Sara still stood directly in front of me,

but a new light shone in her eyes. Swallowing, I thought the word, instead of saying it. *Sara?*

Yes. Her lips didn't move.

I stared at her, not sure what to say now that the link was established. It was disconcerting to say the least. Davin was right. She was a voice, *in my head.* A clear, distinct voice. Even though I'd never spoken to her, I imagined the tone would be similar to her speaking voice. Soft, high and sweet, the voice of a young woman.

Davin said you were going to try this today, she said.

So they'd already talked. *Um, yeah,* I replied awkwardly. This would definitely take some getting used to.

I've been trying to get through to you since you started.

I realize that now. I always wondered why I got headaches around you.

She grimaced. *I know, sorry about that. Everyone says it's uncomfortable initially until the connection's made.*

I nodded and tried to process what was happening. Neither of us said a word out loud, yet we were having a steady conversation. To say it was strange was an understatement.

Are you okay? she asked.

Yeah, I'm just trying to get used to this.

I know. The Kazzies all said it was weird, initially at least, and then it became no big deal.

Hopefully, after a little while, I'd feel that way too. *Davin said you talk to everyone regularly?*

Sara nodded. *Yeah, more now than ever, since we're all in isolation. Most of my days are spent as the middleman, communicating things between everyone.*

Nobody out here knows you can do that.

I know. And we want to keep it that way. If Dr. Roberts found out… She shuddered. *I don't know what he'd do to me.*

Don't worry. I won't tell him.

She smiled brightly. *I know you won't. I knew from the instant I saw you, and got all those emotions and images, that you were good. You've got a kind soul, Meghan. You're one of those rare people who always tries to do the right thing. I trust you completely.*

Her words took me by surprise. Nobody had ever spoken so candidly and convincingly after having just met me. She spoke like she already knew me, but she definitely had an advantage. She could see into me. My social anxiety wasn't an issue with her. I watched to see if she'd show any reaction to those thoughts. She didn't.

I sighed in relief. Apparently, she couldn't read every thought.

Davin said you're going to Rapid City tomorrow, to see his mom again, she said.

Yes, I have to pass a message for him.

She rolled her eyes. *Code stuff?*

Something like that.

Oh, Davin. She laughed, the sound ringing in my head. *Old habits die hard. That code stuff is how he always speaks to his mother.*

I shrugged. *Either that or he's testing me, to see if I actually pass the message.*

He already trusts you. You know that, right?

Um, I'm not so sure about that.

He does, although he *may not know it.*

How can you be so sure?

She laughed. *Because if he didn't, he wouldn't say a word to you. He'd just get that moody, angry look on his face.*

I smiled. Her bubbly personality was infectious. I found myself relaxing as we talked. But a few minutes later, when I realized the guard in the watch room was eyeing us with a peculiar expression on his face, I straightened.

I better go. I nodded toward the guard. *This probably looks really weird.*

Oh. Sara glanced his way. *You're right. This is the first time I've ever spoken to someone other than a Kazzie. Normally, he has no idea we're talking to one another, but I suppose with us just standing here, staring at each other, it looks odd.*

Very odd, I agreed. I said goodbye and returned to the lab, and as Davin stated, I shut the door to my connection with Sara. And just like that, she was gone.

23 - BACK TO RAPID

I leaned back in my seat. The landscape flew by as I drove toward Rapid City. All that happened yesterday sloshed around in my mind like toys in a child's bathtub.

I was still getting used to it. The connection with Sara. Davin's comment about me being different. Me berating myself for being overly sensitive.

But one thing bothered me more than any of that. When I went home last night, I started putting two and two together, which made me question everything about Davin and the Kazzies.

Sara and Davin had been in touch and talking the entire time I'd known him.

I'd told Davin things in confidence, and since I didn't know he'd been in contact with six other Kazzies, I hadn't asked him to keep that information to himself.

Does Sara know about Jeremy now? About how I pretend he's alive so I can talk to him? Did Davin tell her everything he and I spoke about?

I bit my lip. I hoped he wouldn't do that, but in reality, I was just getting to know him. I had no idea if he would or not.

I leaned my arm against the door as the miles ticked by. Solitude, a long drive, and nothing to keep me occupied meant I had four more hours to mull over this stuff.

Ugh.

I felt Sara make several attempts to contact me as I drove, but I hadn't opened our connection. I needed a minute, or rather, a day, to think this all through. The logical part of me knew this could all be cleared up with a conversation, but I wasn't ready for that. Not right now at least.

With each passing mile, it became increasingly apparent that my mental connection with Sara far exceeded city limits. The scientist in me was curious. I could still feel her, just waiting to talk on the other side of the mental door that separated us. It was possible I'd feel her anywhere in the world.

I shifted uncomfortably in my seat but then reminded myself I'd never felt anything but good vibes from her. I didn't regret making our connection and hoped I never would.

Still, I couldn't talk to her right now. I needed a little time to hash everything out on my own. Taking a deep breath, I did my best to settle back into the drive.

I PULLED NEXT to the curb outside Sharon's house a few hours later. There was actually life in her neighborhood this time. A couple raked their leaves. An old woman sat on a porch, sipping something in a mug. A few kids rode their bikes in the streets.

When I stepped out, the air smelled like autumn. I hurried to Sharon's door. After knocking, I stuffed my hands in my pockets until the door cracked a few inches before swinging open.

"Meghan!" Sharon's bright, blue eyes lit up. She wore jeans and a sweater with fluffy slippers on her feet.

I smiled sheepishly. “Hi. Davin thought you’d be home now.”

She smiled brighter. “Come in.”

I stepped into the small entryway, taking off my shoes while she took my coat. “I just made a pot of tea. Come into the kitchen and join me.”

Her friendliness warmed me. It was amazing how I’d only just met her the previous weekend, yet she greeted me like an old friend. I could see why Davin loved her so much. He was lucky to have a mother like her.

“I have sugar this time.” She smiled over her shoulder while I followed. Her auburn hair was swept up in a loose bun, a few tendrils escaping. Only a few gray hairs streaked through it. I was once again struck at how different she looked from Davin, if I ignored the eyes.

I sat at the kitchen table while she busied herself at the counter. Everything was the same as last weekend. The environment was worn yet clean, tidy, and very homey feeling. Sharon whisked away the old teacup that was sitting on the counter and pulled out the cherry blossom china set.

I bit back a smile.

“There,” she said, a few minutes later, setting the tray down in front of us. “Milk and sugar?”

“Yes, that’d be great.”

She poured my cup and handed it to me. Her fingers didn’t shake this time. “Were you able to get the picture to him?”

“Yes, on Monday.”

She smiled. “Did he like it?”

“He loved it.”

She practically glowed. “I thought he would.”

A comfortable silence fell between us. I was surprised she didn’t ask what brought me here, but I remembered a few things Davin had told me about her. Sharon was a very patient, unassuming person.

"So, I'm sure you're wondering what brings me here." I took a sip of the rich brew.

She smiled. "How could I not be?"

I bit back a laugh. *How right Davin was.* "I have a message for you, from Davin."

"Oh?" She leaned forward.

"The thunderbird sings in Sweden."

She raised an eyebrow. "Did he tell you what that means?"

I shook my head.

"But he's obviously speaking to you now?"

"Yes. You were right. The picture worked. I think he's beginning to trust me."

"Good." She sipped her tea again. "The *thunderbird* is Davin. That's the code name we used for him. If he's singing, it means he's happy. And *Sweden* refers to the Compound. So that sentence essentially means that he's happy, even though he's in the Compound."

I set my tea down. My fingers were shaking. *He's happy?* My heart filled. I helped make that happen.

"Thank you for telling me."

Sharon clasped my hand. "Thank *you*, Meghan."

And in that moment, it was all worth it. All the worry. All the anxiety. All of the feelings of isolation, even amongst the Kazzies. The look on her face made everything worth it.

I squeezed her hand back. "You're welcome."

I SPENT THE day with Sharon. Even though I'd only driven out to deliver the message, and had intended to leave within the hour, she insisted it was too long of a drive for me to go back on the same day. In other words, I was spending the night.

We had lunch together and spent the afternoon playing board games. Before supper, we went for a long walk. I was a bit nervous about that. If anyone found out I worked at the Compound, questions would be asked.

But Sharon insisted. "Nobody knows you here, Meghan. Trust me. It will be fine."

The crisp autumn air smelled like wood smoke and cold, and as soon as we stepped outside, I was glad she'd suggested it.

A couple approached us on the sidewalk, going the opposite way. They had a dog and stroller. A baby's chubby hand waved at a toy dangling overhead. Sharon stopped to talk to them for a few minutes.

I smiled as best I could, but as usual, nervousness coursed through me at the introductions, and it was more than just my social anxiety. Luckily, Sharon was smart enough to stick to my first name only and gave no indication that I was anything other than a friend visiting from Wall. There was no way they'd guess I worked at the Compound.

"They live a few streets over from me," Sharon said after we resumed walking. "She lost their first child during the Second Wave after going into early labor. Their doctor couldn't do anything since supplies and hospital personnel were stretched so thin."

It was an all too common story. The Second Wave had caused many tragedies that hadn't been linked directly to the virus. "Do they have any other children?"

Sharon shook her head. "That's their first. She was born six months ago. I was so happy when they told me they'd conceived again. They'd had such a hard time getting pregnant the first time."

"That's nice to hear."

"Have you ever thought about having kids?"

My step faltered, but I quickly righted myself. "Um, well, honestly no, I haven't."

"Do you have a boyfriend? Back in Sioux Falls?"

I almost laughed but managed to keep my face neutral. "No."

I'd never had a boyfriend. I could count on one hand how many times I'd been kissed. In college, I'd gone out with guys a few times, but I'd never counted any as a boyfriend. Our times together had been too brief. *Makanza* naturally made people wary of close contact. My social anxiety wasn't entirely to blame for my lack of experience.

"It's nothing to be ashamed of." Sharon nudged me. We rounded a corner to the next block, and she looped her arm through mine. "Davin's only had a few girlfriends, but most didn't last for longer than a few weeks. Maybe a month or two at the most. There was only one girl he really seemed to love, but she moved away before The First Wave. My guess is she's dead now."

"Oh," was all I could manage. *So Davin's been in love with someone else before?* It was crazy how much that realization hurt.

She continued, oblivious to the knots inside me. "Plenty of women have wanted him, but other than that one girl, nobody's ever struck his fancy long enough to keep him interested."

I bit my lip. Davin had only been eighteen when he caught *Makanza*, so he'd been young enough he'd probably never thought of marriage, but he'd still been old enough to fall in love. I tried to picture Davin with the mystery woman Sharon spoke of. I was surprised at the jealousy that seared through me.

"Is there anyone you're interested in?" Sharon asked.

I tucked my chin so she wouldn't see my face. Davin's face flashed through my mind. There was no point denying to myself or Sharon that I'd developed feelings for him. "Kind of."

She smiled. "He'll be a lucky man if he gets you."

I was amazed at how candidly Sharon spoke. I knew now where Davin got his charm. By the time we returned to her house and sat for supper, Sharon felt like a long lost friend.

"I'm so glad you came out for the day." She dished a small serving of pot roast and potatoes onto my plate. I could tell from the smell that her cooking was immensely better than mine.

"Me too. I've really enjoyed it."

"Have you played any games with Davin?" She settled into her chair and lifted her fork. "I'm guessing there aren't many things you can do in his cell?"

"That's true, but we haven't done anything other than talk."

"Do you play poker?" She took a bite of pot roast.

I shook my head.

"You should ask Davin to teach you. He's an excellent player."

Something stabbed in my heart. *Playing games in his cell is probably all we'll ever be able to do.* Davin was a prisoner of the Compound. He probably always would be. I frowned heavily, remembering his comment yesterday about me being different. I still didn't know what he'd meant by that. And I also didn't know if he'd shared with everyone how I pretended to speak to my dead brother.

"Are you okay?"

Sharon's voice broke my thoughts. I picked up my fork

hastily. "Yes, I'm fine."

She set her utensils down with a disapproving, motherly frown. "Meghan, I raised five children and have seen it all." She paused and then said more quietly, "Do you want to talk about it?"

An ache that had nothing to do with her question came over me. *Has my mother ever asked me anything like that? Have my mother and I ever talked like Sharon and I have today?*

No, not once in twenty-three years. I took a deep breath. Maybe Sharon was right. Maybe I should talk about it. After all, she knew Davin better than anyone.

"I'm not entirely sure what Davin thinks of me."

She clasped her hands, resting her elbows on the table and leaned forward. "Go on."

"I found out yesterday that he can communicate with another Kazzie in the Compound. She has telepathic abilities and can speak with all of the Kazzies silently, and now me too."

Sharon's eyebrows rose so high that it reminded me that most people knew nothing about the bizarre manifestations of *Makanza*.

"I thought it was just him and me talking this week, that he hadn't talked to anyone in months, but that wasn't true. The whole time, he's also been talking to Sara."

"And that worries you?"

I swallowed. "I said some things to him, opened up to him, and I'm not sure I would have done that if I'd known he may be telling someone else what I said."

"So you're afraid he told this other girl whatever you divulged?"

"Yes."

"Have you asked him if he has?"

"Not yet. I just found all of this out yesterday."

"Well, I can understand your concern. I'm sure most people would react that same way."

"So you think Davin told her?"

She smiled but shook her head. "No. I know my son better than anyone, and if there's one thing he isn't, it's deceitful. He wouldn't share your information. He'd view that as a break of trust. He despises people who do that."

"He does?" *So maybe I can rest easy that Davin hasn't shared what I told him.*

But that still didn't clarify my other worry. That I was some weirdo researcher to him, different from everyone else, but I kept that thought to myself.

We continued eating, and throughout dinner, I felt Sara again try to make contact. She'd been doing it all afternoon, but it wasn't until she tried three times in five minutes that alarm raced through me. It suddenly occurred to me that something may have happened and that was why she'd been trying to get a hold of me.

"Would you excuse me for a minute?" I tried to keep the panic from my voice as I stumbled out of my chair and raced to the bathroom.

I closed the door behind me, set the lid down on the toilet, and sat. The half bath was small and cramped, but at least it gave me privacy. I closed my eyes and tried to relax. I pictured the mental door in my mind, my link with the twin. I pretended to knock on the door while thinking, *Sara?*

The link clicked. It felt like someone tied an invisible thread around my cerebral cortex before giving it a tug. It was the oddest sensation. *So much for distance being a concern.*

Meghan? Her word came through right away.

Yeah, it's me. Is everything okay?

I swear I heard Sara sigh. *Meghan, are you okay? Did you make it to Rapid City?*

Yeah, I arrived early this afternoon. Why? Is something wrong?

I heard another sigh, this one more exaggerated. *No, other than Davin practically screaming in my head all day, asking if I've connected with you. He's really worried.*

He is? I frowned. *Why?*

He's worried you got in an accident, or you got caught somehow after you left the lab. I know something else is bugging him too, but he won't tell me.

Oh. I'm sorry, I didn't realize.

That's okay. Have you talked to his mom?

Yeah, I'm with her now.

Really… I felt her pause.

Sara?

I'm here. I just…

I couldn't be sure what I felt from her, but it felt like she was thinking about something. *Sara?*

Sorry. She shook herself. *It's just… I have an idea. It's something I've tried before, but it's never worked.*

What are you talking about?

Just… hold on. I think if it's going to ever work with anyone, it would be you.

Huh?

I felt her put some mental distance between us. It was weird. I could still feel her, but it seemed like she moved farther away. At least a minute ticked by. It felt like forever, but then I felt a new presence in my mind. My breath stopped.

Meghan?

My heart beat harder. I'd recognize that timbre tone anywhere. *Davin?*

I was glad I was sitting down. I was pretty sure my knees

would have given way if I'd been standing.

What happened to Sara? I finally managed. I could still detect her presence, but it was like she'd gone into another room, close to us, but not near.

She's giving us privacy. I think.

How is she doing this?

I have no idea, but I think she's channeling us somehow.

I was quiet for a moment, still reeling that I was talking to Davin, in my head, even though I was hundreds of miles away from him. *How are you?* I finally asked.

Better, now that I know you're okay.

My heart rate increased. *I'm fine.*

His tone changed, becoming gruffer. *Why wouldn't you talk to Sara? She said she's been trying to reach you since this morning, but you wouldn't respond.*

I… ah… I guess I just needed some time.

Oh. Right. I felt his guard go up again, just like it had yesterday before I'd left.

But I'm okay now. I remembered what Sharon said, about how Davin was a lot of things, but deceitful was not one of them. *Your mom helped me see a few things.*

I felt him relax. *Like what?*

Ah, nothing, just… Everything's fine.

I could tell he didn't know how to interpret that.

Are you still with her? Is she there now? His tone turned hopeful.

She's in the kitchen. We're having supper. Speaking of which, I've already been gone a long time. I should go back.

Where are you?

In the bathroom.

The one that's so cramped you can barely sit on the toilet without your knees touching the wall?

I looked at my knees. They were two inches from the wall. *That's the one.*

He paused. *Do you think I could talk to her?*

Talk to who?

My mom?

I cocked my head, not sure what he was asking, but then it suddenly dawned on me. *Oh…* I nodded but then realized he couldn't see me. *I get it. You want to try to talk to her through me?*

If you don't mind.

We can try.

I returned to the kitchen. Sharon was still at the table. It looked like she hadn't touched her plate since I left. Our food was probably cold.

"Is everything okay?" Her bright blue eyes looked worried.

I sat. "Um. Yes."

She raised an eyebrow.

I twisted my hands. "Well, yes and no." Before she could ask what I meant, I rushed on. "So you know how I told you that Sara and I made a telepathic connection?"

Sharon nodded.

"Well, as it turns out, Sara's put me in contact with Davin. Just now."

"She's put you in contact with Davin?" The confusion on her face told me she had no idea what I meant.

"Yes, so I am talking to him right now, in my head."

She balked.

"So if you want to, you know, say anything to him, now's the time."

I heard Davin chuckle. *You're doing just fine.*

You heard me say all that?

Yes.

Weird.

Tell her I'm really happy I got the picture.

"He said he's happy he got the picture."

Sharon just sat there, her skin pale. She finally cleared her throat. "So anything I tell you right now, he can hear?

"No. I have to tell him. He doesn't have complete access to my senses." *Fortunately.*

I heard that.

I rolled my eyes.

"Can you…" Sharon paused. The shocked expression still hadn't left her face. "Can you ask him what his favorite toy was when he was ten? He'll know what I'm talking about."

So, she was going to test this. I couldn't blame her. This was definitely bizarre. It was hard to wrap my head around the situation too.

She wants to know what your favorite toy was when you were ten.

I felt him smile. *The mountain bike they bought me for my tenth birthday. It was blue.*

"A mountain bike you got him for his tenth birthday? A blue color?"

Sharon's mouth dropped. Her hands flew to her cheeks as tears sprouted in her eyes. "It really is him. Can you ask him what he did today? How's he feeling?"

I relayed that message too, and Davin replied, telling her he just finished a crime novel and was feeling fine.

"How are they treating him? Has anything bad happened this week?"

I again passed on the message.

I can honestly say for the first time in six years, I've been treated very well, all week.

Davin's reply, as happy as he sounded, made my stomach drop. Six years and only now was his treatment humane.

"What about the other Kazzies? Do you still talk to

them?" Sharon asked.

Yes, was his reply.

Their conversation continued for over an hour. It felt strange being the middleman, but both Davin and Sharon seemed to relish the little contact they had. They spoke about all sorts of things after Sharon finished asking about the Compound, mostly things I had no idea about. After a while, I stopped trying to follow along. It was kind of like listening to someone's conversation on a public bus. You could understand what they were saying since you spoke the same language, but you didn't really understand it since it was completely out of context and involved people and places you had no idea about.

By the time they said goodbye, it was well into the evening. The potatoes on my plate had cooled into gooey mush while the drippings on the pot roast were gelatinous pearls. I'd tried to eat while I'd relayed the conversation, but it took too much concentration. It was worth missing dinner, though, even though my stomach growled in protest. I'd never seen Sharon smile as she was now.

"That was the best gift anyone's ever given me," she stated.

"I'm glad you two were finally able to talk."

"I really can't thank you enough." She clasped my hand. "Just a week ago, I thought I'd never talk to my son again, and now I've given him a photo I've held on to for years, and I've talked to him, almost in person. You have no idea what that means to me."

If I hadn't formed such a surprisingly close bond with her, I would have squirmed in discomfort from her praise. "You're very welcome. I'm glad I've been able to help."

At just that moment, my stomach let out another big

growl.

Sharon smiled. "How about I reheat our plates and we actually finish supper?"

"Good idea."

AN HOUR LATER, Sharon led me to one of the bedrooms. "I hope this will do."

She opened a door, revealing a room crammed with three beds and mountains of stuff. "It was the boys' room. Davin slept in the single twin while Lars and Elliot shared the bunk beds."

My mouth opened and then closed. "Sharon, I can't sleep in here." It looked like nothing had been touched since they'd all gone. It felt wrong disturbing it since she'd obviously kept the room as it was.

Sharon however, just waved her hand and smiled. "Please, it's fine. A few years ago, I realized this room is not a mausoleum. I come in here sometimes now and look through their things, but it's not a tomb. Things have been moved. I dust when I can be bothered. Besides, I already threw Davin's sheets in the wash when you were in the bathroom earlier. It's all ready for you."

I wrung my hands. "I could sleep on the couch."

"No, don't be silly! You're staying here. Bathroom's down the hall on the left. I hung a fresh towel for you."

We each said goodnight.

After brushing my teeth, I padded into the bedroom. Moonlight shone through the curtains, and the silence seemed to echo. It wasn't a large room, but the three boys had made use of every inch. Knicknacks, books, CDs, and other various things were crammed wherever there was room. I didn't want to snoop, but it was hard not to notice the clothes jumbled into the drawers. The dresser was so crammed, a few drawers wouldn't even close. Sleeves and pant legs hung over the edges.

It was a room of teenage boys, even though Davin hadn't lived here for over six years and was well past being a teenager. Sharon obviously kept it similar to how it had been. I knew both Lars and Elliot had been living at home when *Makanza* infected them. Davin said Lars was only fourteen and Elliot had been twelve when the Second Wave struck.

I changed into some sweats and a t-shirt before pulling back the sheets. The pleasant scent of laundry detergent wafted around me when I burrowed under the covers. I wondered what Davin would think if he knew where I was sleeping.

The irony of it made me smile. A few weeks ago, he'd hated me. Now, I was sleeping in his childhood bed.

Who would have thought?

24 - POKER

I was surprised at how hard it was to say goodbye to Sharon the next day. She'd been more of a mother to me in two days than my own mother had been to me in twenty-three years. I knew I'd see her again, but I didn't know how long it would be. It was strange. I already missed her.

"You're welcome here anytime." She hugged me tightly as I stood by the door. She smelled good, like soap and lavender. "I always leave a key under the green pot out back. If I'm not here, and you come to town, just let yourself in. I'm never gone long."

"Thanks, Sharon. Take care until then."

She waited at the front door, still in her bathrobe, waving goodbye until I could no longer see her in my rearview mirror.

I drove slowly through the neighborhood, settling in for the long trek as I headed to the interstate. I took a chug from my water bottle as my thoughts inevitably drifted toward Davin. I propped my elbow against the window and leaned my head into my hand as the rising sun blazed through the windshield. I wondered what he smelled like. *Will I ever know?*

Sara knocked on our mental door as I merged onto I-90. I opened my mind, grateful for the distraction. The connection clicked instantly.

Hi, I said.

Good morning, Davin wants to know when you're coming back to Sioux Falls.

Right now. I just got on the interstate.

Sara sighed. *Thank God. He's been driving me crazy all weekend. Just get back here. I have a feeling when he sees you, he'll calm down.*

My pulse leaped. I could picture exactly what she meant. Davin was not someone who waited patiently. *Tell him I'll see him tomorrow,* I said.

I will. Drive safely.

GOING TO WORK the next day was much different than how it had been one week ago. After my first trip to Rapid City, I'd been convinced everyone knew what I'd done. Today, that was far from my mind. I just wanted to see Davin and talk to him.

I hurried through security and went straight to the Sanctum.

When I reached Davin's hallway, a smile spread across his face, softening his angular features and making him look almost boyish. Since it was almost eight in the morning, he'd probably been up for a couple of hours.

Well-worn jeans hung from his lean hips. A form-fitting shirt accentuated the hard angles and planes of his chest. Heat cascaded to an area of my body that left me squirming. *Seriously, Meghan, get a grip!* This was beginning to get ridiculous. I was his researcher after all. I should act like it.

"Good to see you, Dr. Forester," Sergeant Rose said when I stepped up to the control panel. "Good weekend?"

If you only knew. "Yes, it was nice. How about yourself?"

"Can't complain. Are you going in today?"

I looked out the window. Davin stood on the other side. He'd followed me from his bed to the watch room. His blue eyes were bright and intense. I made myself breathe slower. "Yes."

"Then let's get you suited up."

It didn't take long to get my suit on.

Sergeant Rose cocked an eyebrow. "I think he's happy to see you. He spent most of the weekend pacing. He was pretty edgy all day Saturday from what the weekend guard told me."

"So you're not here twenty-four hours a day?" I joked after clicking the external speaker on.

Sergeant Rose chuckled. "No, although my wife likes to point out that I work too much. What can I say? Five twelve-hour shifts a week is good pay. Besides, I find this job interesting."

He exited the containment room a few moments later. I waited at the door to Davin's cell, straining to see through the tiny glass window, but it was hard in the bulkiness of the suit.

My feet itched to move. I wanted to see Davin, to talk to him. Nothing I could say to myself minimized that.

"Ready?" Sergeant Rose's voice sounded in my earbud.

I tried to calm my pounding heart. "Yes."

In front of me, dials turned as the room depressurized. With a hiss, the door to Davin's cell opened.

HE WAITED FOR me on the other side. His body was tensed, an anxious smile on his face. Once again, I cursed the bulky awkwardness of the biohazard suit. It made my movements clumsy.

Davin took my hand, steadying me.

I paused, my eyes going to his large hand that engulfed my smaller one. His body heat was warm through the gloves. I subtly rubbed his fingers, wishing I could feel the texture of his skin.

"Hi." His voice was deeper than usual. "Do you want to sit down?"

"Sure."

He led me to the chair by his desk, holding my hand the entire way. I didn't know what to make of that. After I sat, I turned to Sergeant Rose. I didn't have to say anything. His voice sounded in my earbud. "Turning off now." The speaker clicked.

I was alone with Davin once again.

He released me after I was safely seated in the chair. My shoulders drooped. Perhaps that was all the hand holding had been – good manners as he helped me to the chair.

"How was the weekend?" He sat on the bed, his hands clasped in his lap.

"It was good. Fun."

"You took long enough to let us know you got there," he said gruffly.

I tucked my chin. "Sorry about that."

"It's okay, but you seemed a little… off… when you left last week. I wasn't sure if I'd done something."

I shook my head. "No, it was nothing really. Your mom helped me see that."

He frowned. "See what?"

I gripped my hands tightly together and shrugged. "It seems dumb, what I'd thought."

"What'd you think?"

I took a deep breath. *Just say it, Meghan. Get it over with.* After all, I promised myself I'd always be honest with him.

"When you said I was different from the other researchers on Friday, I got a little sensitive."

A pause stretched between us. Davin just sat there, a confused expression on his face. "Why? It was a compliment."

"It was? Oh… I guess at the time, I didn't see it that way."

"Then how did you see it?"

I told him a little more about my upbringing, about how my abilities in school made me different from my peers. That, along with the frequent moving and school changes, made me very isolated.

"You thought I was saying it in a negative way," he stated, after I finished explaining. "That being different was something bad."

"Yes."

"Meghan…"

I tried not to react to the sound of my name on his lips.

He continued. "I thank the spirits every day that they sent you to me."

My eyes widened. I just stared at him. When I finally gained control of my senses, I could only manage two words. "You do?"

"Yeah. Meghan, you connected me with the only family I have left. I'll always be grateful for that."

"Oh, right, of course." My stomach plummeted. *He's your friend, Meg, nothing more.*

"What did you and my mom do?"

"Oh, um." I mentally shook myself. "We played some games and went for a walk, but for the most part, we just talked."

"About me?" He grinned devilishly.

I couldn't stop my smile. "A little."

"Did she reveal anything embarrassing?"

I laughed. "Hardly."

"Did you ask her about the thunderbird singing in Sweden?"

I nodded. "She said you're the thunderbird, and if you're singing, you're happy."

"Correct."

"Why a thunderbird? For your code name?"

He leaned back on his elbows, his strong chest evident in his shirt. "The thunderbird is a legendary Sioux bird. The *Wakinyan* is the guardian of truth."

I assumed *Wakinyan* was Lakota for thunderbird. "You guard the truth?"

Davin cocked his head. "I've been known to value truth and honor above all."

I thought about what Sharon said, about how being deceitful was not a trait in Davin's personality. Thankfully, his time in the Compound hadn't changed that. "That's what your mom said."

"She knows me pretty well."

"That must have taken a long time to formulate a code with her."

"We had nothing but time back then." His gaze dropped after he said that.

His look made me ache to touch him. I wasn't sure what it was about the Kinders, but they brought out a side of me that hadn't existed with anyone else. A side that wanted to touch and be touched. For the most part, I never touched anyone, besides the occasional hug from Jeremy, but that was a long time ago.

"So what games did you play?" Davin asked, changing the subject.

I shook off my thoughts and told him about Monopoly

and Trivial Pursuit. "She said you were pretty good at poker."

"She did, huh?"

"Yes, and she also said you should teach me."

"That's a bit hard. You need more than two people."

"What if we make up additional players, or ask Sergeant Rose to join in?"

He cocked his head. "I suppose that could work."

"You want to teach me then?"

He grinned. "I'm not sure that's a good idea. I've never played with anybody as smart as you. Poker is a strategic game. You'll probably beat me."

Now it was my turn to grin. "Sounds like fun."

He laughed.

"So are you going to teach me?" I asked.

"I suppose, but only because I don't have an ego. You'll no doubt crush it."

"You give me too much credit."

"We'll see."

Luckily, Davin had a deck of cards. He retrieved the deck from his desk in one of his blurred movements. "Okay, we'll play Texas Holdem. It's fairly easy to learn." He shuffled the deck just as fast. The cards disappeared in the quick movement.

"You certainly wouldn't want to teach me anything challenging."

He chuckled, the sound rumbling in his chest. "All right, now pay attention."

I tried to salute him, but the effect failed miserably in the bulky suit. He just chuckled again. "To start with, each player is dealt two cards."

He dealt out hands to myself and four imaginary players. He went on to explain all of the rules, telling me various things to be aware of.

"Right, I got it," I said when he finished.

"I was afraid of that."

I bit back a smile. The entire time he'd been dealing cards and showing me things, I'd watched his hands. He had beautiful hands. Large palms. Long, strong fingers. I swallowed. I felt my cheeks flush. Clearing my throat, I said, "Should we ask Sergeant Rose to join in?"

Davin's eyebrows drew together but then he shrugged. "Might as well."

I glanced at the watch room. Sergeant Rose watched us with an amused expression on his face. I tapped my hood. The speaker clicked on. "Do you know how to play Texas Hold 'em?" I asked.

"Doesn't every man?" he replied.

"Want to play with us?"

"With only three players?"

"I know, I know. It'll be short and sweet."

"Sounds like fun," he replied. "But it may be challenging since I can't hold any cards."

"We'll hold them up to you, and we won't peek," Davin said.

Sergeant Rose's mouth dropped. I wondered if in all the years Sergeant Rose had been his guard, if this was the first time Davin had willingly spoken to him.

"Works for me." There was a catch in the guard's voice.

Davin told me to stand so he could move his desk and bed beside the watch room's window. In a flash of movement, it was all done. "Show off," I murmured.

He just grinned.

THE NEXT FEW hours were some of the most enjoyable

hours I could remember in a very long time. We played poker until lunchtime. It probably wasn't anything like a legitimate game. Three players definitely had its limits, but I laughed more often and longer than I had since Jeremy died.

Davin had such a serious poker face, yet I couldn't keep mine straight. I kept laughing and smiling, which turned infectious at every hand. A corner of Davin's mouth would quirk up or he'd give me a look, pretending to be annoyed, but I could see the amusement in his gaze. Despite how fun it was, I still had to work for the hands I won.

Davin was smart. His mother hadn't been kidding when she said he was good.

"I think I'm done," Sergeant Rose said around noon. "I can only take so many losing hands."

So far, he'd lost every one. Davin and I were about fifty-fifty. As much as he said I'd beat him easily, I hadn't.

"And Meghan," Sergeant Rose continued, "you really need to learn the definition of a poker face."

Davin grinned. "I don't think I've ever played with anyone who laughed at every hand."

"Didn't stop me from winning," I pointed out.

"Touché," the guard replied. "I've got my replacement coming in an hour for my lunch break. Just want you both to know in case you want to wrap things up." He paused. "I'm not sure he'd be as understanding about giving you privacy."

"Right," I replied. "Thanks." The speaker clicked off in my earbud. "He's signed off," I told Davin.

Davin nodded and moved the furniture back to its original location.

"Did you have fun?" he asked when he was done.

"Yeah, we should do it again sometime."

"We should." He eyed Sergeant Rose through the glass. A

long speculative expression followed. "He's all right, isn't he?"

"Yes. He's been accommodating for everything I've asked."

Davin frowned as if thinking about something. "Yeah."

We were quiet for a minute, and then I brought up the subject I'd been avoiding for the last two weeks. "Davin? You know I'm going to need to get a sample from you at some point. Dr. Roberts gave me a month to get one. Otherwise, he's going to send Amy in, and I won't be allowed to work with you anymore."

"I knew you'd have to get one sooner or later."

"I'm in no rush. We still have two weeks."

Davin looked me in the eye, all joking gone. "You can have one anytime you want. All you have to do is ask. Besides, it's not like I'm not used to it." He lifted his shirt revealing hard abs littered with scars.

My breath caught in my throat. When I was finally able to speak, it came out in a furious whisper. "He did that to you?"

Davin dropped his shirt. "Remind me to not show you my legs."

I just stared where his shirt had been lifted, trying to get myself under control. I hadn't felt a surge of adrenaline like that since the day I'd seen him forced into the Chair. Seeing all of those scars reminded me of something I'd always wondered. Something I'd never had the courage to ask.

"What did Dr. Roberts do to you that week he had you in the Experimental Room? Before I started here? Amy said no one else was allowed in."

Davin's gaze hardened. He glanced away. "Don't worry about that."

"Davin, tell me."

He let out a harsh sigh. "Let's just say there was a lot of

cutting and no anesthetic, more so than usual."

Fire burned in my gut. "That bastard!"

His gaze snapped to mine. "Meghan, it's okay. I'm used to it, but that week was pretty bad. I couldn't control myself for a while. I think that was his goal all along – to make me lose control. Usually, he's not able to."

"Nobody should be treated that way!"

"I agree, but I can't change it, so please, don't worry about me. I'm fine."

It all seemed backwards. I should be the one comforting him, not the other way around.

"I'm going to do everything I can to get you out of here," I said.

He reached out but then dropped his hand. If my hood hadn't been in the way, I felt fairly certain he would have laid his palm across my cheek.

"I know you will."

25 - SAMPLE

True to his word, Davin willingly gave me a sample. It was near the end of my month-long deadline. Every working day, Monday through Friday, I'd gone into his cell, and each day it became harder and harder to say goodbye.

I knew I couldn't put it off forever. I only had a few days left before my deadline, but I was afraid once Dr. Roberts found out Davin's sample had been collected, he'd put an end to our daily visits, telling me they were no longer needed.

And the thought of not seeing Davin, or not talking to him, left a hole in my heart that at times felt so big, I thought I'd disappear right into it.

So I kept finding an excuse for why it wasn't needed yet. Why it wouldn't hurt to wait a little bit longer. Yet each day my deadline loomed, and there was nothing I could do about it.

I think Davin knew I was putting it off, but I think he also knew I needed the sample. None of the other samples taken from Kazzies in Compound 26, or Compounds throughout the nation, had been viable. Twenty minutes – the longest stable sample taken in Washington – still held the record, but twenty minutes was not long enough.

We needed a more stable version if we were going to beat *Makanza.*

It was at the end of the day on Friday when Davin laid his hand over mine. We'd been visiting for over five hours, yet it felt like minutes.

He peered at me closely, his bright blue eyes drawing me closer like a moth to a flame. "Come on, Meg. You can't put this off forever. Take my sample. Please."

I sighed in acceptance that the time had finally come and gathered my supplies.

I worked as gently as possible and made sure the area was completely numbed. Cutting into him still hurt – me, not him. He reached out to steady my hand, murmuring that it was okay. His heat and calm words steadied my racing heart.

When the intramuscular sample was in the airtight vial, I carefully stitched him back up. Only two stitches were needed, but it would still leave a scar.

Tears rolled silently down my cheeks as I stared at what I'd done.

"Meghan, really, it's okay." He reached out as if to touch me again. When his fingers encountered my hood, he cursed quietly. "I stopped being vain a long time ago," he joked. "A centimeter long scar is nothing."

Tears still burned my eyes despite his reassuring words. "I'm sorry. I'm sorry I did that to you."

He held my gaze. "If anyone's going to do it to me, I'd rather it be you."

I resisted the urge to wrap my arms around him. I wanted so badly to bury my face in his neck, to feel his hard chest pressed against mine, to burrow into his scent that would surely be uniquely his.

Of course, that wasn't possible.

Touch was not something we'd ever experience.

Instead, we both stared at one another. An emotion so deep it felt like the ocean swirled in his eyes. It was an emotion I'd seen before, but he'd usually look away, but today, he didn't.

Today, that emotion swam in his gaze, and he didn't try to hide it.

"I should get this to the lab." I held up the vial.

He nodded. "I'll see you Monday."

With a heavy heart, I exited his room into the containment area. Fifteen minutes later, I was carrying the vial with Davin's sample back to the lab. Time right now didn't matter. In the airtight vial, the sample wouldn't degrade during my walk to the lab. It would only be when we opened it that the clock would begin ticking.

Only time would tell if this sample was able to survive the harshness of traditional DNA testing.

Emotions weighed me down, making my steps feel heavy. Despite holding a sample that could potentially be more stable than any we'd ever extracted, that wasn't where my thoughts lay.

Instead, bright blue eyes swam through my mind. I was falling in love with Davin. I had been for weeks.

It was so unbelievably stupid for me to let my feelings get to this point. And regardless of how he felt, nothing could ever come of it. Even if we found a vaccine, even if the entire country was inoculated, it was possible the MRI would still refuse to let the Kazzies out. If someone like Dr. Roberts made the decisions, it was possible they'd be imprisoned forever.

"What have you got there, lil' Meghan?" Mitch's voice

startled me.

I'd almost walked right into him. I hadn't realized I'd entered the lab. "Oh, um. It's the sample Davin just gave to me."

His eyes widened. "A sample willingly given to you from a happy Kazzie?"

I pictured Davin's face and his touch while I'd cut into him. *Happy?* Maybe, but I didn't think so. *Accepting?* Definitely, but it was more than that. His touch had been so gentle, his words so warm. I wasn't sure what his emotion was when I'd taken his sample, but it was definitely positive. "Yes, he willingly gave it."

Mitch clapped his hands, his light blue eyes aglow. "Charlie! Amy! Get suited up! We have work to do!"

Mitch's excitement soon took hold of all of us. The love that ached in my chest fell to the background as fierce determination once again bloomed inside of me. The only chance Davin had of being free was if we developed a vaccine.

Charlie and Amy danced when they suited up. This was it. Dr. Hutchinson's theory of mind-body genomics put to the test. We could only hope she was right.

IT WAS NEAR the end of the day. The four of us had spent the afternoon working with Davin's muscular tissue. After suiting up, we'd entered the sterile lab attached to our main lab and sliced his sample into dozens of sections. It had been hours now since we'd placed Davin's muscle tissue into the various solutions required for traditional DNA testing.

We were currently at the final stage, the sequencer. All four of us hovered around the screen.

"This is it, guys." Mitch rubbed his gloved hands together, his words muffled through the hood. "Let's see what this puppy's gonna show."

The loud hum of the machine reverberated around us. It was the only sound in an otherwise quiet room. "Come on," Amy murmured. "Work!"

A dot appeared on the screen.

Then another.

Then another.

Then another.

"Holy shit," Charlie murmured.

The loud humming continued.

I just stared, my mouth falling open. Those dots only meant one thing.

Davin's DNA was intact.

Amy, Charlie, Mitch, and I watched as pictures of Davin's DNA slowly formed. The sequencer continued to hum, loud ticking coming from it at times. It was the sweetest sound I'd ever heard.

"No freakin' way." Mitch was shaking his head back and forth, a bewildered expression on his face.

"I don't believe it." Charlie peered closer at the screen.

"Is this really happening?" Amy put her hands on her hips. "Do we really have an *intact* Kazzie sample that has been exposed to the harshness of labs using traditional DNA testing, and it's still *intact?"*

Twenty-four hours ago, that had been impossible.

"Mitch, you and Charlie stay in here." Amy headed to the decontamination room where we removed our suits. "Meghan, come with me. We have to tell Dr. Sadowsky. Now!"

The urgency in her voice said everything.

OUR BOSS AND the Compound's Director marched into our lab thirty minutes later. Amy and I stood outside the containment cell, waiting.

"You need to see this." Amy waved them closer to the window.

They peered into the containment room within our lab, where Charlie and Mitch still stared at the screen. Thousands of dots stared back.

"Meghan collected an intermuscular sample from Davin this morning under positive circumstances. We put it through traditional DNA processing, and this is what's coming out." She tapped on the window.

Mitch moved so we could all see the screen. Neither Dr. Roberts nor Dr. Sadowsky said anything for a minute.

"Dr. Hutchinson was right," Dr. Sadowsky finally murmured.

"Within twenty-four to forty-eight hours, we should have his entire genome mapped out." Amy crossed her arms and tapped her foot. "We can then start looking for variations. Hopefully, within a few weeks, we'll have some answers."

"We need to run this through the night." Dr. Sadowsky straightened. "There have been rumblings about samples being more stable, but not to this extent." He turned toward me. "Dr. Forester, can you replicate the environment in which you extracted this sample?"

I swallowed uneasily. "I think so."

"Good. I'll set up the conference. Be prepared to join me. I want you telling the scientists nationwide what you did."

What I'd done? What I'd done couldn't be replicated by just anyone.

I'd fallen in love with our Kazzie. I couldn't say for sure, but I was fairly certain he had feelings for me too, even if it was only friendship. *How in the world can anything like that be replicated?*

"Dr. Forester?" Dr. Sadowsky repeated.

The lump in my throat grew. "Yes, sir, of course."

THE CONFERENCE WAS scheduled for the next day, even though it was Saturday. As much as I hated to leave the Compound Friday night, there was nothing else we could do. The sequencer would work through the night, doing its job. All we could do was stare at it. Not very productive.

"This never happens," Amy informed me as we walked to our cars that evening. "Nothing has ever been found that was worthy of bringing everyone in on the weekend. You've really discovered something, Meghan." She gave me a squeeze.

I couldn't reply. How could I admit that the secret to unlocking the Kazzie's DNA appeared to be love? Love your Kazzies, have them care for you too, and poof! A stable vaccine was possible.

The next morning came much too quickly. Memories of my first day at the Compound, when I'd been a nervous wreck, came tumbling back. *I'm about to leave my apartment to go to work and present my findings to hundreds of researchers. Maybe thousands.* Who knew how many workers throughout the Compounds would listen to my presentation. I didn't even know how many researchers were employed by the MRI.

"Oh God," I murmured. It was already after six in the morning. I was supposed to be leaving, but instead, I ran back to my bathroom. I barely made it to the toilet before I threw up. *How am I supposed to do this?*

I splashed cool water on my face and rinsed my mouth. *I'll go see Davin. That's what I'll do. Maybe he'll give me the courage to do this.*

When I finally slid into my car, it was already half past six. The conference was scheduled for nine. If I hurried, that would give me thirty minutes with Davin before I'd have to leave his cell.

DAVIN SMILED WHEN I walked into his hallway. I tried to smile back, but bile still rose in my throat. I'd never felt so sick in my life.

His smile vanished.

I walked stiffly down the hall to the watch room. When I stepped inside, I almost jolted back. Sergeant Rose wasn't there. A different guard sat on the stool. *Of course, it's the weekend.*

"Um, hello," I mumbled when he turned.

He was young. Probably mid-twenties, with sandy blond hair and a square jaw. He had military written all over him. The guard looked down at my badge. "Ah, Dr. Forester, nice to meet you. Sergeant Rose said you may come on some weekends. He said not to be surprised if you showed up."

"He did?"

The guard nodded. "I'm Private Anderson."

I took his hand. It felt hot. Of course, the reason for that was my icy palm. A sheen of cool sweat erupted across me, and my breath caught in my throat. *Keep it together, Meghan!*

Davin stood on the other side of the window, watching me. I let his comforting gaze and presence wash over me. My heart rate slowed.

"Do you mind helping me suit up?"

Private Anderson nodded. "Yes, ma'am."

He led me into the containment room. It took longer to suit up than normal. Private Anderson didn't have the practice Sergeant Rose had. My blood pressure rose as time ticked by. I'd been here so long, and I still hadn't spoken to Davin.

When the light on my wrist finally flashed green, I turned

on the external speaker. "Sergeant Rose usually gives Davin and me privacy. He usually takes a bathroom break and grabs a cup of coffee."

Private Anderson's eyes widened. "He does? That's against policy."

"Dr. Sadowsky okayed it." It was a lie, but I needed to speak to Davin privately, and I didn't know if I could trust Private Anderson to not listen in. "You can call him if you want." I held my breath, not sure if the guard would call my bluff.

The guard studied me for a moment, as if he wasn't sure what to do. I bet my life he'd never spoken to Dr. Sadowsky.

"We need to hurry." I nodded toward the clock. "I'm due up in the auditorium in an hour. Surely you've heard of the breakthrough I've made with Davin?"

The guard cocked his head. Of course, he had no idea what I was talking about. Only the researchers would know about our breakthrough.

"Right." He shuffled his feet. "I'll get you in there."

He hurried out of the containment room. I waited anxiously until the door opened to Davin's cell. When it finally did, Davin appeared on the other side, his face a mask of concern. He took my hand and led me to the chair at his desk.

After I sat, I turned toward the window. "Now would be a good time to get that coffee. Call Dr. Sadowsky if you need to."

I actually saw the guard swallow. A part of me felt guilty. He could be fired for leaving his post, but what were the chances that anybody would find out? Nobody else was in the Sanctum other than the guards, and they were all stationed at their posts. Who would tell?

With stiff movements, he left the watch room. I let out a

sigh of relief. Davin smiled, a gleam in his eye. "I'm impressed." He chuckled.

I took a deep breath. Just his presence calmed me. "With what?"

"That tone of your voice. I've never heard you so... authoritative before."

I laughed, my anxiety slowly melting away. "I haven't either."

He kept smiling.

"What?" I asked.

"It's Saturday. I've never seen you on a Saturday. I thought you wouldn't be in again until Monday."

"Oh." I realized Davin had no idea what we'd discovered yesterday. "I should tell you what we found."

A few minutes later, I finished summing up everything we'd discovered and the reason I was here on the weekend.

Davin just stared at me when I finally finished, his breath coming fast. "So this means a vaccine may be possible?"

"Yes, or, we hope so."

"Meghan... I..." Hope grew so strongly in his gaze that my heart squeezed. "I don't know what to say. If a vaccine is possible, that means someday I may get out of here. I could go outside again."

A click sounded in my earbud, but I barely registered it. The excitement in Davin's voice made me smile. More than anything, I wanted all of that to be true.

"I could go back to Rapid City. I could see my mom. You could come with me. She'd be so happy to know she was a part of this. If you hadn't brought me that picture from her, I don't know if I would have trusted you. She would love knowing what she did helped, and she'd love to see me so–"

He abruptly cut off, his eyes on the watch room. All

excitement left his face. A look I never wanted to see again coated it.

Rage.

I took a step back. A voice sounded in my earbud. A voice that stopped me cold.

"Dr. Forester, get out of there, *now*." The fury in the tone said everything.

With slow movements, I turned and looked at the one person I hoped to never see down here again.

Dr. Roberts.

He stood in the watch room with his hands on his hips. Private Anderson stood beside him. Fury coated my boss' face. Dr. Roberts had heard everything Davin said.

26 – SHATTERED

I began shaking. I shook so hard my teeth chattered.

I had no idea what Dr. Roberts would do.

"You don't have to go out there." Davin grabbed my hands tightly, his eyes still on the glass. "I won't let him hurt you."

Dr. Roberts laughed. The dark sound echoed in Davin's cell.

My boss had turned the speakers on. *That's what that click had been in my earbud.* I squeezed my eyes tightly together. *So stupid of you, Meghan! You should have been more careful!*

"Meghan!" Davin gripped my shaking hands tighter. "You can stay in here. You're safe with me."

"You seem to forget what I can do." Dr. Roberts lifted a plastic cover on the control panel. The gas.

"No!" I lunged toward the watch room and tripped. I almost fell, but Davin caught me, his arms going around my waist. He lifted me back to my feet, his chest pressed against my side. He'd never been so close before.

For a brief moment, I leaned into him. He pulled me

tighter to his side. I could feel him, actually *feel* his arms through the fabric.

"I should go," I said.

Davin's voice grew lower. "I don't care if he gasses me. I don't want that bastard anywhere near you."

Never mind that Dr. Roberts could hear everything we said. Davin obviously didn't care, but I knew what kind of authority my boss carried.

I chose my next words very carefully. "It's crucial that I'm not late for the conference. What we discovered is possibly the biggest breakthrough we've seen. I should get to the auditorium."

Davin let go. It felt like a part of my body had broken away. I felt cold and empty. Not complete.

"Be careful," Davin said quietly.

Emotion surged through me. I actually felt I would choke if I spoke, so instead, I nodded. I walked to the containment room.

Dr. Roberts' gaze followed me the entire way.

BACK IN THE watch room, I couldn't meet Dr. Roberts' eyes. Private Anderson stood in the corner, looking guilty. He'd obviously ratted me out to Dr. Roberts.

Davin stood on the other side of the glass. Fury lined every muscle in his body. I could practically feel his rage.

"Dr. Forester," my boss said coldly. "Follow me."

He turned on his heel and marched out of the watch room. I gave Davin one last desperate look before picking up my bag and hurrying after him.

Dr. Roberts marched ahead. I didn't dare walk at his side. From the steeliness of his shoulders and tense set of his jaw, it was obvious he was angry, but I had no idea *how* angry.

When we exited the Sanctum, I guessed he'd go right, toward the auditorium. Instead, he veered left, back toward the labs. The conference was coming up. We'd be late if we didn't go to the auditorium now. I didn't ask, though. I just followed.

Dr. Roberts marched through the labyrinth of corridors, never once turning to see if I kept up. He seemed to assume I'd follow.

It was only when we approached the outer perimeter of our wing that I realized where we headed: the lobby. When the blinding white walls disappeared, turning into the blueish hue that adorned the lobby's walls, I finally got the courage to ask a question.

"Dr. Roberts, aren't we going to be late for the conference?"

He turned.

I stopped dead in my tracks when I saw the gleam in his eyes. He'd never had friendly eyes, nor any hint of warmness to his face, but now his gaze held something that made me feel sick.

Glee.

He held out his hand. "Give me your access badge."

"Wh… what?"

"Give me your access badge. Now. You're fired."

My stomach dropped. *This must be some kind of joke.* The work I'd done with Davin had been a major breakthrough. Yes, I'd broken MRI policy to obtain it, but surely that wouldn't matter now, not after the results we'd achieved.

"But what about the conference?"

"That's no longer your concern. You broke MRI policy by visiting Davin's mother *and* by bringing him something from the outside that was not approved through the appropriate channels. You knew what would happen if you got caught.

Immediate termination and prosecution."

My heart rate sped up when he mentioned prosecution, but I knew I'd done nothing illegal. "But our results, surely that makes up for it."

He laughed darkly. "Do you think results make you immune to the rules of this facility?"

"No, of course not, but I thought–"

"You thought that you could do what you wanted with no repercussions?"

"No, it's not that. I just thought since we obtained such promising results, you may give this an exception."

"An exception?" His look told me exactly what he thought of that. "Do you know anything about how a facility like this runs? Do you think it would be safe to contain *Makanza* here if people did as they wished? What if everybody decided to break the rules and do as they pleased? Then what? Would we be safe from those… *Kazzies*?" He sneered the word.

For the first time, I saw the depth of his hatred toward them. It went deeper than I imagined. Every pore in his body seemed to ooze malice.

He continued. "You seem to think that results are more important than following rules. Or that making Davin *happy* is more important than anything else. You're young and naïve, Dr. Forester, and I'll be damned if I have someone, who's done what you've done, work here again. Now, give me your badge. You're *out!*"

My mouth opened and closed. "But… my results… nobody else can replicate it. If you just let me explain–"

"Amy will get results. Davin's DNA is obviously stable enough if he's happy. I'm sure we can mimic that."

"But you can't! If you would just let me explain–"

"Guards!" Dr. Roberts barked.

"Please!"

I knew I was begging. If he fired me, I'd never see Davin again. Ever.

Tears filled my eyes. I hated that I was about to cry in front of my boss, but what he was proposing was unfathomable. *To never see Davin again? To not even say goodbye? No. It's not possible. He can't do this.*

"Your badge, Dr. Forester." He held out his hand again as the guards approached.

"Please, don't do this. Let me explain. Let me talk to Dr. Sadowsky," I begged as the guard's hands closed over my upper arms.

Dr. Roberts smiled. "It's too late for that. You're through here."

27 - SURPRISE VISIT

Davin's gone, lost from me forever, and it's all my fault.

I stood in the parking lot as the two guards flanked my sides. They prodded me toward my car since my feet had frozen. A cool autumn breeze rolled across my cheeks. I barely felt it.

I was just fired.

That was the last time I'll ever see the inside of the Compound.

This is the last time I'll be on the grounds.

Once I left the gigantic gates, I'd never be admitted again.

I pushed away from that fact, burying it, denying it. I couldn't think about that right now. Not seeing Davin again…

That wasn't a reality I could live with.

I shook the guards loose and slid into my vehicle. The rest passed in a blur. Starting the motor, leaving the Compound, entering my apartment.

Time stood still.

It was like I detached from my body as if I was watching everything from above. I saw myself lay down on the couch and pull the covers up. I still wore my jacket and shoes. It was all surreal, like a bad dream. *Yes, a dream. That's what this all is. A dream.* I hadn't been fired. This was all just a nightmare and tomorrow it would go away. Davin would be back. I'd see him again.

This couldn't possibly be my life.

A KNOCKING ON the door invaded the quiet, heaviness in my mind. I ignored it and pulled the covers higher, willing myself to sleep. All I wanted was unconsciousness. Nothingness. Sleep was the only way to achieve that.

The knocking came again, sharper this time. I burrowed deeper, but it wouldn't stop. "Meghan? Meghan, are you in there? Open up, it's me!"

The voice penetrated the fog, begging me to surface, but what was the point? I'd failed. Davin was gone. Nothing I could do would bring him back. I shut my eyes tighter, willing myself to lapse into oblivion.

Sleep would make it all disappear. Just like after Jer died. Six years ago, sleep had been the only way to get away from it all. The first few weeks after Jer's death had been more painful than anything I could bear. It would be the same this time. Davin may still be alive, but he was lost from me forever. Already, the raw, aching sensation filled me, constricting my lungs until I couldn't breathe.

"Meghan, I'm going to break this door down if you don't open up! Get up and get out here! Now!"

Amy. But I didn't want to listen. I didn't want to get up.

"Meghan, I mean it. Answer the door! I know you're here! Your car's in the parking lot!"

I knew she wouldn't leave. Forcing myself, I sat up, the blanket falling away. The clock ticked steadily on the wall. It was six in the evening. *Have I really been lying here for eight hours?*

"Meghan?" This time the yell was laced with concern, followed by another round of rapid knocking.

"Amy, I'm coming!" Somehow, I managed to stumble to the door and unlock it. When it finally opened, Amy practically burst through. A guy I'd never met before, followed her.

"What are you doing here?" I shoved hair out of my face.

She pushed past me into the entryway. "Are you *kidding* me? Do you really think I wouldn't come here after what happened today?"

Amy took her coat off and threw it on a kitchen chair. Her hair was wild. Red curls flew everywhere. She looked ferocious and angry like a lioness come to protect her cub. The guy beside her just stood there, hands in his pockets.

"Are you okay?" she asked. "I've been worried sick. Nobody knows what the hell's going on. One minute, everyone's in the auditorium, waiting for you to show up, and the next Dr. Roberts is there, telling us you no longer work for the Compound, and he'd be presenting the findings."

I covered my face with my hands. I didn't want it to be true.

Amy stepped forward. "Meghan, are you okay?"

"I'm fine," I replied automatically.

She snorted. "Like hell you are. You look like crap."

My hands fell from my face.

"When did you last eat?" she asked.

Eat? Who cares about eating. "I don't know, last night?"

"I'm making you food." She pulled a chair out. "Sit down."

I looked again at the guy Amy brought along. Converse sneakers adorned his feet. Straight-cut jeans, which looked stylish in an old-fashioned way, sat on his lean hips. I glanced back at his shoes and felt a brief twinge of curiosity. I wondered where he got them. I hadn't seen Converse shoes in years.

"Meghan, this is Ben. Ben, Meghan." Amy waved the introductions.

Ben had a crop of light brown hair. Dark rimmed glasses sat on his nose. I studied him. Something about him looked familiar. I welcomed the diversion. Anything to keep me from thinking of Davin.

"Do you recognize him?" Amy asked, her tone worried.

"Yes." Even though I couldn't place him. "Do I know you?"

Ben stuffed his hands in his jean pockets, his expression sheepish. "I told you we couldn't fool everyone, Aimes."

The distraction helped bury the pain even deeper. I felt a twinge of my old self return.

Amy bit her lip. "He works at the Compound." She ran an agitated hand through her hair. "Crap, if you recognize him, others might too. At work, he dresses like a lab geek so people won't recognize him in public, but maybe that won't work."

Everyone knew it was strictly against policy to date others within the Compound. The MRI prohibited intimate relationships among co-workers, worried that confidential information might get shared. The only way to work as a couple in the MRI was to come into your jobs already married. That was the only exception.

I wasn't sure where I'd seen Ben before, but I guessed it was in another lab. Definitely against the rules for him and Amy to be together.

"How long have you been dating?" I asked.

"Six months." Amy reached for Ben's hand at the same time he reached for hers. I watched the small, intimate gesture.

A pang of envy filled me. I'd never get to do that with Davin.

"Nobody's found out yet," she added.

I hated seeing the worry on Amy's face. I was also surprised. I'd had no idea she had a boyfriend. She'd hid it well.

"You'll probably be okay," I mumbled. "I had no idea, and I don't think Mitch or Charlie do either. If you could keep that from us, and if you've been out in public together for the last six months and nobody's reported you, I'm sure you'll be fine." I hoped I was right. Sioux Falls wasn't a big town, and since the Second Wave, it was even harder to stay anonymous.

"Anyway, sit down." Amy hurried to the cupboards and fridge and made a face when she saw the meager selection. "When did you last go shopping?"

"I can't remember." Weekends I usually shopped. Lately, my weekends had been rather busy. I'd spent the last two with Sharon.

"Come on, Ben." Amy pulled him over. "Give me a hand."

I sat back and watched as they moved around my small kitchen, working quickly and efficiently. It was obvious they'd cooked together before. Fifteen minutes later, Amy put a plate of steaming pasta in front of me.

"It's all I could do with what you had." An empty jar of canned tomatoes sat on the counter, and I was pretty sure that was the last of my pasta. It smelled good, even though I wasn't hungry.

"How'd you do this?" I eyed the steaming food. As much as I tried, the best I managed with Italian was overcooked noodles and burnt tomatoes.

Amy shrugged. "You'd be amazed what seasonings can do. Now, eat."

I ate, only because I knew she wouldn't stop pestering me until I finished. It was awkward. The entire time I ate, Amy and Ben sat across the table, watching me. Amy wouldn't shift her gaze until I swallowed the last bite.

She nodded in satisfaction and stood, whisking my plate away before I could protest. She returned with a full glass of water. "Drink."

I rolled my eyes but did as she said.

When my belly was uncomfortably full, Amy finally let up. She sat and clasped her hands. "Okay, now tell me what happened."

The morning came crashing back. Talking to Davin openly and honestly as if we were the only two people in the world. We should have known better. It was the weekend, unfamiliar territory. *I should have been more careful.*

"It was stupid," I finally said.

"So it's true? Dr. Roberts actually *fired* you?"

"Yes."

"Word is that you were alone with Davin in his cell and the guard was nowhere to be seen. Is that also true?"

I nodded.

"And you and Davin were holding hands or touching or something like that?"

I nodded again. It was amazing how news traveled so quickly within the Compound, especially since everything was supposed to be so secretive. *How does anyone even know that stuff? Did a researcher overhear Dr. Roberts telling someone?*

"And Dr. Roberts caught you? Talking about… something?"

"Yes."

Amy sat back, crossing her arms. "That's where the news gets fuzzy. No one's sure what you were talking about."

At least something Davin and I shared was still private. "It's nothing, really. Besides, it's probably best you don't know. I don't want you getting in trouble."

Amy rolled her eyes. "Please, I'm not going to get in trouble. They can't fire all of their researchers for being curious. The labs would be freakin' empty if they did."

Ben chuckled. From the amused glance he gave her, I could tell he liked Amy's feistiness.

I shrugged. "I broke the rules, simple as that."

"Which rules?" Amy leaned forward.

Knowing she wasn't going to let it go, I told her everything. About how close Davin and I had become, how we visited in private with the speakers turned off, how I'd gone to Rapid to meet his mother, how I'd smuggled things in from the outside since I was so desperate to get him talking. I told it all.

The only thing I kept private was my connection with Sara. I would never subject her to more testing. If Dr. Roberts found out about her ability…

I cringed at what he'd do.

When I finished, Amy gaped. "Are you kidding me?"

"It's nothing to be proud of."

Amy shook her head. "You've got balls, Meghan. I'll give you that."

I sighed. "Not that it did me any good."

The entire time I'd told them my story, Ben had sat quietly, listening. I had a feeling he did that a lot. Stood in the shadows, picking up on the things around him, drawing little attention to himself. That was probably the trait that had kept others from recognizing him in public.

Amy was a personality that was hard to miss, and if that didn't catch your attention, her hair surely would. But Ben had a blandness about him that one could easily overlook.

"I guess I understand now why Dr. Roberts sounded furious," Amy said thoughtfully.

I grimaced at the way she said *furious*. I could picture my boss, well, former boss, throwing a tantrum. "Was it that bad?"

Amy sighed. "He'll get over it eventually."

"Do you know how Davin's doing?"

She shook her head. "None of us do. Dr. Roberts closed the Sanctum this morning, to everyone."

AMY AND BEN stayed another hour. Even though the dark spell that wound around me this morning had disappeared, Amy wouldn't leave until I showered and changed clothes. I did it simply to appease her.

She gave me a fierce hug before they left. "Call me tomorrow."

My wet hair stuck to her chin when she pulled back. I hastily swept it away. "I will, promise."

After the door closed behind them, I turned around to face my empty apartment. Except this time, that emptiness didn't weigh me down. Amy's visit reminded me how driven I'd become to fight for the Kazzies, yet for eight short hours, I'd been reduced to a shell of what I was.

That had happened after Jer's death too, but I'd been younger then. I hadn't known I could survive something like that. I was older now, wiser if only a little. Curling up into a ball, wishing the world would go away, wouldn't help Davin, and it wouldn't help me.

I wasn't sure what I could do now, but I'd be damned if I didn't figure something out.

28 – NEGOTIATIONS

I spent the evening pacing my apartment as I tried to formulate ideas to get my job back. When the clock struck midnight, I finally called it quits. I had a few ideas, but until Monday morning, when the Compound administration offices opened, there was nothing I could do.

It was early Sunday morning when a scratchy feeling in my mind aroused me from a deep sleep. I bolted upright in bed. Pale morning sunlight peeked through my curtains. Pushing long, dark strands of hair from my eyes, I gripped my head and concentrated as hard as I could.

Sara?

Our connection clicked.

Meghan? Yeah, it's me. So, you're okay?

Yes. My head slumped into my hands. I'd completely forgotten about our connection amidst the whirlwind yesterday. I berated myself for not checking in with her earlier.

Are you okay? I asked.

I felt her nod. *I'm fine. We're all fine, but…* Her nervousness strummed through our connection. *There's a rumor going through here that the Sanctum's closed.*

I grumbled in disgust. The MRI obviously hadn't informed the Kazzies of their plans. *Yes, that's right. Didn't somebody tell you?*

Nobody tells us anything, but Victor overheard his guards at handover this morning. They must have forgotten his speaker was on.

What did they say?

That nobody's allowed into the Sanctum right now, except for the guards and Dr. Roberts. Davin told me what happened yesterday, so I'm guessing that's why it closed?

Yes, that's why.

Sara sighed. *I was worried that was the reason. Are you sure you're okay?*

I rubbed my eyes. *I'm okay, but I got fired.*

What!

Sara's loud response made me squint. *Dr. Roberts found out I visited Davin's mom and brought him that picture. He fired me on the spot.*

A long paused followed. *Holy crap. Davin's gonna freak.*

It was possible he'd fly into another rage. I sighed. I didn't know how severely Davin would react, but I *did* know he wouldn't take it well. *I'm hoping tomorrow after I talk to Dr. Sadowsky, I can get this all straightened out.*

Sara perked up. *So maybe you won't be fired?*

That's my hope. Davin and I had a major breakthrough. That can't be ignored regardless of what I did.

Okay, then we won't tell Davin. Not yet at least. Things are pretty tense right now. If he flies off the handle, I don't know what Dr. Roberts will do.

My stomach lurched. *Yes. I agree. Let's not tell him.*

Do you want to talk to him? I can try channeling you again.

More than anything, I wanted to hear Davin's voice, but I

also knew I couldn't lie to him. If he asked me what happened, I'd have to tell him. I didn't want to take that chance.

Not yet. Let me get my job back first.

Okay. She paused. *Hey, Meghan?*

Yeah?

Good luck.

IF ANYONE HAD the power to get me back into the Compound, it was Dr. Sadowsky. Since I didn't have his number, I had to wait until Monday to call him. To burn time, I went grocery shopping Sunday morning and for two runs in the afternoon.

Each mile that passed under my shoes only drove me more. I couldn't sit still. Pacing in my apartment only made it worse. Thoughts of Davin being hurt burned my mind. I needed to keep moving, so I ran and then ran again.

My muscles protested angrily when I picked up the phone first thing Monday morning. Even that little movement hurt.

I had to go through several channels to reach Dr. Sadowsky. His secretary, Emma Lehmann, answered promptly on the second ring. It was only eight in the morning, but she sounded bright and fresh.

"Dr. Sadowsky's office. This is Emma. How may I help you?"

"Hi, Emma. This is Dr. Meghan Forester. I need to speak to Dr. Sadowsky. Is he in?"

She paused. "No, he's not, Dr. Forester. May I take a message?"

"Oh… yes." I left my contact information along with a note that it was urgent. When we hung up, I sat at my bedside, willing the phone to ring. It didn't. I spent the next two hours pacing around my apartment. Waiting.

Every little sound made me jump, but it was never my phone, only a neighbor slamming their door, or someone walking by on the street. By ten in the morning, I still hadn't heard from Dr. Sadowsky, so I called back.

Emma answered again on the second ring. I told her it was me and asked if he was free yet.

"No, I'm afraid he's still busy."

"Is he in the office today?"

"He's busy, Dr. Forester."

In other words, it was none of my business. Frustrated, I hung up and turned on my computer. *Maybe an email will be better. He'll get that for sure. Right?*

I typed one up, using my personal address since I didn't have access to my MRI email anymore.

> *From: mforester@connect.sd.net*
> *To: Sadowsky.Ethan@mri.gov*
> *Subject: URGENT*
>
> *Dr. Sadowsky,*
>
> *I've called several times this morning. It's urgent that I speak with you.*
>
> *I'm sure Dr. Roberts told you what happened Saturday morning. I can't apologize enough for my actions, but if you'd let me explain, you'll know why I did everything. It's also important that you know another researcher will not be able to replicate the sample I withdrew. Please call me. I'll explain why.*
>
> *Thank you,*
> *Dr. Meghan Forester*

I reread the email three times, mulling over how he would interpret it. I eventually hit send and proceeded to bite off all of my fingernails as I sat by my computer, waiting for a response.

The clock ticked steadily in the living room, reminding me of time passing by. Each *tick, tick* solidified that the world kept turning, oblivious to my turmoil, as if mocking that my life was on hold.

The universe didn't care. I was just another peon, nobody important, just another fleck in the space-time continuum. I glared at the blasted clock and considered throwing it out the window.

When early afternoon rolled around, and I still hadn't heard from Dr. Sadowsky, I called Emma again.

"He's still unavailable, Dr. Forester." Her tone wasn't as friendly this time. I hung up and paced around my living room, stopping every ten minutes to check my email. I called Emma again when another two hours passed.

"Yes, Dr. Forester?" Emma asked, bypassing a greeting.

I was a little startled she knew that it was me, then realized she obviously had caller ID. "Oh, I just wondered if he's free yet?"

"Like I told you before, he's busy."

"You'll let him know I need to talk to him?"

"Yes."

"Can you let him know it's urgent?"

She sighed audibly. "Yes, Dr. Forester. I'll let him know that as well. Just like I said I would every other time we've talked today."

"Thank you, Emma."

She hung up without responding.

When I climbed into bed that night, a sinking pit formed

in my stomach. I never heard back from Dr. Sadowsky. He obviously didn't view me as a priority.

I thought for sure Dr. Sadowsky would call me right away or at least email me back. The data we'd collected from Davin's sample was the MRI's first major breakthrough. Common sense said that wouldn't go unstudied.

Or will it?

THE REST OF the week passed in a blur of worry and pacing. More phone calls. More emails. All unanswered. Amy came over a few times to make sure I was eating. Unfortunately, she didn't have any information either. Every time she'd tried to speak to Dr. Sadowsky, she'd been shut out too.

Desperation claimed me Friday night. For the first time, I wondered if I'd ever return to the Compound.

As I climbed into bed, I closed my eyes, tuning into the door that connected me to Sara. We'd spoken daily, her making up excuses each time to Davin for why I couldn't speak with him. I knew it was wearing on her. She sounded more tired every day.

I lay back on my pillow, closed my eyes, and concentrated on the door. I mentally knocked, but it was distant feeling, fuzzy almost. That hadn't happened before. Worried, I concentrated harder, urgently knocking and willing Sara to hear me. The connection felt weak.

Breathing harder, I squeezed my eyes tightly shut, pouring every bit of energy into our mental link. Eventually, the door pried open. *Sara? Are you there?*

Yeah, hi, Meghan. She sounded quieter than usual and not as clear. As if she was far away. Worry strummed through me.

Hi. Are you okay? You sound so distant.

I'm fine.

Are you sure?

I felt her nod. *It's just been a while since anyone's been in here, other than the guards. Things have been tense.*

A paused stretched between us. *I wish you were here,* she said.

Me too. You sound tired.

I'm exhausted. Everyone's wanted to talk today. I don't think I've ever had so many conversations telepathically in a twenty-four hour period. It's tiring.

I'm sorry, and here I am, wanting to talk too.

No, don't be. I'm glad you got in touch.

I didn't tell her how hard getting in touch was. She sounded stressed enough. *Are you sure you're okay?*

She sighed. *I'm struggling today with all of the connections. I keep getting people mixed up and then I'm accidentally telling one person what I was supposed to tell someone else. I let a secret slip.*

You can't blame yourself for that. It's a lot to juggle.

Try telling that to Sophie. She has a crush on Victor and now he knows.

I sat up more in bed and leaned against the headboard. *She'll forgive you.*

Eventually, maybe, but right now she's mad at me.

I grimaced. *I'm sorry.* I took a deep breath. *How's Davin doing?*

Not good. He's blaming himself for everything. I've never seen him beat himself up like this.

But he's not being unruly?

No, only because he thinks he needs to be on his best behavior to see you again.

That comment made me pause, my eyes popping wide open. *Sara, I have an idea, but I'm going to need all of you to help if it's going to work.*

SARA KEPT BUSY over the weekend, organizing our plan with the Kazzies. I had no idea if it would work and dreaded the consequences if it didn't. I fell asleep on Saturday night, worried over what may happen. Dreams plagued me. Vivid, haunting dreams of the virus and Kazzies.

But those dreams triggered something.

They latched onto a memory in my subconscious, some part of science that had been there all along, but I'd only just found.

I bolted upright in bed early Sunday morning, the idea coming to me as harshly as a flash of lightning. I scrambled from my tangled sheets and raced to the kitchen table to map out my thoughts before the idea left.

I scribbled the chemical reactions so quickly they were barely legible. When finished, I stared down at them, knowing it was only the beginnings of a possibility.

The world around me disappeared as I continued to sketch and brainstorm throughout the morning, the idea growing in my mind. I spent the entire day there, at my kitchen table, thinking and writing.

For the first time since leaving the Compound, I didn't need to run. I didn't need to distract myself. Instead, hour after hour passed in a blur as my idea solidified on the paper in front of me.

Late that night, I called Amy. I told her everything I'd been working on. She listened, stunned, and promised to find Dr. Sadowsky first thing in the morning.

"I'll get him to talk to me, Meghan. I can promise you that. I won't leave until he sees me."

Her fierce words gave me hope, but I also knew it may not change anything. They didn't need *me* for my theory, only the idea. I may never be allowed into the Compound again, but at least a vaccine may be possible.

And at the end of the day, that was all that mattered.

After Amy and I hung up, I knocked on the mental door that connected me to Sara. Again, it was hard to get in touch with her. Mentally, I was exhausted, and I knew she was too, but I needed to talk to Davin. I couldn't put it off any longer. Even if the MRI listened to my idea, that didn't mean they'd let me back in.

It was time I faced reality.

I'm going to put you through, Sara said. *But I'm not sure how long I can keep you connected.*

Don't worry, I'll keep it brief. Already, tears formed in my eyes.

I'll do my best, but I think you're right. You need to tell him, she replied.

A minute passed. A strum of anxiety pounded through me, like a tidal wave slamming a shoreline. It had been so long since I'd heard his voice or seen his face. Some days, it felt like a lifetime.

I felt his presence enter my mind. My heart sped up. My stomach twisted into knots.

Meghan? he said.

A tear rolled down my cheek. *Hi.*

He let out a deep sigh. A moment passed where neither of us said anything. I started to cry in earnest, hoping with all my soul he didn't know.

It's good to hear you, he finally said. *It's been a long time.*

I know. How are you doing?

Fine. I've… He stopped and took an audible breath and then cleared his throat. He continued in a hoarse voice. *I've missed you,* he whispered.

More tears rolled down my face. *I've missed you too.*

He cleared his throat again. *So, how did it go after you left last Saturday? I've been worried about you. I know what that bastard is like when he's angry. Hopefully, he didn't make you too nervous for the presentation. Did it go okay?*

I grimaced, guilt pummeling me for keeping the truth from him. He had no idea how monumental the last eight days had been. Only Sara knew.

Davin, I need to tell you something. I paused, wringing my hands.

What is it?

After I saw you last Saturday, when Dr. Roberts took me out of the Sanctum and sealed the doors, I didn't go to the conference. He…

What did he do? His voice was so cold, an icy chill blew over my mind.

He fired me.

WHAT? His roar made me wince.

I've been trying to get my job back. I'm doing everything I can. Hopefully, I'll find a way, but if I don't, I want you to know–

The connection broke. I felt it break, like a taut string being cut.

Davin? I called. *Sara?* My voice rose, but there was no one there. I tried to connect with Sara, but it wasn't working.

Something had happened.

SEVEN DAYS PASSED.

Seven agonizing days. As another Sunday rolled around, it had officially been over two weeks since I'd been fired. The most gut-wrenching part was that I hadn't heard from anybody since Davin and I were cut off. Not Sara, not Amy, and not Dr. Sadowsky.

I had no idea if Amy had passed along my idea. It had been a week since we'd spoken. I even went to Sean's Pub, hoping to run into Amy since I didn't know where she lived. Nothing.

I then drove to the Compound and parked outside the gates, hoping to connect with her on her way home. But the guards told me I'd be arrested if I stayed, so I left there too. It was awful. Absolute radio silence. I had no idea what was going on, and it was driving me crazy.

Despair wanted to claim me, pulling me into her icy grip, refusing to let me go. On some level, I knew Sara had to be okay. I still *felt* the connection, but I hadn't been able to get through to her.

As for why Amy wouldn't answer my calls, I didn't want to think about the reasons. My mind went in a million directions, none of them good.

Pulling on my running clothes, I set out for another run. It was the only thing keeping me sane.

It was just past nine in the morning. November had arrived with a vengeance. The sky was a crisp, icy blue when I stepped onto the sidewalk. Cold winds whipped through the trees. An early dusting of snow covered the slushy streets.

I set a fast, furious pace. The more I pushed, the less I thought. Running hard required breathing bordering on gasping, but it was what I needed. With each mile that passed, the only thing I thought about was getting air. By the time I returned to my apartment building, I could barely walk, let alone, think.

As I was about to go inside and attempt to walk up the stairs, I noticed a strange car in the parking lot. It was brand-new, expensive, and clean. Any car like that drew attention since new cars were rare, but that wasn't what caught my eye.

Instead, it was the MRI license plates.

I sucked in a mouthful of cold air, expelling it in a misty

cloud around me. With shaky limbs, I opened the door and climbed the stairwell. Whoever was here was here for me. Nobody else in the building had ever worked for the MRI.

I reached the second floor and hesitantly opened the stairwell door. Outside of my apartment, a man stood in the hallway with his back to me. He turned. My breath caught.

It was Dr. Sadowsky.

"Dr. Forester," he called. "I was hoping to have a word with you."

I stared, unblinking. *He's here? At my apartment?* Since I'd still hadn't heard from him, I assumed I never would.

Taking shaky steps, I walked forward. If he was here, that meant I could tell somebody my theory. I still hadn't heard from Amy. I had no idea if she'd passed it along.

My hands were unsteady when I brought my keys up to the lock. He hovered behind me. Scents of soap, aftershave, and wool clung to his long, expensive looking coat.

He followed me inside, and for a minute, I didn't know what to do. I was a mess. Sweat dripped off me, and I was in desperate need of a shower.

"Can I take your coat?" I managed as I held out my hand. He shrugged it off.

Since I didn't have a closet, I folded it carefully and draped it over a kitchen chair. "Would you like a drink?"

"No, I'm fine, but perhaps we could sit."

Melting, slushy snow dripped off my shoes, so I leaned down to take them off. He followed my lead. I was about to tell him he didn't have to remove his shoes, but he already stood back up in his black, trouser socks, looking dignified while I was sure I looked ridiculous.

He followed me into the living room and opted for the lone chair while I sat on the couch. My pulse raced uncontrollably. I wished I'd known he was coming. I would have dressed presentably and had a speech rehearsed for my theory.

Instead, my muscles ached, sweat pooled between my breasts, and my limbs shook from my vigorous run.

Oblivious to my inner turmoil, Dr. Sadowsky leaned forward. "I know you've been trying to reach me."

"Yes. Every day."

"I'm aware of that, and I'm sorry for ignoring you, but I had to address more pressing issues before I could even consider speaking with you."

"Oh."

"I also know you've been speaking to Dr. McConnell."

I swallowed. "*Oh.*"

"I asked her to stop contacting you until I reached a decision on what to do."

So that's why I haven't heard from Amy. "Is she in trouble?"

"No. From what the lie detector test revealed, she's being truthful when she says she was not aware of any of your actions while you were employed at the Compound."

My mind raced. So much had happened without me being aware of it. A lie detector test? Did that mean Amy had gone to Dr. Sadowsky on Monday, like she'd promised, only to be interrogated?

"For the past two weeks," Dr. Sadowsky continued, "we've interviewed all of the guards, your co-workers, the other lab groups, and Davin's mother to ensure you weren't doing any other illegal activities."

My eyes bulged. *They visited Sharon too?*

"You have to know what you did was entirely unacceptable."

"I know. I can't tell you how sorry I am."

"I also know that you obtained a sample from Davin that yielded extraordinary results."

"Yes, I've wanted to speak to you about that–"

"I'll get to that in a minute." He held his hand up. "Right now, I need you to know that we *cannot* allow a researcher to stay employed within the Compound who does not follow the rules. Keeping Kazzies within our facility is a major risk. If exact policy and procedure are not followed, there's a risk of the virus escaping."

My heart plummeted. I hung my head. "I know. I know all of that. Please believe me that I would *never* do anything to jeopardize anyone's safety."

"I know that from what our investigation concluded, which is the only reason you've never been arrested." He sighed heavily. "Dr. Forester, right now, I'm between a rock and a hard place. Nobody's been able to replicate your results. However, I cannot employ someone I do not trust."

My head shot up. "Does that mean–"

"Let me finish."

I shut my mouth.

"And on top of that, I currently have a Sanctum full of Kazzies causing mayhem. They are demanding we allow you to return. In all of the time that the Compounds have been running, I've *never* heard of anything like this."

I swallowed, thinking of the plan Sara and I had formulated last weekend. The plan where all of the Kazzies became unruly, demanding to see me again. It was a selfish plan. I knew that, but I'd been desperate, and Sara agreed it may be the only way to get me back in. We'd both wanted to try.

"Are they okay?" I asked.

Dr. Sadowsky pinched the bridge of his nose. For the first

time, I saw how tired he looked. "Yes, but they've become so unruly we've had to sedate them. Davin especially. Sunday night, he became incredibly violent."

Sedate them? Perhaps that was why I couldn't get through to Sara. And Sunday night. That's when Davin found out I got fired. "But they're all okay?" I persisted, my heart rate picking up.

"Yes, Dr. Forester. They're fine. But perhaps now, you can see my dilemma. I cannot have a researcher who disrespects the rules, nor can I have a Sanctum with Kazzies who are a danger to themselves and to those around them. I realize you are an incredibly talented scientist, but that alone cannot guarantee your employment."

I clasped my hands together, nodding. "Dr. Sadowsky, please, I understand all of that, but please, just hear me out. You have to understand my intention while working with Davin was only to further our understanding of the virus and work toward a vaccine. Dr. Hutchinson's theory works. However, the last sample I collected from Davin cannot be replicated by another researcher. I tried to explain that to Dr. Roberts, but he wouldn't listen. I know it was unprofessional to behave as I did, but Davin means more to me than almost anyone in my life. He gave me that sample willingly with an open heart. Davin and I share something. A bond has formed between us. I believe that's why his sample was so stable. Please, just let me return to work with him. I'm confident I can obtain more samples that are just as stable. If I'm allowed to do what's needed, I won't need to hide anything. The only reason I ever hid my actions was because I knew Dr. Roberts would never allow it, but I *never* did anything to jeopardize safety, and I never would."

Dr. Sadowsky studied me, silent for a long time.

He eventually sighed and took a deep breath. "Even if I

did let you back in. And even if forming this bond, as you put it, was the reason for your success, what about the other Kazzies? How would their samples be taken? We have forty-one variations of *Makanza*. Each variation needs a vaccine, which means every Kazzie needs to produce a sample like the one you took from Davin. Dr. McConnell said you had developed a hypothesis on how that could happen. Perhaps, you'd care to enlighten me?"

I smiled, my hands shaking as I straightened. "Yes, I do. I think I know how we can retrieve samples like that from every Kazzie in the U.S."

For the first time since Dr. Sadowsky arrived, I felt him truly listen to what I was saying. I launched into my theory, thanking the stars that Dr. Sadowsky was more interested in finding a vaccine than he was in following the MRI's rules.

29 - BREAKTHROUGH

After a lengthy discussion about my theory, Dr. Sadowsky agreed to negotiate my reemployment.

In other words, I was returning to work.

He stated that I would be allowed to work with Davin, but my whereabouts would be monitored twenty-four hours per day for the next six months. I could tell Dr. Sadowsky wanted to believe that I was trustworthy, but he couldn't jeopardize the safety of his workers or the public.

I completely understood and took the terms in stride. Essentially, I was on parole, but I'd be working with Davin again and sharing my findings with the rest of the Compounds. With any luck, in a few months, we'd be on our way toward a vaccine.

When he left, I bounced around my apartment in absolute glee. Come tomorrow, I'd see Davin again.

"MEGHAN!" AMY GRINNED when I strode into the lab the next morning. Mitch and Charlie flanked her sides. All of them came forward.

"What have you been up to, troublemaker?" Mitch lifted me into a hug. "This place has been insane since you left."

I smiled, hugging him back.

"No suit for your first day back?" Charlie assessed my blouse and slacks before giving me a quick squeeze.

"I'll admit I have a suit jacket in my office. I'll wear it at the conference." I was amazed at how far I'd come. Just three months ago, I would have been a nervous wreck at the attention, but now I felt confident and sure. Amy was right. I'd come a long way.

"The conference, about time," Amy muttered. "I'm glad Dr. Sadowsky is a reasonable man. Dr. Roberts certainly isn't."

At the mention of my boss, I tightened. I had yet to see him.

"Have you seen Davin yet?" Mitch asked.

"No. I'm going to the Inner Sanctum now before I go up to the auditorium."

"I'm guessing you want to see him in private and have us meet you there?" Amy asked.

"If you don't mind."

They all nodded and gathered their things.

I walked to the Sanctum alone. It was the longest walk of my life.

WHEN I ROUNDED the corner into Davin's hall, he stood waiting. He had to know I was coming. Sara had probably told him.

When we finally saw each other, we both stopped, frozen in time, staring at one another. He looked exactly as I remembered. Tall, strong, and ready to conquer the entire world.

It was what I admired most about him, loved about him.

Davin was a warrior. Those warrior traits ran in his blood and could never be banished. Hundreds of years ago, he would have been astride a stallion, galloping across the plains, fearlessly hunting the wild buffalo. Now, he stood ramrod straight. Proud, distinct, the last Sioux warrior to roam the land.

Sergeant Rose helped me suit up. Never had I felt so much anxiety at seeing Davin again. When I was finally ready to go in, my heart raced, and my breath came in short gasps.

The door opened to his cell.

He stood waiting, his blue eyes shining.

Grasping my hand, he led me to his chair. I sat while he perched on his bed. A few feet separated us, yet I'd never felt so close to another human being in my life.

"Did you and Sara really hatch out that plan to get you back in here?" he finally asked, his voice husky.

I nodded. "We needed to do something to get the Director's attention. Otherwise, he may have never let me back in."

He clasped my hand. Heat seared through my gloves. I looked down, wishing so much that I could feel his skin. Touch him. Love him.

"I'm going to get you out of here, Davin. If it's the last thing I do on earth, that will be it."

"I know you will."

WHEN I FIRST saw Davin, he'd been a blur of a human being. Whizzing, throwing, and fighting too quickly for me to see him. How little I had known when I entered the Compound on my first day. I would have never guessed what was to come, or how much this Kazzie would affect me.

Davin's soul was as strong and unyielding as the *Makanza*

strain within him. He had a heart filled with goodness and honesty, but a backbone made of brick and mortar. His touch and laughter sang to my soul, and just a glance from him sent shivers to my toes. I had no idea what was to come when I first laid eyes on him. Not only would he capture my heart, but he'd be the breakthrough for the vaccine to come.

As he held my hand, I explained my theory to him, a variation of Dr. Hutchinson's theory on mind-body genomics. I told him that we needed to bring families and spouses of the Kazzies into the Compounds. If we wanted to collect samples that were stable enough to synthesize into a vaccine, we needed to fill the cells with love. The uniqueness of *Makanza* was that it was tied to a Kazzie's DNA, similar to the way an unborn child was tied to his mother.

They were one.

Breathing, feeding, and growing together. One could not be detached from the other unless the body was ready. Just the way an unborn child, forced from the womb,. came into the world with an abundance of complications, so was the way of *Makanza*. However, when love and acceptance filled the environment, when the virus was coaxed and not forced, when it was caressed and not beaten, it was stable.

The conference that afternoon opened the door to the next phase of ending *Makanza*. In a few short months, we'd have our vaccine. We would have the beginnings of the path to recovery, to healing, to making us a global community once again.

I held Davin's hands and gazed into his bright blue eyes as I explained what we endeavored to overcome. I felt his awe, fear, and hope. He knew just like I did that a vaccine was only the beginning. It wasn't a guarantee, but it was a start.

For with a vaccine, only then would the real work begin.

CONTINUE THE STORY

Reservation 1, book two in The Makanza Series

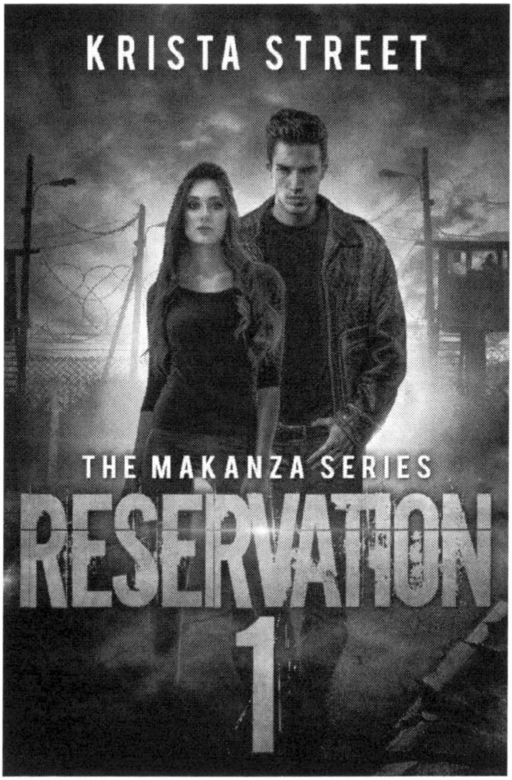

To save the only man she's ever loved,
she must pay a price.

AUTHOR'S NOTE

If you're reading this, you probably just finished the entire first book in The Makanza Series *and* you stuck around long enough to read this too. Wow, thank you! :)

I hope that you enjoyed *Compound 26*. It was a book that I began writing a number of years ago, but then I put it on hold to finish *The Lost Children Trilogy*. I came back to it in 2017 and finished it, along with books two-four in the series. The entire series will be available in 2018. I hope you enjoy it!

Lastly, I'd really appreciate it if you'd leave a review on *Compound 26*. Goodreads is great, but a review on Amazon is even better. Amazon has a ranking system for its authors – the higher you rank, the more visibility you get. And guess what helps ranking? Reviews. So if you enjoyed *Compound 26*, please consider logging onto Amazon to leave a review. I'd very much appreciate it if you did!

I'll end my note here. Thank you again for reading my work. You can connect with me more using the links below. In the meantime, happy reading!

Website: www.kristastreet.com

Bookbub: www.bookbub.com/profile/krista-street

Facebook: www.facebook.com/authorkristastreet

Twitter: https://twitter.com/Author_K_Street

Instagram: www.instagram.com/authorkristastreet/

ACKNOWLEDGMENTS

There are many people I need to thank. To Bruce Eckloff for giving me a tour of your lab and explaining genetic basics to me. Seeing the insides of a lab, hearing its sounds, and smelling its scents gave me great material to work with.

To my editor, Mike Kalmbach – thank you for not only editing this book but for sharing your scientific knowledge. Any misrepresentations about genetic science in this novel are my mistakes and mine alone.

To Jesikah, Mark, Charis, and Jaime Lea for beta reading and proofreading. Thank you all for your time and help with this novel.

My cover artist, Deranged Doctor Design. You've once again blown me away with your amazing talent and artwork.

And of course, thank *you*, my reader. Without you, I'd have no reason to publish. Thank you for reading my work!

ABOUT THE AUTHOR

Krista Street is a Minnesota native but has lived throughout the U.S. and in another country or two. She loves to travel, read, and spend time in the great outdoors. When not writing, Krista is either spending time with her family, sipping a cup of tea, or enjoying the hidden gems of beauty that Minnesota has to offer

THE LOST CHILDREN TRILOGY

Krista Street's bestselling series on Amazon.com

Four months ago, Lena woke up in a dark alleyway with no recollection of who she is. The only clues to her past are a mysterious tattooed symbol and a supernatural power: the ability to see evil in people.

While struggling to regain her memory, she follows a strange guiding instinct to a small Colorado town. There she finds other young men and women with similar stories, similar tattoos, and a multitude of superhuman powers. Among them a man she's intensely attracted to, yet with no memories of him, she has no idea why.

As Lena and the others explore their powers and try to figure out who and what they are, they make a frightening discovery. Those who know the answers to their questions are hunting them. And if they find them, these superhumans may not survive.

34434447R00195

Printed in Great Britain
by Amazon